Janey Year of Surprising Triumphs

GEORGIA HILL

A catalogue record for this book is available from the British Library

Published by Goldcrest Books International Ltd
www.goldcrestbooks.com
publish@goldcrestbooks.com

ISBN:978-1-913719-13-5
eISBN: 978-1-913719-14-2

For Gilly, who blossomed for too short a time
but made life sweet and who gave me the idea
for this book a very long time ago.

Chapter 1

'What on earth is that woman doing?'

Will stared from his centrally heated, double-glazed office on the top floor of Cheney House. The woman in question was doing something quite extraordinary. She was dancing in circles under the large chestnut trees, near the lake. Thankfully, as it was early in the day and they hadn't been open long, there were few people about. And that was the nub of the problem. According to his grandmother, there were rarely any customers around. Her garden centre was haemorrhaging money. It was why he'd volunteered to help.

He watched, fascinated, as the woman leaped and pirouetted. She held up her hands to the sky as if supplicating to the thin February sun. The wind tugged at her autumn-coloured hair and, as it flew wildly about her face, she laughed without inhibition.

'It's barely above freezing out there,' he muttered into his espresso.

The woman didn't seem to care.

Will was at once disturbed and strangely attracted. She was so not his type. He always went for the quiet ones, the ones he could take to a work function and rely on not to put a foot wrong. They certainly wouldn't dance like a wild thing under trees. He couldn't want a woman like that. Could he? His brain said one thing but, as he shifted uncomfortably, there was no doubt his body was saying quite the contrary. There was something so free and sexy about her. Earthy. He stared fascinated as, obviously getting warm, she took off her coat. 'Voyeur!' he accused himself and turned away, determined to begin on the accounts. But his gaze was tugged back. Now without her scruffy, faded denim jacket, he could see she wore dungarees underneath. Unflattering but no doubt practical, they were the Cheney House Garden Centre uniform.

Will groaned. 'Surely you don't work here?'

It couldn't continue. She'd frighten the customers off. If any turned up. He was just about to go out and have a stern word when he saw a member of staff go over to her. They had a laughing conversation, as the man picked up her jacket and slipped it around her shoulders. They walked towards the house and then the strange woman in dungarees disappeared into the plant sales office. Definitely worked here then.

Weird. The whole thing was weird. He turned away. He needed to start ploughing through the till readings. He'd promised his grandmother he'd get to the bottom of why her finances were in such a mess. Trying to scour the image of the dancing woman from his mind, he sat at his desk and rubbed his hands together in anticipation. Studying the list of figures on his computer, he pushed his glasses further up his nose and grinned. There was nothing like the thrill of chasing those numbers down. And people said the job was boring. How little they knew. Gulping back the remains of his coffee, he felt the caffeine hit and got stuck in.

Breathless and rosy-cheeked from the exercise, Janey slumped in her desk chair, sulking. She was stuck inside the office when she could be scrubbing around in the woods for a new snowdrop, or seeing if the primroses had come up, and it was the most glorious fresh, sappy day. It was all the new accountant's fault. She didn't care if he was Clare's grandson. Fancy asking her for the monthly takings on a day like this. As if her mind was on numbers and turnover when the wind was seething through the chestnut trees and the first daffodils were dancing.

'Ruddy accountants,' she muttered. 'Never get their hands dirty. Never even get the wind in their hair.' She reached over to the keyboard, sending a pot of pencils flying. Clicking the email on its way, she leaned back, unaware that her muddy jacket was staining the chair. The recipient was only a few hundred yards away, in his office in the big house, and she could just as easily have taken the information round but she didn't want to face him. She sucked in a slurp of cold coffee and thought it was just as well the new garden centre manager was starting today. Becca Woods could flamin' well take over the boring admin, Janey thought, and leave her to do the important plant stuff.

Idly, she surveyed her surroundings. The plant sales office was little more than a shed tacked onto the side of the ramshackle series of buildings that housed plants, garden furniture and equipment, and all the other merchandise customers expected from a garden centre. At the back was Graham's domain: sheds, fencing, containers and aggregates. Displayed on the large cobbled courtyard, which separated plant sales from the rear of the Georgian Cheney House, were water features and ready-planted-up pots bursting with spring colour. As Janey pondered on what change a new manager might bring, she could just about see, through the smeared windows of the office, the cheerily bobbing *Narcissi* she'd planted up yesterday. Turning back to the computer and wishing she was outside; she began to type. This month's blog was late. Again.

The Galloping Galanthophile: February

Welcome to this month's blog from Cheney House Garden Centre. Chilly out there, isn't it? Let's talk snowdrops. Galanthus. Candlemas bells. Or, if you prefer but it's far less romantic, the white bulbous violet – what a name for such a pretty flower! These tiny white blooms, with their delicate grace, drooping heads and slivers of leaf are also occasionally known as fair maids of February or white ladies. I love them for their sheer optimism. Arriving in the dull, dark days after Christmas, they're a welcome harbinger of longer days and better weather. Hardy. Unshowy. Quietly beautiful. Rewarding. So worth getting to know. And grow. Even within the limited white and green theme, there is surprising variety. Some are leggy, some have a creamier hue than others. Some have green within the flower or are double-headed, and there are even variations in leaf colour. They are a subtle flower, admirably low-key. For some, and I count myself among their number, they become an obsession. Galanthophiles, as we snowdrop fanciers are called, hunker over bulbs in potting sheds, desperately trying to create something new. People pay hundreds of pounds for a new type of snowdrop – you could make your fortune! But, for many, the real kick comes from being the first to create a brand-new variety.

History records other such obsessions with flowers, just think of the tulip fever in seventeenth-century Holland but, in my opinion, snowdrops are a fairy flower compared with the stolid petals of the garish tulip! In the Victorian language of flowers, the snowdrop is synonymous with hope and consolation, it's easy to see why. As well as being decorative, they are useful too. Did you know, although poisonous, Galantamine, a substance derived from the flower, is used to treat Alzheimer's patients? Amazing, isn't it? It's not hard to see their appeal. They appear when the ground is hardened by frost, when precious little else is in flower. The white of the flowers contrasts against the fresh green of the leaves and they always seem to me to epitomise new beginnings. Snowdrops thrive in the sandy, well-drained soil here, a tribute to Graham's regular mulching, and we have lots of different types in stock, including the easy to grow Galanthus nivalis. Come and buy some – all at affordable prices. Best planted up 'in the green', you can then look forward to your very own display of brave little Galanthus flowers this time next year.

As ever, happy gardening!

GG

Just as she'd finished and was stretching stiff shoulders and blinking eyes so tired they were beginning to cross, Graham came in, banging the door behind him against a gust of wind.

Coming to perch on the edge of the desk, he peered at the screen and at the blog she'd just spent an hour crafting. 'Blimey, better cut that by half, my lovely. Customers don't want a history lesson; they just want to know what's on offer this week. But keep the mention of me in, I like that.'

Janey saw him shiver.

'Brass monkeys out there today. What do you know about this Becca Woods woman, then?' He picked up Janey's coffee mug and drained it.

'Oi! Get your own.'

'Cold anyway.'

'And unfinished. And mine!'

Graham shrugged. 'Not for long. The rate you get through mugs. Come on, who's this Becca Woods?'

Janey snatched back her mug and glared. It was her new favourite. It had a picture of snowdrops on it. Graham had given it to her for Christmas. He always claimed she was so clumsy she needed regular replacements for all the mugs she broke. Anything he gave her was cherished but she'd rather die than let him know. 'Used to manage the Somerset division of Country Xteriors.'

'A supermarket?' Graham's derision was clear.

'More like outdoor hypermarkets,' Janey corrected him.

'Is that what they want to turn us into?' He scowled, his good-looking face closing down in anger. 'A bloody leisure retail outlet?'

Janey tried to suppress the longing, which habitually went through her whenever Graham was near, even when he was on a major sulk, and forced a nonchalant shrug. 'Don't know, reckon we'll find out at the next staff meeting. Clare's going to unveil her masterplan then.'

'Just hope she knows what she's doing. This place has been in her family for as long as I can remember.' He swung a moody foot. 'It's always been somewhere a real plant lover can come for advice and healthy stock. A proper nursery. I can't be doing with somewhere that piles up petunias and geraniums just to shift them quick.'

'Clare's not like that, Gray,' Janey said, loyally, hoping it was true.

'Have you met these two? This Becca and this accountant bloke? They might have other ideas. It's all about profit and loss nowadays.'

'Will? Nah. Keeps sending me requests for numbers, that's all. I reckon he's fat and bald. And boring. Isn't that what accountants are like?'

Graham snorted. 'Yeah. And that Becca will be all power suits and snotty attitude.' He blew out a breath and crunched up an empty seed packet. 'Oh Janey, why did this have to happen? We've been doing all right for years. Selling a few plants, doing the open garden days.' He turned and focussed his startlingly blue eyes on her. 'We were okay weren't we? A good team?'

Janey tried to catch her breath but her heart was tumbling any old way. He was so very dear to her and he didn't have the first clue about how she felt. Recovering, she went for a reassuring tone, 'It'll be all right.' For a minute she let herself gaze back and wondered if this crush would ever fade. Then reality bounced in. Graham had only ever seen her as a best friend and work colleague and nothing seemed likely to ever change that. The fact she was head of plant sales and head gardener and therefore, technically, his boss made things even more awkward. She forced herself to be matter of fact. 'But even you have to admit that ever since that big garden centre opened in Yeovil we've been losing custom.'

'Help yourself to cheap bedders and buy a load of fudge and greetings cards at the same time? Can't compete with our knowledge, Janey,' he said, gruffly.

'No. But we can't compete with a big chain's prices either. That's why Clare has been forced to expand. Wanted to really, ever since her husband died.'

'Ah, now Gerald. He would never have let this happen.'

'No, he wouldn't. But then if it had been up to him, we'd still be selling stuff in pounds, shillings and pence. Not one to accept the march of progress was Mr Gerald,' Janey said it fondly; they'd all loved Gerald Cheney.

It brought back a smile to Graham's face. He straightened. 'Well, enough of the chit-chat,' he said, abruptly. 'I'll get over to the side drive and put that new gravel down.'

Janey watched his departure fondly. He never could stand around idle. Graham was a man of action, not talk. He strode out towards the car park and was stopped by a trim blonde in an immaculate trouser suit and stilettoes. Janey got up and went to the window to see more clearly. It could only be one person. This must be Becca, their new boss. She studied Graham's body language as he and Becca held an animated conversation. She knew him so well she could instantly judge his reactions. There was no doubt. Despite what he'd just said, despite Becca's power suit and possible snotty attitude, Graham fancied the well-cut trousers off her.

'Oh Gray,' she murmured, her whole being sinking under the weight of jealousy and disappointment. 'How could you fall for a blonde in too much make-up and stilettoes? For someone so obvious. I mean, *stilettoes* in a garden centre?' It wasn't the first time she'd played witness to Graham's love-life. And it wouldn't be the last.

Bracing herself, she reluctantly turned her attention back to the computer and to editing the blog. Graham had been right; it was far too wordy. Her phone pinged. Reaching into her dungarees' pocket, she saw it was a text from Will. A demand that she go to his office later that morning. She pulled a face at the poinsettia on the windowsill, where it had sat, unsold and dejected, since Christmas. 'Looks like I've been summoned.' Tracing over the snowdrop image on her mug, she whispered, 'Give me some of your strength and bravery, little *Galanthus*. I think I need it.'

Chapter 2

The main administrative offices were housed in Cheney House itself, the Georgian red brick pile that served as the show piece for the garden centre. At present, customers could only gain access to the café, which took up the ground floor, but Janey knew Clare had plans for the rest of the house. A stylish garden furniture showroom had been suggested for the first floor, with a dedicated gift shop on the second. Currently gifts shared an awkward space with plant sales. Clare had an apartment on the top floor, alongside the offices. But that was into the future. In between the newly revamped café and the top floor, the middle floors currently yawned empty.

As Janey trudged up the stairs, failing to notice the mucky footprints she was leaving, the ball of tension knotted tighter in her stomach. She hated having to deal with numbers, always had. It just wasn't her strong point. Show her a planting bed overrun with weeds, or a huge lawn that needed over-seeding and she was in her element. But she had a blind spot when it came to anything to do with maths and numbers. She even had trouble remembering her car registration number and hadn't the first clue what her mobile number was. For her, an accountant's job would be torture. She simply couldn't imagine having to pore over the tiniest financial detail looking for discrepancies. Sheer hell. What made her tick was breathing fresh air, smelling the earth as it was dug over, getting the rich mixture caked on her hands and grimed into her nails. She hated being indoors, away from her precious plants. Pausing on the half landing, she stared through the arched window, longing for the meeting to be over and she could get back to what she loved. It was gorgeous out there. Crisp and green and springing with new life.

'Beautiful,' she murmured.

'Miss Trelawney?'

Janey swung round. Behind her, on the stair above, was a tall lean man dressed in a neatly tailored grey suit. It was one of those trendy ones, with narrow legs and a short jacket. Janey always thought they looked too small. They certainly looked uncomfortable. Couldn't shovel up a load of manure in one of those. She sighed a little thinking of Cary Grant in *Bringing Up Baby*. Now there was a man who could wear a suit. A proper suit. She blinked. The man in front of her reached out a hand but, as she hadn't moved, he let it hang awkwardly at his side, embarrassed. He pushed his tortoiseshell specs up his nose.

'Will Cheney-Mortimer. I don't think we've met before. I asked you to come and see me,' he added, as Janey still didn't respond.

'Yes,' she stuttered, dragging her mind from Cary Grant. He'd somehow escaped Katharine Hepburn and the leopard and had taken her for a romantic stroll through Cheney House's snowdrop woods. That dimple in the chin! Grudgingly, she forced herself to focus on Will. He wasn't her idea of an accountant. Far too young, far too fit and actually, if you looked closely, quite good-looking. Although there was definitely a distinct lack of Cary Grant's charm. Will Cheney-Mortimer seemed downright stuffy and awkward.

'Shall we, um, go into the office? This way.' He gestured in an old-fashioned way to the open door at the end of the corridor and gave a tight smile. 'Would you like some coffee? I expect you're cold after working outside on such a chilly day.'

Janey found her voice. 'Chilly?' she exclaimed, as she followed him into the office. 'It's absolute heaven out there today.'

Will seemed to recoil at the vehemence in her voice. 'Really?' he said mildly. 'I haven't been out since first thing. Paperwork you know.'

'Paperwork, smchakerwork,' snorted Janey and, without being asked, slid into a leather chair in front of his desk. She watched as he filled two cups with coffee from an expensive-looking machine in the corner. Long legs, she noted, and a nice bum. Actually, very nice considering all he did was sit on it all day.

'Yes, paperwork. It's what I do.' Will handed Janey a cup of steaming coffee. 'Biscuit?' He offered a plate of plain digestives.

Janey's stomach rumbled. Gwen in the café had promised some of her homemade chocolate and hazelnut cookies but she'd been too busy to go and get them. Accidentally slurping her coffee, she took three biscuits.

'Thank you,' she mumbled through a mouthful. Graham

was always on at her to mind her manners but she was too hungry to care. Besides, eating squashed down some of the anxiety she was feeling.

If Will was taken aback at her lack of social graces he took pains not to show it. 'Right, Miss Trelawney,' he said, sitting at his desk and carefully placing his cup of coffee on a coaster. 'Shall we begin?'

Janey flicked a glance at her watch as she left Will's office. Far too late for cookies and coffee in the café. In fact, at this rate, she'd nearly miss the lunch serving. For someone like her who undertook hard physical labour most days it was a mistake not to eat, especially in cold weather. She needed her energy. As she hurried down the stairs, in the hope of begging a sandwich and bowl of soup off Gwen, she reflected that the meeting with Will hadn't been all bad. While he was clearly frustrated with her lack of understanding, or indeed interest in anything financial, he had gone through the last month's till readings with painstaking patience and clarity so that even Janey, maths dunderhead that she was, could understand some of it. Mainly, the bit that they weren't making enough money. But she'd known that already and hadn't needed a smart Alec accountant in a fancy suit to tell her that. They agreed the till readings didn't add up. Janey defended her staff robustly and said they were all honest to a fault. She did agree, however, that any discrepancies were highly likely to be a case of them sometimes forgetting to ring through a sale on the till and promised to take them to task on it. She'd left, relieved she could, from now on, leave the more complicated number crunching to the new manager. She just had to send in a basic record of plant sales and leave the rest to Will and Becca.

'Thank goodness,' she muttered to Gwen, as she grabbed at the dregs of today's potato and leek soup and hunk of homemade granary bread, 'that I don't have to number crunch ever again.' She gobbled her food down and raced outside before the best of the light had gone. Not much to be had at this time of year and it was too good to waste.

From his office, Will watched her energetic figure stride across the carriage drive and disappear along the side of the lake. He admired how her chestnut hair bounced and flew in the breeze. He shook his head. He'd never met anyone quite like Janey Trelawney. Straight talking and without any hint of feminine guile whatsoever. She was a breath of air, as fresh as that outside. The picture of her dancing under the trees stayed with him. Such a completely unselfconscious act. But she wasn't going to be easy to manage. He didn't envy Becca Woods that job. Not one little bit.

Chapter 3

'A whistling woman and a crowing hen are neither fit for God nor men,' her dear, departed nan always used to say. Janey stopped herself abruptly before getting too sad. She'd often thought her nan was the only person who'd properly understood her. It was too cold to whistle anyway. The temperature had dropped to minus seven in the night and a heavy frost rimed the outbuildings into an icy white. It was just beginning to get light, with a glimmer of a muffled pink sunrise in the east. She jogged from the car park to the plant sales office with only one thought in mind: coffee. It was the only way to start a working day as cold as this. As hot as hell and as strong as—

The thought was interrupted. She could hear shouting. And splashing. Breaking into a fast run, she headed, full pelt, to the lake. She halted, breathing heavily, shocked by what she saw.

Graham!

He was in the water, desperately trying to grasp the reeds at the edge but missing. 'Janey woman, help!' His next words were lost in a gurgle as he sank under.

'Swim, Graham,' she yelled, 'swim to the shore!'

As an answer he flailed his arms and splashed some more.

Janey looked about her, thinking hard. Her first impulse was to jump in after him but she knew that was the wrong thing to do. She began to take off her sweater to act as a rope and then changed her mind. It wouldn't be long enough to reach him. Graham had stopped shouting. He'd stopped doing anything, apart from gulping at the air and spitting out lake water. She was running out of time. Think woman. Think! Casting about, her eyes lit on the lifebuoy hooked onto a post half-hidden by the boathouse. It was mildewed and ancient but would have to do. She lifted it off, hands slippery and numb with cold. Twisting the rope end around her wrist, she threw the buoy into the water. It landed too short. Fighting to keep calm, she tugged on the rope and wound the lifebuoy back in. It came back covered with some disgusting kind of black, half-rotted pond weed. Oh God, Graham was deeper down in the water and bobbing under it more often, she was sure of it. His thick work clothes must be soaked through and too heavy for him to cope with the weight. Taking a deep breath, she mustered all her strength and threw the buoy once again. This time it landed nearer.

'Grab it. Gray, grab it. I'll pull you in.'

She jumped up and down on the bank helplessly, watching as he registered what had happened. He seemed to be losing the fight. It must be the cold water. With a monumental effort, he reached out a frozen hand and caught hold of the buoy. But it was too wet and his grip too weak. It floated just out of reach.

'Graham!' she yelled, 'you have to grab it. Grab it and put your arm through.' She swore long and hard and vociferously. It seemed to get through. Graham tried to grasp the buoy again and a swell of water nudged it closer. He got his arm through.

'I'll pull you in,' Janey shrieked, by this time her voice hoarse and sore. She yanked on the rope and began to pull him in, getting him as far as the bank. However, even her digging-heavy-clay-soil-honed muscles weren't up to lugging a thirteen stone, six-foot man in sodden clothes up out of the water. There was nothing for it. Eyeing the cold, dark water with distaste, Janey waded in. Holding him around the waist, she manoeuvred him to the boathouse next to which were some rickety steps. Half dragging, half pushing him, they eventually reached the top where they flopped down, exhausted, gasping like just-caught carp.

'What were you doing in the lake?' Janey managed to roll over, ignoring the mud and filth she was covered in.

Graham sat up, coughed and retched hard. When he recovered, he answered. 'Trying to rescue Camilla.'

'Camilla?' Janey stared at him blankly. Camilla was Clare's golden cocker spaniel. Gorgeous but without a brain cell to rub together.

Graham coughed again so Janey thumped him on the back. 'Thanks,' he spluttered. 'She'd got onto the ice. Chasing ducks I bet.' He shook his head. 'I've never known such a stupid dog.'

'Did you?'

'Did I what?'

'Rescue her!'

'No. I slipped down the bank into the water. It was so cold it took my breath away. Literally. I couldn't breathe. I got nowhere near. She'd gone through the ice and swum off.'

Janey sucked in a breath. 'Jeez, if she's drowned Clare will be heart-broken. She dotes on that dog. She was the last thing Gerald gave her.'

Graham shrugged. 'I tried. I did my best.' It was almost a whine. He shivered violently.

If they didn't get out of these wet clothes they'd come down with hypothermia, but Janey couldn't leave without having one last look for the dog.

'Do you think you can make it back to the office? Get out of those wet clothes and put something else on. And turn on the paraffin heater while you're at it.'

As he lurched to his feet, they heard a familiar bark. They stared at one another and then Janey guessed where the sound was coming from.

'The boathouse. The little so-and-so has got into the boathouse!' She began to make her way towards it.

'Janey be careful. The place is rotten. The floorboards will give way.'

'Well then, it had better be me going in, seeing as I'm not as heavy as you.' She stopped, half hoping he'd be chivalrous and insist he go in her place. But he didn't.

'I'll go back and get the kettle on.'

Janey didn't hear him. She'd already begun to open the door of the boathouse.

Chapter 4

It creaked ominously. Like a lot of things at Cheney House, it was in dire need of repair. As her eyes adjusted to the dim light of the interior, Janey could just make out the shivering blob that was Camilla. She was huddled up against the far most wall, soaked to the skin. Janey assumed she'd clambered out of the water onto the wooden platform that ran around the inside of the boathouse. The only trouble was, in the process, she had broken part of it off and only a narrow and jagged spur remained. There was no hope of Janey getting along it to reach her. The broken section floated on the opaque black water mocking her. Ugh, it stank in here. More pond weed but an underlying stench of something nasty rotting.

Janey tried calling her, hoping she would jump back in and swim towards her, but the dog refused to move. She rummaged in her sopping and disgusting dungaree pocket for treats, or the remains of a biscuit, but it was empty. Then she remembered; she'd scoffed the double-choc chip cookies

Gwen had given her as breakfast on the drive in. The dog's head was beginning to droop and her shivering increased. Janey wondered if dogs suffered from hypothermia too. Clare would be distraught if anything happened to Camilla. And Janey would be too. The dog may well be the most stupid spaniel she'd ever come across, but she was affectionate and good company on the days when Clare needed a dog-sitter.

Janey considered what to do. Hearing Camilla's pathetic whimper decided her. After all, she was already soaked to the skin and the water in the boathouse couldn't be all that deep. Wishing Graham had stayed with her, she eased herself in. The cold hit her immediately. Adrenaline had given her some kind of immunity when she'd rescued Graham. The water here was only waist high but that seemed to make her feel the cold more. Her soaked hair clung around her head making it ache. She began to wade carefully towards the dog, her heart thumping and her breath already coming in gasps. She began to shiver. She needed to be quick.

'Hold on Cam, I'm coming to get you.'

Inching towards her, Janey was relieved the dog stayed perched where she was. She even had the temerity to bark as Janey got closer. Clinging on to what was left of the walkway, Janey made a grab for the scruff of the dog's neck.

'Sorry, my lovely. Can't stand on ceremony here. Got to get you warmed up.' Wading back was nigh on impossible with a heavy spaniel to hold, but she made it. Heaving the wriggling dog onto the step by the entrance, Janey was dismayed to see Camilla give an enormous shake and then leg it before she could get herself out. She just hoped the dog would find her way home and not venture onto the lake in a second attempt at a duck snack.

'That's gratitude for you,' Janey muttered as, after three attempts, she hauled herself out. For a second, she lay sprawled on her front, lacking the strength to move. Staggering to her feet, she tried to jog towards warmth and a change of clothes but was dismayed to find her legs were so stiff with cold, all she could do was a sort of hobble. Overcome by vicious shivering, she lurched around the corner of the office and collided full on with Will. He was holding Camilla by the collar.

'What the—'

'You found her! Thank goodness. Thought she'd gone off in chase of more ducks.'

Will stepped back and, with fastidious fingers, picked off a trail of pond weed from where Janey had deposited it on his suit.

'Gran's terribly worried. She sent me out to hunt for her. Why is she soaking wet?' He looked Janey up and down, his lip curling in disgust. 'Why are *you* soaking wet?'

'Camilla decided to dive in the lake after a mallard. She got stuck in the boathouse and I got her out.' Janey decided the short version was best. Her teeth were chattering so much she could hardly get the words out.

'You went in the lake after a dog?'

'Not any old dog. Camilla.' Janey was indignant on behalf of Clare's beloved pet.

'You went in the lake?' he repeated, as if having trouble believing her. 'It's below freezing. You must have had to break the ice.'

'I'm well aware of that,' Janey began to say, but her lips were numb with cold and had stopped working; no actual words came out. She'd explain in more detail at some later point. When she was dry and warm and had some of Gwen's hot chocolate inside her.

Will's mouth opened but, before he could say anything more, Clare tore across the cobbled courtyard and found them. She was dressed in a bathrobe and fluffy pink slippers.

'Oh my darlings,' she cried. 'Graham's just filled me in. My poor, poor Cam.' She bent down and picked up the dog.

Janey wanted to say, 'Be careful, she's filthy,' but her mouth still refused to work. In fact, she was beginning to feel distinctly odd. 'Excuse me,' she tried to croak, but the words fell away as she slumped to the ground.

She half heard Clare insist Will pick her up and carry her to the office.

Janey tried to protest but felt Will's arm around her as he picked her up. Impressions of a solidly muscled chest, and the warm security of his arms, penetrated her frozen mind. He was surprisingly strong. For an accountant. She fought against an urge to burrow into him and placed the blame on needing heat. They bumped along and then he gently laid her on the beaten-up leather sofa that served as seating in the plant sales office.

'There you go, darling.' Clare shoved the men out of the way. Janey vaguely heard her order Will to go and dry off Camilla, and Graham was told to get a hot drink. She then stripped Janey's semi-conscious body and wrapped her in several throws purloined from the gift shop. They were cashmere and retailed at over four hundred pounds each.

A dry Camilla bounded in twenty minutes later, with Will in hot pursuit. He looked far from pristine, with a huge grass stain down the front of his shirt, his glasses on crooked and his dark hair spiked up. Graham followed, carrying an enormous mug of cocoa.

'Not too hot,' he said, as he folded Janey's fingers round it. 'Apparently, according to Gwen, that's not the right thing when you've been in cold water. But nice and sweet. Oh, there goes Camilla to keep you company,' he added, as the dog sprang up and snuggled down beside her.

Janey sipped the cocoa and grimaced. 'Far too sweet,' she protested. She was beginning to feel almost normal and hugged Camilla to her. The dog was warm and her golden coat all fluffed up and glossy. 'Not for you,' she laughed, as Camilla's nose strayed too close to the mug.

Clare joined them on the sofa. She patted Janey's hand and pulled Camilla into an embrace. 'Nice and dry now, dear girl, thanks to Will wielding my hairdryer.' She blew him a kiss. 'Thank you, darling boy. Now Janey, Graham has told me all about how he rescued my poor little Cami.'

Janey's eyes met Will's.

'And then you went in to rescue him. So brave.' Clare tucked a lock of silver-blonde hair behind her ear. Usually immaculate, she, too, looked dishevelled, with mud stains all down her robe and pink slippers, which would be fit for nothing after this morning. She caught Janey's stare. 'And just look at us.' She giggled. 'You, dear girl, dressed in finest cashmere, Will with Cam's muddy water all over him, me still in my night things.' She glanced up at Graham. 'Only darling Graham looks anything like presentable.'

All eyes locked on Graham. He'd had time to change into a new uniform and looked his normal self. Janey peered closer. Had he had time to dry his hair into its quiff? Yes. And apply hair gel. All while she was fighting that disgusting water in the boathouse! If he'd had time to do all that, surely he could have come and helped her? The horrible memory of trying to heave herself out of the black water returned and she shivered.

'Let's give Janey chance to get properly dry, shall we?' Will said, noticing. 'And, um, she can get into some clothes.'

'Yes, we must.' Clare rose decisively, gathering Camilla to her. 'Come, dear one. A special breakfast for you. What about sausages, eh? We'll get Janey some too.'

She left, with Will trailing behind. Janey flashed him a grateful look before he disappeared.

'I'll leave you to it then, Janey,' Graham said. 'Think Becca wants a chat about a possible new car park layout.'

Janey pulled a throw around her more tightly and sipped the now tepid cocoa. She watched his departure thoughtfully. Apart from bringing her hot chocolate, he hadn't seemed concerned. He hadn't asked how she was, or even thanked her for rescuing him. And he'd taken full credit for rescuing Camilla. Not once had he mentioned how it had been her who had flailed around in the gloom in a stinking, rotten boathouse after an ungrateful spaniel.

'Nice one, Gray,' she muttered. It wasn't like him. It wasn't like him one bit.

Chapter 5

The following day, the entire staff of Cheney House gathered in the only space big enough to fit them all in – the café. Taking up most of the ground floor of the house, it was a vast space and the only room that had been refurbished recently. With its bamboo flooring and enormous restored sash windows, it usually had an elegant, tranquil atmosphere. This morning, however, the café hummed with expectation. As it was early and before the centre opened properly, Clare had given Gwen orders that hot drinks and buttered toast should be on offer.

'Gran, no wonder you don't turn a profit when you're giving out freebies like this,' Janey heard Will say, as they all shuffled around trying to find a seat.

'Told you, it's all profit and loss with that sort,' Graham whispered in her ear.

Janey elbowed him in the ribs. 'Shut up. The meeting's about to start.' His negativity was beginning to irritate her.

She watched as Clare got up and went to stand at the front. Clare had always been good to her; she'd taken a chance on her when most had given up. She'd continued, ever since, to be supportive of whatever project she dreamed up. The knot of anxiety tightened. She put a hand on her stomach to quieten her nerves. Graham's moaning was getting on her nerves. It wasn't as if she wanted things to change either, she just wanted to continue working at Cheney House. Even if it meant suffering the daily humiliation of unrequited love. Glancing up at Graham's handsome face, she wondered if he'd ever return her feelings. In some ways, she was comfortable with the status quo. At least she knew where she was with him. Routine was what she craved. She knew what to expect from him each day – a few jokes, a bit of gossip and banter. A strictly platonic but friendly hug every now and again. Routine was why she loved working for Clare. Over the years very little had changed. It was also why she was passionate about gardening. Despite the vagaries of the weather, you could always rely on summer following spring and winter following autumn. The turning of the world was predictable. It made her feel secure. And she needed security. She'd worked for Clare since being thrown out of school. Janey shifted in her seat at the memory of how she was back then. She wasn't proud of that part of her life. Clare had taken her on when, at sixteen and truculent, Janey had been trouble. They'd recognised something in each other. Clare had seen Janey's burgeoning skill for gardening and Janey, despite being sullen and closed-off to the world, had glimpsed a glimmer of hope, of what her life could be. Thirteen years later, she was still grateful. She didn't know what she'd do if she couldn't work at Cheney House. 'Please let me keep my job,' she breathed.

'What did you say?' Graham asked.

'Just that I hope we keep our jobs.'

'Yeah, well. Reckon that'll be up to the bean counters, won't it?' He nodded to where Will was sitting on one side of Clare. Flanking her other side was Becca, looking glamorous and ruthlessly efficient in a magenta trouser suit, her hair scraped back into a brutal ponytail and her face a mask of make-up. All three sat at the front, facing their workforce.

How many suits must Becca have? wondered Janey. Her own wardrobe consisted of jeans and sweatshirts; she had need of little else. A night out consisted of an evening in the pub. No need to dress up for that. For exercise she had work, or a long walk with Camilla. Certainly no need to dress up for *that*. Wishing she was crashing through a muddy field with the spaniel right at this precise moment, she forced herself to concentrate as Clare stood up and began to speak.

'My darlings,' she began, to a wince from Will at the endearment. 'Thank you for taking time out from your working day. I hope you've all had tea or coffee and some of Gwen's delicious toast?' A few murmured their thanks. 'Good.' She unfolded a sheet of paper, which fluttered nervously in her hand. 'I've gathered you all here to listen to the new action plan for Cheney House. One that will build on our past and take us into a secure future.'

This didn't sound like Clare. She didn't speak in soundbites, Janey observed. She saw her give a swift glance at the piece of paper in her hand and continue speaking.

'She's reading what Will and Becca have cooked up,' Graham whispered in her ear.

'Well, she did bring them in as consultants,' Janey whispered back.

'Whose side on you on?'

'Ssh, let's listen,' Janey hissed, as she saw Will give them daggers.

'But, before I launch in to explain how things will change, may I introduce two people who will be instrumental in Cheney House's future. First of all, Will, my darling grandson. He's on leave from Keel and Wesson.' Clare named a multinational company, which even Janey had heard of. 'He has very kindly agreed to be our executive accountant for a short while.' She turned to Becca. 'And this is our new general manager, Becca Woods.' Clare gave her a beaming smile. 'She is full of ideas and enthusiasm for our vision for Cheney House and I just know you're all going to love working under her.'

Janey heard Graham stifle a giggle. Really, he was juvenile sometimes.

Clare went on to outline the proposed changes. Rumours had been flying about for weeks and there was little that hadn't been mentioned before. The gift shop was to be moved into Cheney House proper, a garden furniture and craft outlet was going to be established and the café was to be open longer hours. At this Gwen huffed.

Clare heard her. 'We will be taking on extra staff, of course, Gwen. We couldn't possibly expect you to do it all. We may investigate opening in the evening too, looking at themed evenings, world food, that sort of thing.'

Gwen huffed even further. Janey could tell she was torn between being delighted at the thought of extra staff and having to hand over her baby to someone else.

'With the gift shop moving,' Clare added, 'we can create more room for plant sales, Janey. I know that will meet with your approval. Darlings, I know this looks like an awful lot of change in a very short period of time, but I'm hoping you will bear with us and see us through this new little adventure. We need to expand and progress, and that way your jobs, I hope, will be safe-guarded.' Her voice took on an almost wistful longing. 'And Janey, I'd like to talk to you about the garden centre becoming a centre of excellence for a selection of plants. Our USB—.' She turned to Becca and frowned. 'That's not right, is it?'

Becca gave a smug smile. 'Not quite, Clare. It's USP. Unique selling point. It's what will mark us out as different to our competitors. I'll expect to work closely with Janey on this.'

Oh goody, thought Janey, and tried to keep the sarcasm off her face.

'And there's one last thing, although you know where I am if there are any questions' – all eyes focussed on Clare again – 'after yesterday's events concerning the rescue of my little dog,' she beamed at Graham and Janey, 'which I'm sure you've all heard about, I'd like to pursue the idea of opening up the boating lake again. Repair the boathouse, offer boat hire and the like.' She clapped her hands together. 'I want to make Cheney House a destination, a day out as well as a place for meeting gardening needs. I can't think of anything nicer on a warm summer's day than a little punt on the water. And then back to Gwen's for a delicious cream tea. I'll expect Becca to work very closely with our lovely Graham on that. Now, I'm sure you all need lots of time to process this mass of information. Becca will hold regular staff meetings from now on, to keep you all up to date and check progress. We have an awful lot of work to get done before the spring season gets underway, but I know we'll do it.' Clare's eyes sparkled with unshed tears and Janey sensed the audience warm to her; they were all incredibly fond of their boss. 'If only for my dear husband's memory,' she continued. 'I'd like to create something truly special for Gerald.' She left, dabbing her eyes. One or two people even cheered as she went.

Janey sat motionless. Either Clare was the most sincere, rousing public speaker of all time – or she was the most manipulative. Either way, you had to hand it to her. She relaxed her shoulders for the first time since the meeting began. One thing at least, their jobs didn't seem in danger.

Chapter 6

The Galloping Galanthophile: March

Welcome to this month's blog from Cheney House Garden Centre. If you're a regular customer (and if not, why not?) you may have noticed some changes happening around the place. The gift shop was temporarily shut but is now open in its shiny new premises on the second floor of the main house. Don't worry though, our building won't be closed for much longer, as it's being fitted out to be a brand-spanking-new plant sales centre. We're hoping to get it up and going by the end of the month. Just in time for you all to begin thinking about bedding plants for the spring. If you're one of those organised folks and are already doing that, we have some plug plants for sale in the temporary nursery. Don't be going and putting them in that cold soil just yet though. Keep them in a greenhouse or indoors – somewhere not too warm but above freezing.

And speaking of freezing, winter hasn't let go its grip yet, has it? We're still waiting for the next show of daffodils to come out here. They seem deeply reluctant to show their heads and I don't blame them. Our Narcissus 'Jetfire' will be out soon. It's a tall daff with yellow petals and a bright orange trumpet – perfect to add a splash of colour to your beds. Or you might want something daintier, in which case plant up a container with 'Hawera' and enjoy its musky scent. We've got ready-planted up tubs to save you the trouble.

You'll soon spot us wearing new uniforms. More change! Let's hope they're warm and cosy. I might well add a woolly hat to mine. Another way to beat the cold is to pop into Gwen's new-style café. The menu's had a complete makeover but rest assured, hot chocolate with all the trimmings is still on. I insisted!

As we're going through huge changes, we thought we'd offer a few discounts. Come and have a look at what's on offer. Lots of bargains to be had as we stock-clear in time for the new plant sales centre. Those plug plants are three trays for the price of two, and Graham has priced some wonderful containers to make them as tempting as Gwen's Victoria sponge. Yes, she's still doing that. One thing that hasn't changed.

As ever, happy gardening!

GG

Their first proper staff meeting had been a disaster. Janey had argued furiously with Becca over the refurbishment of the gift shop taking priority over the new plant sales centre.

'But it's what we're known for. That's why people come here. To buy plants!' she'd yelled, exasperated. 'Back me up on this, Graham.'

But Graham remained silent and Becca would not be moved.

So, the gift shop had been launched first, with the promised extra plant space taking a lot longer than promised.

It made no sense to Janey whatsoever. Spring was their best-selling season. They were risking losing a large chunk of profit for novelty tea towels and over-priced ornaments.

'It won't stock stuff like that,' Graham said confidently, when she moaned to him about it afterwards. He'd come into the office to ring round for quotes for dredging the lake. Plans for that were steaming ahead as well. All this change was dizzying.

'Oh, you know, do you? Had cosy chats with Becca about it all, have you?'

He put the phone back on its receiver and resigned himself for a chat. 'Yeah, I have actually.' He scratched his ear with his Biro. 'We've been out for a drink once or twice.'

'Oh.' Janey sank back onto the office chair. It wobbled a little so she steadied it with her Dr Marten-shod foot. As far as she knew, Graham's infatuations rarely developed into the going for a drink stage, they usually fizzled out after the first bonk.

'She's really not that bad you know, Janey. Give her a chance. Get to know her.'

'Like you have. Obviously.'

'Well, we talked it over. More profit in the craft goods they're going to sell than from a tray of begonias. And they're only stocking locally made stuff so we can be seen to support the area.'

Words parroted from Becca. They must be. Graham didn't normally talk like that. What was it with this woman being able to put words into people's mouths? Janey didn't challenge him. She wasn't sure how she felt about Graham these days. From moaning for England at the beginning of all this change, he'd instantly become Becca's most staunch ally. Janey wondered which part of his anatomy was ruling the transformation. She doubted it was his brain.

'You've never thanked me for getting you out of the lake, you know,' she said, suddenly.

'Haven't I?' He looked surprised. 'I thought I had. Soz, Janey. Thank you, my lovely. Thank you. I owe you.'

'Yes, you do,' she added, with asperity. 'How about you back me up more in staff meetings? Especially the one coming up next week, where we get our new uniforms.'

Graham fiddled with his pen. He didn't answer for a minute. 'Are they really so bad?'

'Yes Graham, they really are bad!' Janey plucked at her dungarees. 'These might be a pain when they get wet but the material is thick enough to keep out the wind and cold. That polyester stuff is going to freeze us in the winter and sweat us out in the summer. It's been chosen by someone who has never worked outdoors in her life. Just like the decision about the gift shop opening first. I really don't think Becca's got the interests of the plant sales bit of the garden centre at heart.' Janey thought she had gone too far as she saw Graham's expression change. But she was wrong about the reason.

'Haven't I?'

Janey spun round on her chair, knocking Graham's mug flying as she did. Becca was standing in the doorway.

'My office. Now.'

Heart sinking and lower lip jutting in dangerous fashion, Janey followed Becca to her office on the top floor of the big house. Memories of when she'd had to go and see the head teacher at the various schools willing to take her, flooded back. They passed a frowning Will on the way.

Becca slammed shut the door of her office and pointed to the chair in front of the desk.

'Sit,' she commanded. She went behind the desk and perched on the edge of her office chair, fingers steepled and carefully drawn-in eyebrows arched. 'Janey.'

'Yes Becca.'

'I hardly need say I need your support in order to make Cheney House a success.'

'No, Becca.'

'I need especial support from my key players. You in the plant centre, Graham in maintenance and grounds work and Gwen in the restaurant.' She paused and sat back. 'I seem to have Gwen on board and Graham too. It's just you who is challenging my authority.'

'No, Becca. I mean, yes, Becca. I mean no.'

Becca gave a smile, which reminded Janey of a shark she'd seen in Weymouth Sea Life Centre. Just before it snapped up its lunch. Then she surprised her by changing tack.

Leaning forward again she added, 'I can assure you, Janey, that I have Cheney House's interests at heart. I gave up an extremely promising retail career at Country Xteriors for this job and I wouldn't have done it had I not wanted to drive forward its success.' She pouted a little. 'Actually, I rather fell for the place when I saw it. This gorg Victorian house–'

'It's Georgian.'

'Whatevs.' She flapped her hands. 'Victorian, Georgian. Old. Beautiful. And can I confess something to you, just between you and me? I rather fell for Clare. Losing her husband like that. I knew I'd found my calling. To help Clare make Cheney House the best it possibly could be. That's my mission.' She ran a hand over her ponytail and flicked it back, sighing. 'But I can't help Clare on my own. I need you, Janey. I need you to be the best possible plant seller Cheney House can offer. I know you have the expertise.' Becca fluttered her eyelashes. Actually fluttered her eyelashes. Janey watched in fascination; she hadn't known eyelashes could flutter. Not in real life. 'An expertise I cannot confess to have.' Becca smirked.

Janey paused before deciding what best to say.

'But in order to sell plants I need the space promised.'

'And you shall have it!' Becca gave the merest shake of her head. She gave another sigh, a gutsy one this time. She picked up a pen with a fluffy pink thing on the end and played with it. 'You have no idea how let down I've been over the shop fittings. They promised to get them to me by the beginning of the month without fail. And I'm still waiting. What can I say? I have no control over external issues.' Putting her head onto one side, she quoted inaccurately, '*Mea pulpa*. I should know which companies are reliable and which are not. Blame the relocation. When I was working for Xteriors this absolutely would not have happened. But I promise you, Janey, you will have your extra retail space by the middle of April or heads will roll. Trust me!'

'We're missing out on sales, Becca. It's a key selling period.'

'And I'm only too aware of that.' She tutted and tapped the fluffy pink pen on the sheet of paper on her desk. 'The sales figures don't lie. It's not been good lately, has it?' There was only a hint of patronising but it was there.

Janey bit down on her frustration. 'And what about these uniforms? I can't see how practical they're going to be.'

Becca sucked in a breath and rolled her eyes. 'Do you know, I said the exact same thing to Clare. I said, Clare we've got to look after our staff. Keep them warm and dry in the winter, cool in the summer.' She shook her head in a regretful manner. 'I'm afraid Clare went straight ahead and ordered a shedload of them.' She sat back and spread her hands. 'It's a done deal, Janey. And I can't change them. Think of the money it would lose us. Money that we can ill afford. That Cheney House can ill afford.' She rose and came to perch on the edge of the desk nearest Janey. She took her hand. 'Do you think you could try them out, just for now. If not for little old me, then for Clare's sake? We just can't afford any other stuff at the moment. Maybe when things pick up, and I'm one hundred percent positive that it will, we'll all have a little rethink and then I promise you we'll take all feedback on board. I promise you that.' She stood up suddenly. 'And now we've had our little chat I really must get on, and so, I imagine, must you.'

Janey was outside the office door without realising she'd been dismissed. She hadn't said half the things she wanted to. Hadn't established what plant wholesaler Becca had agreed to buy from; hadn't really got a definitive date when the new plant sales centre would be open; hadn't discussed whether the snowdrop project could still go ahead. She'd been working on developing a brand-new snowdrop variety for some years but without success. Clare had always said to take as much time as she liked. Janey was fairly certain that philosophy didn't fit in with how Becca ran things. Quick results, and even quicker profits, seemed to be the order of the day.

Will came out of his office, as she began to descend the stairs. She hadn't seen him since the Camilla-in-the-lake incident. Her mouth twitching, she remembered the last time they'd spoken she'd been half-naked. He'd seemed stern and a bit cross then. He looked marginally more approachable today, in suit trousers and a snowy white, immaculately tailored shirt, his sober navy tie in a neat knot.

'Survived?' He pushed his specs up his nose.

'Survived what?' His question took her by surprise. If anything, she'd half expected him to join in with Becca and tell her off. Except it hadn't been a telling off, more a mild reproof, and not even that. Janey couldn't work it out.

'The invitation into the lion's den. She's quite a player, isn't she?' He smiled and it lit his face.

Janey nodded, not really knowing how to respond. It was only when she was back outside into the fresh March air and could think more clearly, she realised she didn't know how to take the comment. She didn't know if Will was paying Becca a compliment or criticising her. Looking up at the top floor of Cheney House she saw he was watching her from through the arched window on the landing. Ignoring him, she strode around the corner and into the plant sales office. She felt safe there. From what or whom she didn't want to analyse.

Chapter 7

The Galloping Galanthophile: April

A short blog from me this month. I'm sorry to say our new plant sales centre has suffered yet another delay, but I'm assured that it will be open just as soon as possible. Trust me, I'm as frustrated by all these delays as you must be.

Let's look on the bright side, spring has finally shown up and I'm sure you're all itching to get back out in your gardens. Just watch out for those April showers. This month at Cheney House is Lawn Month. Yes folks, it's time to examine your post-winter lawn and see what needs to be done. If you need to re-sow we sell grass seed to cover or repair any bald patches (and netting to stop those pesky birds). It's a good idea to use some moss killer if afflicted, and then give your lawn a really vigorous rake, and then feed. We sell everything you need plus some nice, sharp edging cutters to give your lawn that professional finish.

Pop by if you need advice with any of this, we're always happy to help.

As ever, happy gardening!

GG

The changes continued apace at Cheney House, with one exception. Janey champed at the bit and could only sit back and watch as the rest of the garden centre took shape, while the plant sales centre, the very heart of the whole operation, was running at the bare minimum. The spring sale had been a success, no surprise; she'd had to put the stock out at knock-down prices. Becca insisted on having the old cleared out, so they could start with fresh new stock. The problem being, Janey now had precious little stock to sell and a new plant centre yet to open. Consequently, there was very little for her to do. She hid in her beloved potting shed at the far end of the growing fields, researching techniques for the cultivation of a new variety of snowdrop and quietly fuming. It was now the end of April; if the new plant centre didn't open soon, they'd lose, to borrow a Becca phrase, a shedload of money. To make matters worse, Clare had gone on an extended holiday, claiming she was confident she was leaving the centre in good hands. Janey wasn't so sure. Becca said all the right things but there was very little follow-up action, certainly where plant sales were concerned. Clare had left Camilla in Janey's care and Janey took great comfort in the spaniel's company despite the dog's habit of stealing slippers and humping her beanbag.

Janey and Camilla were holed up in the shed one blustery rainy day, an icy gale biting in from the east, when Will paid them a visit.

He poked his head around the door and let in a howl of bitter wind. 'This looks cosy,' he said, obviously surprised.

Camilla got up, did a downward dog stretch and ambled over to him.

'Come in, come in,' Janey said, shock at his appearance making her irritable. 'You're letting all the heat out.'

'Sorry.' He came in and, with a little difficulty as the door had warped, latched it shut again. Reaching down to scratch Camilla's ears, he added, 'Thought I'd come over and fill you in with this month's takings. Graham said I'd find you here.'

'If I've got to do numbers, I'll need a refill,' Janey grumbled, and with a stretch of the arm, flicked on the kettle. 'Would you like a coffee too?' she asked, as she clocked his hopeful look. 'It's only instant.' She expected him to refuse. Didn't he only drink that posh ground-beans stuff?

'I'd love one. Thank you.' He pulled out the only other seating – a decrepit paint-stained stool – from its hiding place under the bench and sat down gingerly. Camilla immediately scrabbled up and made herself comfortable on his lap.

'Shove her off. She'll cover your suit with hair.'

'I don't mind. I've become rather fond of Cam.' He clucked the dog under her chin and her eyes rolled in ecstasy. 'It's very good of you to look after her while Gran is away.'

Janey levered herself out of the deckchair, which served as the main seating in the shed, and poured boiling water over coffee granules. She hadn't bothered to swill her mug out first and the only other one she could use was an ancient chipped one that had belonged to Howie, her predecessor. It proclaimed: 'Grumpy Old Gardening Git at Work' and would just have to do. She glanced at Will, immaculate as ever in his dark grey suit and a black wool coat, and wondered why he was really here. He could easily have emailed the figures over, which she could just as easily have ignored. She handed him his mug. 'No milk.'

'Then I'll take it black,' he replied, evenly.

Janey plonked herself back into the deckchair. She closed the book she'd been reading and, to her annoyance, Will picked it up.

'The Galanthophiles?' he said, raising an eyebrow. 'Sounds interesting,' he added, not quite sincerely.

Janey snatched it off him. 'I find it so.'

'Galanthophiles? What are they?'

'Snowdrop experts.' Janey didn't mean to be quite so curt. He put her on edge and she didn't know why. Must be the threat of doing numbers.

'Oh. Of course, you're working on a snowdrop project, aren't you?'

'Who said?' she asked defensively.

'Gran.'

Janey relaxed a little. If Clare trusted Will enough to tell him that, he couldn't be all bad. But then, he was her grandson.

'You're trying to develop a new bulb I understand? Gran seemed to think it's not easy.'

'Not easy at all but a new snowdrop variety could make a fortune. There are people out there willing to pay thousands for one. Clare has let me work on it,off and on, over the years. But only when work's slack,' she put in, hastily. 'It could make Cheney House famous.'

'And would you share any profits with the garden centre?' Will asked, a curious expression on his face.

'I'd give *all* profits over to Clare. After all, I'm using her time, her premises,' Janey said, stoutly. 'Besides.' She shrugged. 'I've got all I need. I don't need money. Well,' she corrected herself, 'only enough to live on. I'm not doing it for the money, although lots do. I'd do it to put Cheney House on the map. To make us a centre of excellence for snowdrops.'

'And is that the project over there?' He nodded to the serried ranks of potting trays, all neatly lined up and labelled. 'Looks very organised.'

'I have to be.'

'I like that. I'm an organised person myself. How do you go about it?' he asked, curiously.

'Are you really interested, or winding me up?'

Will laughed. 'I'm really interested.'

'Well,' she began, almost reluctantly, 'I have to be the bee.'

'Okay.'

'You don't understand, do you?'

'Not in the least,' he said, cheerfully.

Janey observed him. 'I'll explain it as simply as I can then.'

'Thank you.'

Janey examined him for sarcasm but detected none. 'So, I have to be the bee and the bee's job is to cross-pollinate. I take the pollen from each of the two parent plants I want to cross, harvest the seed and then plant them out to grow them on to the flowering stage. It's only then I see if I've been successful.' She paused and blew out a frustrated breath. 'Only no luck so far. Sometimes it happens naturally, so I have to keep a lookout in the woods. We get thousands of snowdrops there. People come from miles around to walk through them.'

'Sounds like a good thing to do. Bluebell woods are a big attraction nowadays, aren't they?'

'Yeah. We make a big thing of them too.' She grinned. 'Weather's normally better by then so we get more folk turning up.'

'It's all fascinating. I had no idea.' He looked genuinely impressed. 'Not, alas, my area of expertise, though.' He took a sip of coffee, grimaced and put the mug on the bench.

'Not like your fancy stuff I suppose?'

'Too hot.'

Janey felt ashamed of herself. Okay, he was so different from her as to be from a separate species but, thinking about it, he'd been quite kind to her. Going through all that difficult number stuff at that first meeting. Seeing that she needed some privacy after rescuing Camilla. Interested in the snowdrop project. Maybe he wasn't all that bad?

'I don't really know much about flowers. I collect Bonsai.'

She might have known. Those horrid miniature trees, bent like gnarly old men and sitting in tiny trays of gravel. They bore no resemblance to the trees she loved whatsoever. Her opinion of him plummeted.

'I've a particularly fine Chinese Elm. I see them more as a work of art, I suppose. I find them calming to look at.' He came back to himself and there was a hint of warmth in his pale face. 'Of course, they're not like your chestnut trees. I saw you dancing underneath them on my first day here. Do you ... do you do that a lot?'

'On certain days,' Janey answered, cagily. 'When the wind's fresh and there's sap in the air. You should try it. Can't dance under a Bonsai.' She let a giggle escape.

Will pulled a rueful expression. 'That's very true.' He levelled a look at her from behind his specs. 'I'll leave that sort of thing to you, shall I? I think you do it rather better than I ever will.' He smiled in that devastating way and his eyes twinkled in humour.

Their eyes met and Janey felt the air snatch in her throat. He was quite good-looking when you examined him closely. Sort of Gregory Peck circa *To Kill a Mockingbird*. Same lean cheekbones, same opaque dark eyes, same floppy black hair.

Will gave a little cough and reached for his mug of coffee. He drank and then adopted an efficient tone. 'Shall we get down to this month's figures? I always find it helps if I talk them through with a client rather than shove an email into their in tray. Too easy to ignore.'

Janey's face heated and she shifted uncomfortably. It had been exactly the thing she'd planned on doing.

'Was never any good at maths at school,' she muttered.

'No? I was. No surprise there I suppose. Tell you what though, Janey.' He leaned forward and grinned, impishly. 'I was terrible at dancing! Come on, I'll talk you through it all.'

Will walked back to the main house, hardly noticing the chilly weather. He couldn't believe he'd spent the last hour holed up in a stuffy shed, perched on an uncomfortable stool with a spaniel shedding hair all over his second-best suit, and a grumpy gardener for company. He was already craving a return visit, although he could survive without that chipped, filthy mug. It was as far from his normal routine as could be. And he needed routine; it made him feel safe. There was little about Janey that felt safe but he'd loved every second spent with her. She'd come alive when talking about her beloved snowdrops. Her enthusiasm had shone through the spiky reserve he normally encountered. And that throaty giggle had him rooted to the spot. She reminded him of a stray cat his grandmother had rescued when he was a little boy. Lashing out but curiously needy too. Will still bore the scars on his wrist from his attempts to stroke her. Pippin had eventually settled and learned to accept their overtures of affection with a bad-tempered grace – and then only on her terms. Will grinned. He rather thought Janey might be the same. The bigger question was, did he want to approach her with any overtures of affection? The image of her dancing under the trees flitted into his mind. Despite the heavy denim dungarees, he'd spotted lush breasts and long, work-toned legs. His blood quickened. He remembered, in the aftermath of Camilla's rescue, the tempting curve of Janey's neck as it led to an ivory shoulder, revealed when the cashmere throw was tugged by the boisterous spaniel. And she was so careless about her appearance. Unselfconscious about how beautiful she was. Her hair was inevitably a tangled mess, her fingernails permanently grimed and she always wore a good covering of mud or compost. On top of all of that, she came across as positively gruff. She was unlike any of the overly careful, exquisitely made-up women he usually dated. Her attitude to money was refreshing too. He'd tired of the women he took out. He never missed the quiver of interest when he explained what he did, or who his family were. The Cheney-Mortimers of Cheney House were well-known. Sometimes, he was convinced he'd glimpsed pound signs in his dates' eyes. He longed to be taken on merit, on who he was, rather than where he came from. No fear that Janey was drawn in by his money. And she didn't seem to care two hoots who his family was. He couldn't decide if she attracted or terrified him and thought it was probably both. Striding past the chestnut trees, he grinned even more. Maybe, on the next windy day, when he was absolutely sure there was no one about, he should try dancing under them for himself?

Chapter 8

ITALY

Clare eased herself back on the sun lounger and felt herself relax for the first time in what seemed like years. Certainly for the first time since leaving home for the airport. How had air travel become such an effort? The crowds, the queues, the endless security checks. What on earth had they thought she had hidden in her shoes? It had been awful. It wasn't until she had settled into her plane seat that she realised it was the first time she'd flown since Gerald's death. Somehow, he had smoothed her path through any airport or station so that they seemed to glide effortlessly past all the petty inconveniences that had made her confused and sweaty this time. Gerald had made everyone smile; he had charm and knew how to use it. Not for manipulative purposes but to make everything more pleasant – for everyone. He'd smoothed her path through life in much the same way and she missed him fiercely.

Adjusting her sun hat, she gazed at the view of the island of Capri, shimmering in an azure sky and sea. She and Gerald had gone there for part of their honeymoon and this was as close as she could bear to be. Darling Gerald, her Gem, her diamond, had only been dead for eighteen months and she couldn't – wouldn't – trample her grief-heavy espadrilles over the island and its memories. This hotel, suggested by a mutual friend, had seemed perfect. Not too far from Sorrento should she want something livelier, it hugged the steep Amalfi Coast and afforded spectacular views over the Bay of Naples. Built on a series of terraces, with the public rooms at the highest point, it had a swimming pool and a rocky platform overhanging the sea from which she could dive into the Mediterranean if she so wished. At the moment all she wanted to do was snooze in the sun. It was deemed far too chilly for most to sunbathe, but out of the sea breeze and in a sunny patch by the pool, to Clare's English-wintered limbs it was perfect.

A waiter wandered by and asked if the *signora* would like anything. On the brink of asking for a sparkling water, she changed her mind. She wasn't planning on doing anything more strenuous than reading in the sun today. 'Cinzano soda, *per favore*.' He gave a quick nod and disappeared. For a second she thought he'd been checking her out, and then she smiled. She was sixty-nine, for goodness' sake. She doubted he was much more than twenty. It was just the macho Italian way of making women feel appreciated. And put in their place. She stifled a giggle. In her youth, she would have been outraged, appalled and more than a little indignant. Now she was used to being invisible in middle age. Did sixty-nine still count as middle-aged? It must be. She refused to think of herself as being old. She allowed herself a moment or two to bask in the glow of being appraised as a desirable woman. But was she still desirable? The thought sobered her. Until Gerald had been very ill, towards the end of his life, they had enjoyed an active and affectionate sex life. It had been the thing that had brought them together and had never left their marriage. Blinking and blaming the strong sun for the sudden tears, she hardened her heart. He wouldn't want her to be unhappy. 'Gem, my diamond darling,' she murmured, 'I still love you and I always will, but I want to be happy at this precise moment. I want to lie in the sun in my rather fetching fuchsia-pink halter-neck swimsuit and matching pedicure, and sip a cocktail without thinking of the past or the future. It's too scary.'

She chose, instead, to think about Cheney House. It had belonged to Gem's family since the late seventeen hundreds and, in the usual way with big old houses, had proved far too expensive to maintain. On his inheritance he had been forced to decide whether to sell or diversify – and had compromised. Building on a life-long love of gardening, he'd hit upon the idea of developing Cheney House as an up-market garden centre. He'd had to sell some land in order to achieve his dream but it had all been worth it. At first, he'd even employed the old estate and house staff to help run it. Gwen's mother had been the house cook and had readily adapted to running the café, with Gwen taking over when she retired, and Howard had swapped from being head gardener of the grounds to head gardener of plant sales. He'd flourished in the new role and loved passing on his knowledge to customers. It had been touch-and-go at first but they'd made a success of it.

Mostly.

Clare had been barely eighteen when she'd got the job in the gift shop and met Gem. Gerald Cheney was then a resolute and somewhat eccentric bachelor of thirty-nine. They'd scandalised the tiny village of Bereford when they'd married, but all gossip had shrivelled when it had been proved a love match that had lasted.

Clare picked up her bottle of suntan lotion and rubbed some onto her forearms, her skin always seemed to get so dry these days. Nearly fifty years of happy married life. How had her life flown by so quickly? There were some regrets, not having more children being one. Clare would have filled the house with a whole rugger team of children but it wasn't to be. Regret that she didn't get on better with her daughter. Alicia was a remote creature and had left home as soon as she could and had married her army husband soon after. She wasn't one bit interested in the business but she had provided William, her grandson. Clare sighed fondly. Tightly buttoned up Will, permanently huddled over a computer. And those insipid girls he dated, all so tedious! He needed someone to bring him out of himself, to show him the frivolous side of life. He'd always been such a serious little boy and, as an adult, had done nothing but work. Through his exams and then with Keel and Wesson. She and Gem had always believed in working hard but that company demanded blood. And soon he'd be flying off again. If only she could persuade him not to take up this ridiculous job offer in the States and stay at Cheney House. It was a promotion but would it make him happy? Boston indeed. Why on earth would anyone want to live in Boston? There were times he reminded her so much of her darling Gem, although the charming side of Will was rather more low-key. Just as handsome and loving though. She felt tears threaten yet again.

Her drink arrived, courtesy of the same smiling waiter bearing a silver tray covered in a snowy cloth. He put it on the small table next to her, along with a tiny bowl of nuts.

'*Ecco qui!*'

'*Grazie.*'

'We have veal escalope on the menu, if the *signora* wishes.' He lingered and his presence irritated.

Was this how being a lone woman on holiday was going to be? She just wanted to be left with her thoughts. Oh Gem, I miss you. I don't want to be pestered by well-meaning but annoying waiters.

'Thank you. That is all.' This time she tried English. The clipped dismissal got through and he left. Picking up her drink and sipping it through a straw, she watched as the view of Capri hid itself behind a veil of tears.

Chapter 9

The Galloping Galanthophile: May

Hi everyone. First of all, I must start with an apology. I'm sorry April's blog was so short! Perhaps you've been too busy in your garden to be on a computer, though, and didn't have time to read it? Changes have been happening thick and fast around here and I'm glad to say the new plant centre is now open and just in time for you to stock up on your bedding plants. And why not come on in and try your hand at one of our brand new competitions? They're great fun and you can win some amazing prizes – vouchers to spend at Cheney House or a meal for four in Gwen's new restaurant. You have to try her Thai spiced noodles, they're delish! Treat yourself after a walk around our bluebell woods. The flowers are amazing this year and the fragrance is from heaven itself.

Top tips – you should have deadheaded your spring bulbs by now, although everything's a little late (on a similar note, protect your tender plants from the late frosts we're still having), dig in your summer flowering bulbs and plant up your onions if you're a veggie enthusiast. It's also a good time to get your patio planters sorted and your hanging baskets planted up – but only if you've got somewhere frost-free to keep them. We've got gazillions of all of the above if you want to mosey on down and spend some pennies. Graham also has new stocks of glazed patio containers in a stunning range of colours; the deep blue ones are gorgeous and a steal. Prices begin from as low as £15.99.

As ever, happy gardening – oh and keep an eye out for our brand-new website coming soon!

GG

Janey pressed return and entered the piece onto the blog. She could kick herself for not making more of an effort with the previous month's. Swearing volubly, she closed down her laptop and stretched her aching shoulders. Funny how she could dig all day and not notice the effects but a morning slaving over a computer knitted her muscles into four-ply. Becca had jumped on her about the lack of content in April's. She'd also hinted that the new website was something she would take full responsibility for and the Galloping Galanthophile blog would no longer be needed. Although Janey would be the first to admit she wasn't a natural at blogging, she'd miss doing it. She loved the customers' reactions to it when they came in, even if they assumed it was Graham who was the

Galloping Galanthophile and not her. Lots of her regulars were of the generation to remember *The Galloping Gourmet* on the television. He'd been a favourite of her grandmother's too. 'Ooh, that Graham Kerr,' she used to say. 'I'd casserole him anytime.' Some of the customers said much the same about Graham, although not to his face. He was popular with the older women; he was popular with everyone as he was easy-going and laidback. Janey didn't mind, she had no reason to feel precious over the blog, it was only a glorified advertisement feature for the garden centre after all. It amused her, more than anything, that they should think the Galloping Galanthophile was Graham. Maybe it was the G clue they picked up on? Her phone pinged. It was a text from the man himself to say she was late for the staff meeting and Becca had something important to announce. Janey swore some more. Becca always had something important to announce.

Opening the door to the office, Janey was greeted by her manager's sour smile and a sheepish grin from Graham. It seemed to sum him up at the moment. It was as if he had something he wanted to share with her but couldn't. She wondered if his relationship had progressed with Becca and felt queasy at the thought. Surely dating your boss wasn't a good idea. Will followed her, bringing in a chair from his office for her to sit on.

When they'd all passed around coffee and settled, Becca paused dramatically, sucked in a deep, shuddering breath and then began speaking.

'Now we are *all* here,' she said, with a barely concealed sneer in Janey's direction, 'I can begin the meeting. Graham, what news on the lake dredging?'

Janey saw him consult his scribbled notes.

'Dredging company finished two weeks ago so I've now got to plant up sections and make good the bank. The blokes made a bit of a mess with the digger and all their equipment, but it couldn't be helped. I've more or less finished upgrading the boathouse, just got to paint it, and the punts are arriving on Friday.'

Becca winced visibly. 'Cutting it a bit fine, Graham. I wanted a soft launch of the boating lake as soon as.' She glanced out of the window at the light patter of rain which was falling. 'Or should I say when the weather improves?'

'Forecast is good for next week,' Graham answered, cheerfully. 'The lake won't be perfect but folk'll be able to take a boat out. Won't look established until next year.'

'There's nothing more you can do?'

Graham shrugged. 'Can't force plants to grow.'

'Can't we buy some established ones in? For more impact?'

'Yeah. At a price. I've exceeded the budget as it is. And no point planting anything until the banks have stabilised. They'll just wash away otherwise.'

Becca's nostrils flared. 'Well, it will have to do,' she said, sharply. 'And what about safety equipment?'

'All sorted.'

'Good.' She turned her laser glare on Will. 'Financial report please.'

Will cleared his throat. 'Restaurant's up by fifteen percent compared to this time last year.'

'Excellent, Will. That'll be the new themed menus I suggested,' Becca said in a complacent tone. 'Wattana working out?'

'Yes. Seems to be. Gwen says she works incredibly hard and the new Thai specials are popular.'

Wattana, or Tana as she preferred to be known, was a tiny, exquisite woman who was a powerhouse in the kitchens. She'd won Gwen round instantly.

'I thought they'd be, despite Gwen's protestations.' Becca sniffed.

'To be fair to Gwen,' Janey put in, 'she was more worried about workload than different menus. She can turn her hand to cooking most things but I agree with Will, Tana is proving to be a real asset.'

'Thank you, Janey,' Becca said, with a tight smile and narrowed eyes, 'but perhaps you can restrict your comments to your area of expertise? Will, I'm so sorry about the interruption. Please continue.'

Janey felt her cheeks heat at the humiliation. She gave Becca the finger underneath her notebook. Bitch! She felt Will glance at her before he continued.

'Gift shop sales have taken a slight dip.'

'Only to be expected, Will,' Becca said, smoothly, 'with the relocation and everything. I'm positive things will improve along with increased footfall. And once we have the garden furniture salesroom established, that will impact. Graham, when's the first delivery expected? Next week?' At his nod, she blew out a relieved breath. 'Good. Good. Everything seems to be taking shape as planned.' Her head gave a smug wobble.

As *you* planned, Janey thought, mutinously.

'And plant sales?'

Janey felt Will shift uneasily. 'Drop of fifty per cent,' he said, eventually, 'compared to the same sales period last year.'

Becca sat back and steepled her fingers together. She gazed

at Janey. 'Well, well, well,' she said, softly, 'and what have you to say to that, Janey?'

'Well, well, well, Becca,' Janey began, anger flaring, 'what I have to say is this. It's hardly surprising seeing as for nearly two months I've hardly had any stock to sell and what stock I have had has been sold at knock-down prices. Plus, the plant centre not opening on time and being in a complete mess hasn't exactly encouraged customers. Or do we call them *footfall* now? And I'd like to discuss the wholesaler you've chosen to use. I'm knee-deep in complaints about plant quality. What sales I have had, I've had to refund a third.' While being a slight exaggeration, this was true. Since Becca had insisted on over-ruling Janey and using an unknown and cheaper wholesaler, plant quality had deteriorated.

'Then perhaps you should think about your sales advice. Selling the wrong plant at the wrong time for the wrong spot in the garden will only result in complaints and poor return custom.'

Janey's resentment bubbled over. This was too much. 'There is nothing wrong with my sales advice and there never has been in the last thirteen years I've worked here. During which time, I'd like to add, I've built up a loyal customer base. One with a good rate of return. Perhaps, Becca, you should restrict *your* comments to *your* area of expertise? If I'm selling rubbish, our customers will notice. And they have.'

Becca's eyes glittered. 'We will continue this discussion after the main meeting. And I would appreciate it, Janey, if you address your comments in a manner appropriate to a professional meeting.'

'I will if you will, *Becca*.'

There was a tense silence. Will and Graham shifted uneasily and then Will began speaking again, adding detail to his financial report. The others listened but the atmosphere remained fraught. He concluded by saying quietly, 'And I rather think Janey has a point, Becca. Takings are down because there has been little stock to sell. I predict a rise next month with an increase in seasonal sales.'

'Mmm. We shall see. Thank you, Will. Thank you, Graham. And now, if you wouldn't mind leaving us, Janey and I have other matters to discuss.' Becca stared Janey down. 'Don't we, Janey?'

Chapter 10

When the men left, Becca didn't speak straightaway. Instead she let Janey fume silently while she wandered around the office, tweaking the Roman blind at the window, brushing an imaginary speck off her trouser suit jacket. Janey's unease prickled. What was the woman up to? She was just about to remind her boss that she had to get back to work when Becca poured them both fresh coffees.

'I don't know about you,' she said, her demeanour softening, 'but I could do with this. Always find these meetings such a trial, don't you?' She blew out a breath and collapsed onto her desk chair. Smoothing a hand over her immaculate hair, she went on: 'It's so hard being a woman in a man's world, Janey.' She put a hand to her forehead and exhaled dramatically. 'Always having to play the tough guy.' Raising beseeching eyes, she added, 'And I'm really not. Not once you get to know me. I'm a big soft mushy thing inside. Terrified most of the time. I so want to do a good job for Clare. I feel the weight, the burden of responsibility so heavily. This is why I need you on my side, Janey.'

It was the first time Clare's name had been mentioned. With her whole heart Janey wished she was back from holiday. She owed her employer a huge amount and she was sure Clare wouldn't have approved of the plant sales being side-lined like this. Clare was always adamant that plants, research and advice was at the heart of what they did at Cheney House. She sipped her coffee suspiciously; she wouldn't have been surprised if there was weed killer in it. As she drank she thought through her approach. She was still seething but instinct told her it wasn't the tactic to use on Becca. It had only got her angry too, and now, with the men out of the way, it looked as if she was playing the nicey-nicey game. Well, two could play at that.

'I can see how seriously you take running Cheney House in Clare's absence,' she began. 'I'm sure she will applaud your efforts. After all, we're like one happy family here.' Or were, Janey added in her head. 'Clare always appreciates hard work and loyalty and she'll see, when she comes back, just how much change you've put in place.'

Becca allowed herself to preen a little. 'Well, thank you, Janey.'

Janey wished she wouldn't keep using her name. Was it some kind of management technique? Whatever it was, it was profoundly irritating.

'Is there any news on when she's coming back?' She tried to keep the hope out of her voice.

'No idea, I'm afraid. Touring Italy and having the most wonderful time. Lucky thing. I'd love to take a holiday but there's so much to do. It was very good of you to take on

Camilla. I do hope she's not proving a nuisance. Stopping you working? Getting in the way? We could always kennel her.'

Janey sat on the anger, which threatened a return and to spiral out of control. No one was going to put Camilla in kennels. She'd hate it.

'She's absolutely no trouble whatsoever. In fact the customers love her.'

'Well, I suppose that's all right. I just don't want the place looking unprofessional. We're here to do a job, after all.'

'And Camilla helps,' Janey defended the dog, stoutly, 'I make sure she goes nowhere near the restaurant or the gift shop and she's too lazy most of the time to jump up at anyone. I had strict instructions she shouldn't be kennelled from Clare herself.' Janey gave Becca a level look. 'And you know how Clare dotes on her dog. She wouldn't be at all happy if she found out we'd gone against her wishes.'

'Indeed,' Becca said, faintly. 'We wouldn't want to do that.'

Janey could see Becca thinking through her next response; her thin mouth was working as if desperate to say something. If you touch one hair on that dog's head, I'll do acts of unspeakable violence to you, Janey thought, as she glowered at her boss. Or, at the very least, I'll throw you and your scrawny little arse into the lake. And make sure there's no lifebuoy anywhere near. Luckily, Becca had glanced down and was studying Will's report and didn't notice the death glare.

'You know,' she said softly, 'the figures from plant sales really are a little worrying, Janey.'

'And, as I've said, not surprising considering the constraints the plant centre has been under. As Will said, and I agree with him, sales will pick up now we're into our busy season. I've just got things sorted in time. We've missed part of the peak sales for early bedders but, as the weather has been so cold, I'm confident it will have delayed buyers coming out. As soon as the sun shines and the days warm up, folk will flood in looking for ways to brighten up their gardens.'

Becca put the report to one side. 'I hope you're right, Janey. I really do. After all, neither of us wants to let Clare down, do we?'

'And the other thing,' Janey said, ignoring the blatant attempt at emotional blackmail, 'I'd like to go back to our original wholesaler. The plants from Jardeen-Heffler really aren't good enough. Our customers know their stuff, and they know sub-quality stock when they see it.'

Becca made a little moue with her perfectly pink-glossed lips. 'I'll look at the figures and consider it.'

'After all, it's no good selling plants if we only have to give refunds all the time, is it?' Janey tried not to hiss the response through clenched teeth. The woman was insufferable.

'True.'

Janey's shoulders relaxed a little. Had she won the meeting?

'I'd best get back then. Things to do. You're not the only one working hard.' She rose to leave. She was wrong about winning the meeting. Becca had saved her best until last.

'Just before you go, Janey. I have to share a direct message with you from Clare. It's an email. It actually came last week but I was finding the right time to tell you. Clare wants you to stop with all this snowdrop nonsense. She wants us to become a centre of excellence for fuchsias. Or maybe hostas, or something. Anything, in fact, apart from snowdrops.' She fluttered her lashes. 'I know only too well how much of a wrench this will be, but can you give it some thought? Close the door on the way out, will you?'

Will watched Janey as she ran, like a thing possessed, towards the chestnut trees. He'd hated the meeting. Hated Becca's snide put-downs, hated having to deliver numbers which, no matter how hard he tried, couldn't lie about the dire returns from the plant sales. He'd hated most of all leaving Janey alone with Becca. Janey could defend herself but she was no match for Becca's expert manipulation. He'd listened from his office next door for raised voices, ready to barge in if necessary. Who was he kidding? It was hardly his style. But he would have knocked on the door and interrupted if he sensed things were getting too tricky for Janey. But all he'd heard was a muted conversation and then the door close quietly.

For the hundredth time he puzzled over just how Becca Woods had come to be employed by his grandmother and just why she had been left in such a position of authority while Clare was away. His grandmother's most recent text had been last week. Full of wine and Italian sunshine, it sounded as if she was having a wonderful time. He certainly didn't begrudge her a holiday; goodness knows she had had a hard time caring for his grandfather, but it couldn't have come at a worse time for Cheney House. It wasn't that Becca was doing a terrible job exactly, most of her decisions had been firmly based in sound financial sense. It wasn't even that he disliked her management style – he'd experienced far worse. There was simply something about the woman he couldn't quite trust.

And, like Janey, he couldn't understand why she'd prioritised other things over plant sales. A boating lake and a few local crafts were all well and good but plants were at the core of Cheney House. Should he get in touch with Clare and risk ruining her holiday? What point would it serve? He could handle the situation. But the Becca–Janey dynamic worried him. It was beginning to feel like workplace bullying. And it wasn't fair. Should he go and talk to Janey? He hovered in an agony of indecision; he wasn't sure how welcome he'd be.

He watched as Janey emerged from behind a tree. The hand she scrubbed over her eyes and her distraught face decided him.

Chapter 11

Janey was startled to discover Will waiting for her in the plant sales office. Becca had renamed it the Designated Plant Sales Administration Room. A grand title, which was completely belied by the reality. While the plant sales centre looked spick and span with its new, navy-blue glossy racks and plant troughs, and white-tiled floor, the same couldn't be said of the office. Same old leather sofa, beaten up office chairs and chipped desk. Will looked out of place in his immaculately pressed trousers. Inconsequentially, Janey wondered where his jacket was. The rain had stopped but it was still chilly. Spring was stubbornly refusing to put in an appearance. It was about time they had some consistently good weather. At least then, sales would rise. And Becca might just get off her back. She couldn't see what Graham saw in her and, to be honest, he was welcome to her. It was about time he recognised the woman he really needed had been working alongside him for the last ten years. Ooh, she wasn't thinking straight. Sitting down abruptly on the arm of the sofa, she plucked at her clammy polyester shirt.

'God, I bloody hate this thing.'

'The new uniform?' Will nodded. 'I agree. Much prefer the dungarees.' There was a pause, then he added, 'Have you been dancing under the chestnut trees again?'

Janey felt her face heat and tears threaten. 'No,' she croaked.

'I'm sorry, I didn't mean to upset you.' Will said, seeming shocked. He came to stand nearer her and didn't seem to know what to do with his hands. 'I saw you come out from behind them. Please don't cry. She's not worth getting upset over.'

'I'm not upset. I'm furious. Fucking furious!' Janey shot to her feet and began to pace. 'How could that woman do it? I can't give the project up.' She whirled around to face him and jabbed a finger at him. 'I will not give up the project!'

'Give up what?' Will asked, nonplussed. 'And who's asked you to give it up?'

Janey scrubbed her hands through her hair. It made it stick out any old how. 'My snowdrop project. That Becca. That cow Becca, that's who has asked me to stop it.'

'But you've spent years on it.'

'Seven to be precise. Seven years.' Janey held up the right number of fingers to make her point. 'Did you know it can take up to five years to get a snowdrop to flower from seed?' She flung herself back onto the sofa. 'All she cares about is profit and instant results. Well, it doesn't happen like that in the world of plants and someone ought to tell her.' She crossed her arms and blew out a frustrated breath. 'Seven years,' she repeated. 'Wasted.'

Janey watched as Will began making tea. 'My sainted mother always said the one thing you need in a crisis is a pot of tea.' Once made, he took a mug over to her.

She accepted it without thanks and stared gloomily into its contents. 'Not enough milk,' she muttered, holding it back out to him.

Will tried again and took the now milky tea over to Janey. Holding his own mug, he slid in next to her on the sofa. 'Surely Becca can't be serious about you giving up the snowdrop project?'

'Oh, I think she is.' Janey swallowed tea, noisily. 'Can't be measured you see. Can't make dinky little financial reports on it,' she sneered, missing his flinch. 'Can't be allocated targets for me to fail at.' She sat up suddenly, spilling tea all over her navy shirt. 'That's it!' She turned a glowing face to Will. 'The bloody woman wants me to fail. She wants me out.' Janey's gut clenched in panic. She didn't know what she'd do without this job. There were few other garden centres and nurseries around and none like Cheney House. 'She wants to get shot of me. Why?'

'I don't think that's true.'

'You do! I can see you thinking the same. Okay, I'm a difficult woman to manage but I'm a skilled member of the team and even if she does want me out, it makes no sense. It would take months to recruit and train up someone new, even if they found a replacement straightaway.' She sighed. 'No, I'm trouble. Always have been. Same at school. They couldn't wait to get rid of me either.'

'Why didn't school suit you?'

Janey huffed. 'No good at maths. Reading and writing okay, but too clumsy at P.E. to get on any team. Never fitted in,' she added, gloomily. 'Never found my thing until I was sent to a garden project on the edge of Bridport. And once I felt the compost under my fingernails, once I picked my first peas in the summer and ate them straightaway out of the pod, I knew I'd found my home. My tribe. Clare knew the project leader. Interviewed me, got the job here and have never left.'

'Gran could see your potential. I had a friend at school a bit like you. Fantastic artist, prolific reader, brain like a knife but rubbish at anything to do with numbers. He was diagnosed with dyscalculia. Once he found that out, it stopped him feeling stupid.'

'What's dyscalculia?'

'Put simply, it's when you have problems with numbers. You can't hold them in your head to calculate with them, can't remember them. It's a bit like the number's version of dyslexia. I bet anything you can remember the letters part of your car registration but not the numbers.'

'Too right,' Janey snorted. 'It's WUS.'

Will laughed. 'I don't think anyone would call you a wuss, Janey.'

'Well they wouldn't and live.'

'It doesn't mean you're stupid, far from it. It's just that you have a bit of your brain that works differently from other people's. If anything, you're probably more intelligent than most, as you've had to learn strategies to cope.'

Janey was silent for a moment, digesting the information. 'Sounds like me,' she admitted.

'You can get yourself tested, I believe.'

Janey repressed the shudder that went through her. The word 'test' brought back too many awful memories of school. Even so, the thought was intriguing. 'What, even as an adult?'

'I think so, yes.' Will looked puzzled. 'I'm amazed school didn't look into it for you.'

'I never stayed in one long enough for the paperwork to catch up.'

'Okay. I'll get in touch with Prakash then. He might know.'

'Is that your pal with the dyscalculia?'

Will nodded.

'What does he do now?'

Will grinned. 'Shit-hot defence lawyer. Told you it's nothing to do with I.Q.'

Janey managed a laugh and then immediately sobered. 'So, if I'm not stupid, why does Becca want to get rid of me?'

'We still haven't established that's what's happening.'

'Don't think it takes an Einstein to work it out. And do you know what else she suggested?' Her anger enflamed again, as she remembered what Becca had suggested. 'She wants to put Camilla in kennels!'

'What? Why?'

'Thinks she makes the place look unprofessional.'

'Bollocks she does. And Cam would hate it. There's no chance of that happening. If necessary, she can come home with me.' He stopped. 'Although it might be tricky. I'm in a no-pets-allowed apartment at the moment.'

Janey glanced at Will, amused. He couldn't be all bad if he was willing to risk his tenancy agreement. 'Don't worry, she's staying with me, right by my side where I can keep an eye on her. Don't want to give Becca any excuses to get rid of *her*!' She twisted to face him. 'Can you get hold of Clare? Becca said the request I stop the snowdrop project came directly from her, but it doesn't sound like your gran to do anything like that. She was the one who encouraged me in the first place. There's something about all this I'm not happy with. I'm sure Clare would have forty fits if she knew what's been going on.'

'I'll have a go.' Will sighed. 'She's being a bit evasive at the moment. But I promise I'll try.' He got up and put his mug on the desk. He stared at it, thoughtfully, for a moment. 'I agree though, Janey. There's something about all this I don't like either. Call it instinct.'

Janey slurped back the remains of her tea. 'You know something, Will?'

He turned and smiled at her. 'What's that?'

'You're not half-bad. For an accountant, that is.'

He grinned ruefully. 'For a Bonsai-owning accountant, you mean?'

'Well, I might have to overlook the Bonsai. What do you see in them, by the way?'

'I don't know.' Will gave a short laugh, looking embarrassed. 'They're a neat, quiet sort of a plant I suppose, don't need all that much looking after.'

Janey roared. 'Nothing like me then.'

'No, Janey,' Will said, and gazed down at her with shuttered eyes. 'They're nothing like you.' He gave an enigmatic smile and left.

Janey stared after him. He could be awfully James Stewart-like sometimes. He had the same deeply moral and utterly decent quality. A quiver of something unidentifiable and rather wonderful ran through her.

Chapter 12

ITALY

She hadn't seen him in years! She'd always thought him the spit of Rock Hudson in *Pillow Talk*. And there he was, sitting alone on the hotel's breakfast terrace, gazing, as everyone did, towards the magnificent view.

Clare was assailed by a sudden fit of shyness. Would Leopoldo remember her? It had been, she thought for a moment, over thirty years since they'd all shared that incredible yachting holiday around the Adriatic Coast. He was the youngest of a trio of brothers who had been at the same school as Gem. All three had been Italian by birth, gregarious by nature and, in later life, wealthy in pocket. She took the moment to appraise him. In his forties he had been incredibly good-looking, almost too much so, with luxurious black hair and a wide face with movie-star symmetrical features. Now he must be well over seventy. He had weathered, in that annoying way men do, to become less showy but infinitely more attractive. The black hair had been replaced by a silver mane, still thick and shiny and much more distinguished. The oh-so-smooth olive-toned skin was creased by age and showing the humanity of the man.

Clare began to back away. Leopoldo wouldn't remember her. They'd only met about half a dozen times. He'd come to their wedding and they had shared his yacht for a few weeks. He had been partnered by the woman who would become his wife, an arctic blonde named Carla. The women had not got on and Gem had used it as the excuse to cut short the holiday and fly on to Malta.

Conscious of her hair, which was in desperate need of a colour, and lips bare of even a hint of lip gloss, Clare turned to head down to the pool. After all, what would she say to him, even if he did recognise her? She backed into the cocktail waiter, the same one who had been so overly solicitous the other day – it would be him – and trod on his foot. He dropped the tray he'd been holding, thankfully empty, with a tremendous clang on the terracotta tiles.

'*Scusi signora,*' he said with a smile, and used it as an excuse to hold her by the waist for a second.

Clare bent to retrieve the tray and gave it back to him. 'Oh darling, I'm so sorry. I hope I haven't hurt you?'

The disturbance was enough for Leopoldo to look over. He stood up and strode across the terrace to greet her. 'Clare! *Amore mio.*' He clasped her hands and kissed her on both cheeks.

The waiter gave a graceful nod, as if to acknowledge the older man's prior claim, and disappeared.

'Leo, I can't believe it's you!' She allowed him to lead her to his table, the best one on the terrace of course, and sank down on the rattan chair. She felt the pattern of the weave press into the back of her thighs and plucked, self-consciously, at her thin robe. 'I was on my way for a swim.'

'*Bravo!* I will join you later but first we have coffee, *si? Che ne dici?*'

His Italian accent had thickened over the years. She remembered his English being practically perfect back in the day. He poured coffee from an elegant silver pot and she watched as the aromatic liquid slid into the cup. She had not the first notion of what to say. During their brief acquaintance Leopoldo, his good looks and extravagant European lifestyle, had bewildered and alienated her; it was so different to how she and Gem lived. She'd always puzzled over why he and Gem had been such great friends. Gem had always considered him one of his closest, although they hadn't been in contact for years. Sipping the hot, strong coffee enabled her to collect her thoughts. Placing the cup carefully back on its saucer, she said, 'Leo, what are you doing here? It's such a coincidence. If I remember rightly, you don't come from this part of Italy. How on earth have you ended up here? It's not a particularly well-known hotel.'

'Ssh, my love, you will hurt Angelo's feelings. He prides himself on providing discreet luxury that is well-known, but only to those who choose to seek it.' Leopoldo smiled and well-grooved lines etched themselves around his eyes.

A man who smiles a lot, Clare observed.

'And, no, I am not on holiday but,' at this he spread his hands, 'here I would come for relaxation, so maybe I will stay, eh?'

'What are you really doing here, Leo?' she asked. 'It's beyond coincidence.'

'Ah, and so it is.' He steepled his fingers together in an arch and shrugged. Pure Italian. 'I cannot lie. I rang Cheney House and spoke to your grandson.'

'Will?' Clare half rose in alarm. 'There's nothing wrong is there?'

'Be assured, all is well in England. I wanted to see you and,' another little shrug, 'when I found out you were in Italy, how could I resist? Will told me where you were staying. I sailed the *Chiara* down yesterday.'

'You didn't come to Gem's funeral.' Clare let the blunt words hang. She had been bitterly disappointed that one of her husband's best friends hadn't bothered.

Leo chewed his lip, tears glistened. He reached over and clasped her hands. 'I was distraught, trust me. I am so sorry I could not be there. Business, you know. Stuck in Alaska in a snow-bound airport. Carla was in no hurry to reach me, possibly did not want to reach me. Things were, by that point—' He released her hands and sat back, letting the sentence trail. 'Well, we are divorced now.' He gave Clare a tight smile.

'I'm sorry.'

'I am not.' He gave an evil chuckle. 'She married me for my money, she got it.' He lifted his coffee cup in salute. '*Po, po, po*. And now it is gone!'

Clare thought she knew Leo better than that. She gave him an old-fashioned look. 'Apart from the lot you had stashed away without her knowledge.'

He remained silent, adopting a dignified air. '*Possibilmente*,' he said finally. 'But Clare, what is a man without a yacht or two, a hideaway in Monaco, an apartment in Paris?'

She laughed. He looked so hurt and innocent that she couldn't help herself. It was the first time she'd laughed in a long time. She hadn't laughed since Gem had been diagnosed with cancer, hadn't laughed through the roller coaster of his treatment. Hadn't laughed in the eighteen months since his death. Not properly. Not like this. A real bellyaching, rib-squeezing laugh.

'*Bene.* It is good to hear you laugh.'

Clare was aware of him studying her intently.

'I am truly sorry about Gerald. My friend. Your Gem. He was a fine man. *Magnifico.*'

'Thank you.'

'And you, Clare, *amore mio*, how are you?'

'I'm fine.'

'Oh you English!' Leo rolled his eyes. 'So – how do you say it, *impassibile*?' He drew a finger across his lips in a dramatic gesture. 'So tight-lipped.'

'I think you mean stiff upper-lipped,' Clare said, on the remnant of a laugh. How had she forgotten the man's ability to make her roar with laughter? Then she sobered. 'It's been hard. We were married for nearly half a century.'

'You were soul mates.'

'Yes.' It came out on a long, heart-wrenching sigh. 'I miss him so much, Leo. I still reach for him in bed, still look round for him. Sometimes I think I can still smell his aftershave lingering in the flat. As if he's just splashed some on and popped out for a minute. But he hasn't popped out, he's never coming back.' She clenched her jaw and screwed her eyes shut to stop herself from breaking down. The laughter had swerved into tears in a second.

'Cry, Clare. Let it come out. It is only natural you should grieve for your beautiful husband.'

She snatched a paper serviette off the table and pressed it against her eyes, refusing to sob in front of a man she hadn't seen for thirty years and, even then, had hardly known. Not really. 'No. It's not the right place or time.'

Leo swore harshly in Italian under his breath. 'You English,' he repeated. 'There is no right place or time for grief.' Giving her time to recover, he ordered more coffee and some pastries. When they came, he poured them both fresh cups and wolfed down an almond croissant.

'Sorry,' she said eventually, not able to meet his eyes.

Leo spread his hands. 'For what? For loving your husband? For mourning the man and the life you had together?' He shook his head. 'Do not be sorry. The depth of your grief shows the extent of your love.' He broke off a fragment of croissant. 'Here, eat.' Nodding to the coffee, he added, 'Drink.'

Despite herself, Clare smiled. 'The power of food?'

'What can I say? I'm Italian!' Leo pursed his lips and pulled a face.

She thought he'd pursue the subject of Gem, but instead, he asked, 'And how is the business? How is the *bella* Cheney House?'

Clare swallowed some coffee. The pastry, delicious though it was, had stuck in her tear-enflamed throat. 'I can't lie. We've been through some difficult times but I've put in a new general manager and have high hopes for her, and I've got a darling team working for me. They're all bursting with new ideas, which I'm hoping will breathe new life into the place. We're relaunching soon.'

'You won't give up on the place?'

Clare looked shocked. 'Never! It's my life's work, and Gem's.'

'It is the perfect season in *Inghilterra* now,' Leo added, wistfully. '*Primavera*.'

'Spring,' Clare echoed, thinking of walks around the lake with her beloved Camilla.

'Oh, there is nothing like an English spring. I miss it.'

'What made you come back to live in Italy?' Clare asked, although with the Bay of Naples spread before them it seemed a ridiculous question. She knew he and Carla had lived in England for some time.

'Carla,' Leo said, simply. 'She did not like the dull wet winters. She liked the sunshine, the lifestyle. The shopping in *Milano* and *Roma*. Staff were cheaper, also.'

Clare was beginning to get a picture of what Carla had been like as a wife. She tried another bite of almond croissant and this time found it palatable. More than palatable; it was delicious.

'And what after breakfast, eh? A swim?' Leo asked.

'A swim would be nice.' Clare smiled at him in gratitude. She had thought she'd wanted to be alone, but in fact, all she had craved was the right company.

Chapter 13

Becca had been hinting long and hard about the arrangements for the grand reopening. She had someone famous, someone *very* famous, who was going to preside over the tape cutting. Or so she claimed. Rumours had been flying around about who it might be for weeks.

Despite her misgivings about the woman, and despite their fractured relationship, Janey had to admit, albeit through clenched teeth, that Becca seemed to be making a success of Cheney House. There were far more customers about, Gwen and Tana were flat out in the café, Graham was busy overseeing the boating lake, and plant sales were up. Janey was still getting complaints about quality, however, and vowed to tackle Becca again at the next staff meeting. Yawning, she switched off the computers in the office and sat in the soft twilight. It had been a busy day and she had no energy left to confront Becca over anything tonight. It was something else to add to her ever-growing list of things to do. With Graham over at the lake most of the time, it had fallen to her to oversee everything in the garden centre proper, including sales of all the landscaping stock and aggregates, which had previously been his responsibility. She'd had to come rapidly up to speed on everything to do with fencing, paving slabs and summer houses, not to mention grades of gravel – who would have thought there could be so many different types? She shrugged on her fleece, scowling as she did so. The jacket, which was part of the new uniform, was far too thin. In one of those about-turns, at which British weather excels, the weather had turned hot and sunny, but only during the day. The early mornings and nights were still chilly enough to warrant sales of the woolly stuff Janey liked to encourage her customers to use to protect their more tender plants against frosts. Zipping up her jacket, she smiled to herself; the plant fleece, especially the heavy-weight thirty-gram stuff, would be a lot warmer. As she checked through the plant sales area and went out to patrol the garden shed section, making sure no one had been left on the premises before she locked up, she pondered on how best to broach Becca on returning to their original plant wholesaler. A tall shape detached itself from one of their premier twelve-by-eight Forest Overlaps.

'Bloody Nora, Graham, you made me jump! What are you doing loitering in the shadows behind the garden sheds? You nearly gave me a heart attack.'

'Sorry Janey, my lovely. Didn't mean to frighten you.' He looked around. 'Got a bit homesick for the old place, is all. Miss the smell of the timber.'

Janey took a deep breath in and inhaled the rich aroma of untreated wood. She agreed; it was a smell she was fond of too. He looked so forlorn; she immediately forgave him all things Becca but couldn't help being a little impatient with him. He was being pathetic.

'We're only the other side of the car park, Gray. You're free to come and see us any time. Could have blinkin' well done with you today, when a bloke wanted twenty bags of Blue Valley Slate and let me load them all into his pick-up while he looked on.' She ricked her head left and right. 'Think I've done my neck in. Don't fancy a drink down the Star and Garter, do you?' She began to move off adding, 'But you've probably got plans with Miss Fancy-Pants.'

'No, not tonight. And, you know what? A drink in the pub sounds great. Haven't been for ages.'

Graham helped her lock up, and after putting Camilla on the lead, they strolled the short distance to the pub. Like a lot of Devon villages, the centre consisted of the church, a village green and the pub. Luckily, Bereford had kept its pub going, due no doubt to its idyllic setting next to the green, which was complete with a duck pond. Janey settled on a bench outside. The other reason the Star and Garter survived was its reputation for food. With the tourist season coming into sway, even this early in the year, the pub was packed with diners.

'Pint?' Graham asked.

'You bet. Cider please. And cheese and onion crisps. Two packets, I'm starving.'

As there was a cold edge to the breeze, there was no one else sitting outside. Janey took a moment to enjoy the squawk of a late duck scrabbling to get into the duck house. There was a flurry of feathers, a last wag of its tail and then it disappeared. She hoped someone would be along to pull the door secure before it went completely dark and Mr Fox paid a call. Camilla gave a warning throat growl and Janey tightened her hold on her. She didn't want a repeat of the day when the dog dived into the lake. Satisfied there were no more tempting ducks around, Camilla settled down to a lie. Then all was silent, save the wind trembling through the weeping willows on the green. There were three of them, the centre one being the tallest and most graceful. Janey was fond of a *Salix pendulina*. Beautiful trees, especially in summer. Her skin itched to go and stand beneath them and breathe in their shivery murmurs, but she stayed where she was and enjoyed the view instead. It was a truly lovely place. Janey took in a great mouthful of air and forced her shoulders to relax. Yes, it had been a hard day but she didn't want to work anywhere else. Her flat, above a converted stable block, was minutes away. Berecombe, on the coast, provided her with everything she needed and this pub was the hub of her social life. All her life's needs were met within a five-mile radius of Cheney House. Some would consider her boring. Some would think her life dull. But Janey was happy in a small village, in a tight-knit community. She knew everyone, and most people accepted her eccentricities. It was no coincidence that one of her favourite films was *It's a Wonderful Life*. Bereford was her very own Bedford Falls. With a new job would inevitably come a house move, and she didn't want to move. Squashing down the feeling of queasy panic, which was threatening, she realised she didn't want any upheaval. The thought of a new job, new work colleagues, a new part of the country, filled her with horror. It would be like changing schools all over again. Never fitting in, always teetering on the edge of whatever was going on, being the subject of gossipy chatter hidden behind hands and smirks. She'd be buggered if she'd let a jumped-up, stiletto-wearing, overly made-up bitch of a manager make her leave. And to think she'd tried to give Becca a chance at the beginning! For the hundredth time she wished Clare would come back.

'Penny for them?' Graham returned and put their drinks down on the table. He fished out her crisps from his pocket, flung them at her and ripped open a packet of peanuts for himself. 'Packed in there,' he said. Taking a long gulp of lager, he went on to detail his day at work, which apparently involved untangling an errant eight-year-old out of the rope attached to a lifebuoy.

He wasn't really interested in what she'd been thinking. Janey wondered if Graham ever thought of her at all. She ate her way through her crisps and drank her cider in silence, as he droned on about how much he missed selling fencing. He was really quite boring. The thought came unannounced, along with his description, in minute detail of palisade fencing and its advantages over lap fences. She glanced across in the lowering gloom. His face was still the handsome one she sighed over and dreamed of night after night. His sable hair was still in that gelled-up quiff he favoured and of which she was so fond. The entrancing little dimple was still in his chin and he still had the same hands: strong fingers with practical squared-off tips. How many times had she day-dreamed about what those hands could do to her body? There was still that same physical reaction she always had when gazing at him but it had shifted; it felt different tonight. She shrugged her shoulders and drained her pint. Maybe she was just tired. Unsettled.

'Do you want another?' she asked abruptly. Graham looked

surprised and annoyed at being interrupted but nodded. 'Keep hold of Camilla then.' As Janey waited at the bar to be served, she realised he'd not once asked about how her day had been.

Returning to the table and unable to take in any more thrilling snippets about types of wooden boundary, she forced a change of conversational topic. 'So, do you know anything about this celeb who Becca has got fixed up to do the grand opening?' She was confident Graham would share any information he had. He was notoriously loose-lipped after he'd had a few.

'I do actually.' Graham preened a little, a smug grin playing about his mouth. He leaned nearer. 'It's Alina Allen.'

Now he had her attention. 'No! Really?'

Alina was a proper movie star. British by birth, she'd become a huge sensation in the States and had just filmed the latest Bond film. Janey wasn't particularly interested in spy films; souped-up brainless froth with an overload of machismo and explosions were definitely not her thing, but even she had heard of Alina Allen.

'Yep. Bit of a coup on Becca's part. Apparently, they went to school together.'

'Wow!'

Graham sank into his second pint with relish, obviously gratified by her response.

'Oh Gray, she's gorgeous. And so talented. They were fighting over her in Hollywood. And she had a fabulous stage career in the West End before she left the UK.'

'You seem to know a lot about her. Thought you only did black and white ancient creaky films?'

'I keep myself informed,' Janey answered, thinking of the pile of *Empire* and *Total Film* magazines she had at home. 'And my tastes are wider than you think. I don't mind some newer stuff every now and again.'

'Well, that's who's cutting the red ribbon.' He put his pint down with a clunk, looking worried. 'But don't tell anyone, will you? It's hush-hush until Becca has confirmed she can actually make it. Apparently, Alina has some scheduling problems to sort first.'

'What, so she can come here and open a garden centre?' Janey began to giggle. It seemed unlikely that a film star would be clearing the decks just to come to Bereford.

Graham looked affronted. 'Well, she's doing it as a favour to an old friend. It'll be amazing publicity for Cheney House.'

'Can't argue with that.' As Janey finished her second pint of cider, she knew she must be well over the limit to drive. It would be the long walk home. Again. So she might as well have another. 'Your round.' She nudged Graham. 'Come on. You suffering from short arms and deep pockets again?'

He looked more cheerful. 'You up for another? Great. Been ages since we had a sesh. Another pint?'

'Why not? Oh and Gray, bring more crisps. Need something to soak up the alcohol.' Her heart sank. She couldn't deny it any longer – that's how Graham saw her. A mate to have a pint or three with. Was it time to admit to him how she felt? What could she lose? 'Only his total respect and any friendship,' she muttered. Taking her frustration out on the empty crisp and peanut packets, she scrunched them into the tiniest twist possible. Think how awkward it would be, working with him afterwards! No, it just wasn't an option. Until she was certain

– absolutely certain – he felt even vaguely the same way, she couldn't and wouldn't risk it. 'And there's no chance that will ever happen, Janey, old girl. It's probably about time you faced facts. He's never going to think of you that way.'

As Graham sauntered into the pub though, she couldn't help but admire his behind. Taut and muscular, it was perfect. *He* was perfect, except for one detail – he didn't fancy her. Oh, and that fencing obsession. She blew out a gusty breath, wondering why men didn't see her as girlfriend material. A sudden longing for her cosy little flat and her bed overcame her. Camilla lifted her head at the sound of a car and put a sympathetic, if wet, nose on her knee.

The car slid past, its engine purring expensively. It was low-slung and silver. Some type of Jaguar, Janey guessed. She recognised the dark-haired man behind the wheel. Will. She'd bet a hundred pairs of Becca's stilettoes that he wasn't about to spend his evening in the local pub swilling cider and eating crisps. She sighed yet again, causing Camilla to join in. For the first time ever, Janey wondered if change was necessarily always a bad thing.

Chapter 14

Janey was in a foul mood. She had an almighty hangover and Becca had already given her a bollocking for being late. To be fair, she had been, but it was the first time in months. Clare always said she was in so early most of the time that the odd tardiness wasn't a problem. Becca obviously didn't see things that way. To add to her bad mood, Janey had banged into a stack of empty plant trays that should have gone for recycling the day before. Only she hadn't had time. And now, as well as a throbbing head, she had a sea of black plastic to clear up.

Janey and Graham hadn't stopped at three the night before in the Star and she'd overslept. That, and forgetting she'd left her car at the pub, meant she'd rocked up for work thirty minutes late. She'd been given a verbal warning, with the threat that if it happened again, it would become her first written one. Janey was furious, not only at Becca but more at herself for giving the woman another nail to hammer down the lid of the coffin of her dismissal.

Gwen, overhearing raised voices, brought over a huge mug of coffee, a bacon sandwich and a blueberry muffin as soon as Becca had stalked off back to the main house. 'Get that lot inside you, my lovely,' she said, 'that'll do the trick, all right. And take no notice of the woman. You know as well as I do that we don't have all that many coming into plant sales first thing in the morning. The odd late start isn't going to hurt anyone.'

'That's all very well, Gwen, but she's got it in for me.' As she said it, Janey had the image of Kenneth Williams saying the immortal line in *Carry On Cleo*. Only, when it was happening in real life and to her, it wasn't funny. Not at all.

'She's got it in for anyone who don't fit into her master plan,' Gwen said grimly. 'She's got me run ragged over in that café, Tana or no Tana. Ron's on at me to give up. I go home after a shift and fall asleep on the sofa. Would stop tomorrow but I need the money, what with our Elaine's wedding coming up next year. Weddings are expensive things.'

Alcohol-induced self-pity washed over Janey. She'd probably never know how expensive weddings were. She couldn't see herself walking down the aisle in white tulle heading for an emotional Graham any time soon. Any time ever. She tried to imagine him waiting for her at the altar, whip-smart in a morning suit, but his image blurred and wouldn't come right. Instead, all she could see was Will, self-contained and in control at the wheel of his posh car. Pressing her fingers to her eyes, she tried to force sense into her head. Alcohol played terrible tricks with the brain. 'Ooh, remind me never to drink again,' she groaned. 'How could I be late with Becca just itching to find reasons to sack me?'

Gwen gave her an old-fashioned look. 'Do you think Clare would let that happen?' She gave her a hug. Gwen was good at hugs. The best. Janey succumbed and laid her aching head on the woman's shoulder. 'Just don't give her any more excuses to find fault. You're playing into her hands, child. Do your job, keep your mouth shut and hang fire until Clare comes back.'

'Do you think she'll ever come back?'

''Course she will,' Gwen said stoutly. 'Do you think she'd leave this place? It were her and Mr Gerald's dream. She isn't about to give up on that. It'll be his memorial.'

'What if she meets some gorgeous Italian bloke and stays over there?'

'What, our Clare? Isn't she a bit old for all that kind of malarkey?'

'They say you're never too old to fall in love.' Janey blew out a quivering breath. 'And have someone fall in love with you. Well that's what I like to think. I like to hope.'

Gwen tightened the hug. 'It'll happen to you, my lovely. And just when you're least expecting it. Look at my Elaine. Thirty-five and only just now found the right man. Told her to get a shifty on, I did. Want to be a granny while I can still run around after the little buggers.' She gave Janey a little shake. 'Now, come on, buck yourself up. Not like you to be so down in the dumps.'

Janey disentangled herself. She gulped down the coffee, desperately in need of a caffeine fix.

'Thanks, Gwen. You're right. As ever.' As the woman went to go, she blurted out, 'But Gwen, the problem is you see, I don't think men think of me as a girlfriend and I don't know why.'

Gwen turned back and looked Janey up and down. Putting her hands on her hips she said, 'Want my honest opinion, lovely?'

Janey nodded, sniffling a little.

'Well, not that it's really any of my business, and I'm plain speaking here, but maybe have a good hard look at yourself one day, Janey. When was the last time you had a proper haircut? Have you ever worn a scrap of make-up? Had your nails done or even got the grime from under them? Look at them, they're filthy.'

Janey spread her hands and examined them, mystified. True, the nails were rimed with black, but she had her hands in compost for most of the day. And what was the point of having fuchsia-pink painted talons like Becca when she had to hump around bags of sharp sand? She peered closer at them. Maybe they could do with a good scrub though. And they were ragged and in desperate need of a trim. She chewed a bit of skin off and then shoved her hands back in her pockets. Probably ought to give up that habit too.

Gwen was on a roll. Now she'd started, she couldn't seem to stop. 'I been dying to say these things to you for years. Do you even have a dress in the wardrobe? You've got a rare old figure, Janey love, it wouldn't do no harm for it to come out from underneath those jeans and sweatshirts once in a while.'

This was too much. Janey scowled. 'Are men really that superficial? Is that what I need to do, slap on a bit of lipstick? Wear a tight dress?'

'I think men look with their hormones, my lovely.' Gwen

laughed ruefully. 'And yes, now you come to ask me, I think they probably are that superficial. You let me know if you wants a haircut. Elaine'll fit you in. Won awards for her cutting, she has. And take my advice and get yourself tidied up, like. Might make the men take notice but it just might get that Becca to take you more seriously an' all.'

Janey stared at the space Gwen had left. The thought of prissying herself up to Becca's standards left her cold. She wore so much make-up it looked like a mask, with dramatic eyeliner and thick painted-on eyebrows, which looked ridiculous to Janey. And the time it must take and the money! That couldn't be the answer to getting Becca on her side, surely. How stupid would she look unloading a delivery of conifers wearing fake eyelashes and lipliner! And was that really what men wanted? Girly dresses and nail varnish? She shuddered. It just wasn't her. She wanted Graham to love her for what she was, not what she pretended to be. And there was another thing; she had absolutely no clue about make up anyway. Primers were to do with paint, weren't they? Foundations were what you put under buildings, and concealers and highlighters confused the hell out of her. Give her some soil and a pot-bound plant to rescue and she knew exactly what to do. A mascara wand and a blusher brush were things unknown. And terrifying. Glancing at the clock she saw to her horror that it was nearly ten and she hadn't done the watering yet. Shoving the muffin, whole, into her mouth, she raced around the corner of the office only to collide with Will. Again.

'Steady on there,' he said, as he held her by the arms to stop her from going flying. 'What's the hurry?'

'Got to get the watering done. Running late,' she explained, or tried to. The muffin was stubbornly claggy in her mouth and the words came out muffled and accompanied by spat out purple crumbs. Along with a lack of eyeshadow, Janey was pretty sure spewing out a blueberry muffin while talking was high on any list of what men found unattractive in women.

Will took a step back, brushing damp crumbs off his shirt sleeve.

'Ah,' he said, 'I won't keep you then. I just thought you'd like to know I haven't had any luck in getting hold of Gran, but I've left a message with the hotel where she's based in Massa Lubrense. And I promise I'll keep trying her mobile.'

'Where's that?'

Will had the grace to look only momentarily taken aback at her blunt question. 'Where's what?'

'Massa Lubrense.'

'Italy, near Sorrento.'

Janey wasn't much wiser. She promised herself she'd look it up on Google Earth. She might check out Max Factor, too, while she was at it. 'It sounds wonderful.'

Italy! She sighed inwardly. *Roman Holiday*. Dancing by the Tiber. Sight-seeing moped rides through a city shot in black and white. Gregory Peck – handsome and chiselled, and Audrey Hepburn as the incognito princess. Another of her all-time favourite films. She'd always longed to go to Rome but didn't possess a passport and had never been further than Plymouth. Come to think of it, Will definitely had more than a passing resemblance to a young Gregory Peck. She'd thought it before and now she looked closer, she was certain.

The man in question backed away a fraction from the intense scrutiny. 'I believe it is. The hotel faces Capri.'

Janey was lost in her imagination again. She tuned out, imagining the sharp scent of lemon groves and sound of cicadas against a hot night. Pizza slices, real Italian ones with a thin crust, Mediterranean-tanned youths – two to a scooter and wearing Ray-bans ...

'And I'll get in touch with Prakash. I haven't forgotten. About the dyscalculia test.'

'What?' That brought her right back down to earth. The aroma of fresh lemons fled. 'Right. Yes. Thank you.'

Two customers, a well-dressed woman and what might be her daughter, wandered past. They stopped at one of the larger fountains, a water feature with a winged pixie resting against a rock. Janey had always thought it hideous.

'Oh Anouska,' the older woman cried in loud, well-modulated tones. 'Look, how divine. A water feature that, for once, actually doesn't sound like a horse pissing. How much is it?' She peered closer. 'Oh darling, it's a snip. Only seven hundred and thirty pounds. Shall we add it to your wedding list?'

Another happy bride-to-be. She seemed surrounded by them all of a sudden. Janey caught Will's eye and they laughed. 'I'd better go and sell some stuff,' she said, 'even if it fails on the horse-pissing front.'

'I think you better had,' he answered, gravely. 'But maybe wipe the muffin crumbs off your face before you go?'

She dashed a hasty hand over her mouth. That was the last time she'd eat a blueberry muffin. Ever.

'Oh and the other thing I came to tell you is that Becca wants us all to stay late.' He pushed up his specs and grimaced. 'Emergency staff meeting apparently.'

Great, Janey wanted to answer. Just what I want to do today. Stay late listening to Miss Fancy-Pants drone on about how marvellous she thinks she is.

'Righty-o,' she said to Will. And then, seeing the posh woman and her daughter wander off, ran to catch them up. After all, another sale would add to this week's takings nicely.

Chapter 15

For once, the staff meeting was held in the café. Becca had stipulated Gwen and Tana should stay, along with Janey's assistant, Meg. With Graham and Will as well, it would have been too crowded to hold it in an office.

Saying, '*Sawasdee ka*,' to Tana, who performed an elegant *wai* and a beaming smile in return, Janey collapsed onto the nearest chair. It had been a hectic day and she was work-grimed. Looking forward to a long soak in a hot bath and a rerun of *Pretty Woman* later, she eyed the table's contents with interest. There were huge jugs of water bobbing with juicy lemon chunks and tumblers with ice, and a platter of tiny vol-u-vents. Janey bent forward and snaffled one. It was filled with crab meat and delicious. She let it melt on her tongue and then gave the thumbs up to Tana to show her appreciation. Definitely not your average staff meeting then. Becca was nowhere to be seen; Janey guessed the woman wanted to make a dramatic entrance – she had a finely honed sense of the theatrical. In this, Janey was right. Only Becca wasn't alone. Her boss strutted into the café and stood for a second, in order to create the required melodrama. Accompanying her was a tall sliver of a woman; the casualness of her linen shirt and distressed jeans only serving to emphasise her spectacular beauty. Enormous limpid eyes, glowing café-au-lait skin, and cheekbones you could hang clothes off. Alina Allen stood slightly behind Becca and flicked her long, braided hair nervously.

Becca clapped her hands together in a coy and completely pointless gesture; Alina had everyone's attention already.

'Team! Team! I've got an incredibly exciting announcement. You know I said I had someone to preside over our grand reopening? Well here she is. May I present to you, Alina Allen!'

It was something else that was completely unnecessary. Every single person in the room knew who Alina was. Janey glanced around at the group to see everyone staring. Graham's tongue was hanging out and he was practically salivating.

'Alina has only popped by to say hi to you all.' Becca put an arm around the actress and practically dragged her forward.

Alina seemed very unsure of herself and it occurred to Janey that she was shy. Fancy. Top Hollywood star and she's scared of meeting us lot. All very *Notting Hill!* She vowed to lay off the nineties romcoms for a while.

'She's spending some time in the UK before she flies backs to the States,' Becca added in febrile tones. She turned to Alina and gave an obsequious little bow. 'We're very, very lucky to have her. Busy lady!'

A stunned silence blanketed the room, but then Will broke it by standing up, going to Alina and shaking her hand. She seemed relieved someone was acting normally and smiled at him. The effect was dazzling. *She* was dazzling. It was as if a spotlight had been clicked on and caught them all in its glare. It hurt to look but they couldn't tear their eyes away. Janey couldn't stop staring. She heard Graham shift suddenly in his chair and Gwen murmur, 'Oh my.' This was what Hollywood had seen in Alina Allen; the capacity to render mere mortals incoherent by a smile.

'Come and meet the team,' Will said gently. He led Alina over to the table at which they all still sat, starstruck and apparently unable to move. 'Come and say hello to Gwen. She runs our restaurant.' Gwen managed to stand and almost curtsied. Janey heard her croak out a, 'Very pleased, I must say.' Will then introduced Alina to the others, who made about as much sense, and finally came to Janey.

'I think Alina has got to go now, Will.' Becca tapped an imperious pink talon on her watch.

Janey was buggered if she was going to lose out on meeting a real live movie star, so shot out of her seat. Gwen caught the tumbler of water that was knocked over as she did so.

'And this is Janey, our head gardener.'

Janey scrubbed a hand down the side of her trousers and they shook hands. 'I loved *Golden Dakota*,' she said.

Alina looked surprised. 'Oh my gosh, that was one of my early films. One of my first.'

'Kiley Gilmartin is one of my favourite directors. I've loved all of her films, although I have to admit my real interest is in old films. The old black and white classics.'

Alina dropped her shoulders and looked relaxed for the first time.

'Ah, a film buff. I know what you mean. My fave has to be *Bringing Up Baby*.'

Janey clapped her hands together. 'A real favourite of mine too,' she exclaimed in delight. 'So, do you think you'll work with Kiley again?' She ignored Becca who was making strange little strangled noises to their side.

Alina nodded enthusiastically. 'I hope so, if the right role comes along. At the moment I'm contracted for another Bond film, so it may not be for a while. But I'd love to work with her again. She's a genius.'

'God yes. *Adelaide* was a masterpiece.' Janey named the director's last film. It had narrowly lost out at the Oscars.

'It should have won,' Alina said mournfully. 'I was there and we all said she was robbed.'

'You were at the Oscars?' Janey suspected she was developing an enormous girl crush. Not only was the woman stunning, she was a bona fide film star and had been at the Oscars!

Becca gave an annoyed shriek and intervened. 'Now, before our little gardener hogs you anymore, can I remind you that you have an appointment at seven thirty? And we, of course, have to get on with our staff meeting. Some of us have real jobs to do, you know. We may not all be Oscar-going film stars but we have salaries to earn and homes to run. Your driver is waiting outside, Alina, I believe?'

Alina gave Becca a careful look. 'Yes, that's right, I do have to go. It was lovely meeting you all and especially you Janey. I'd love to talk films some more with you.'

The last sentence was said over her shoulder as Becca frog-marched Alina away.

Janey sat down in shock. Whatever she imagined Becca capable of, she couldn't believe her rudeness to someone who had agreed to do Cheney House an enormous favour. If anything, she expected Becca to be crawling up the star's arse. It was all most odd. She watched as Becca shepherded Alina out of the café. At their departure everyone immediately burst into excited chatter.

'I didn't know you were a film buff,' Will said.

Janey nodded, still too stunned to say anything more.

'I've a fondness for Doris Day movies myself.'

That got Janey's attention. It seemed so unlikely.

'I spent a lot of time with Gran when on vac from boarding school and my parents were abroad. She's a huge fan too.'

That made sense, Janey knew Clare was a Doris devotee. 'What's your favourite film?'

'Hard to choose.' Will screwed up his face, trying to decide. '*Pillow Talk* possibly.'

'Bit of an obvious choice but it's my favourite of hers too.'

'Well, there you go. You may be a galanthophile while I'm strictly Bonsai. You may do the plant and soil stuff whereas I'm more of a numbers man.' He grinned. 'But we may have something in common, after all.'

Something sparkled in the air between them as they stared at one another, oblivious to what was going on around them. Janey was just about to launch into, 'Don't you think Doris Day was one of the most iconic stars of her time?' when Becca marched back in, high heels clacking annoyingly on the restaurant's wooden floor, and called the meeting to order.

Chapter 16

To Janey's utter delight and surprise, she didn't have long to wait before meeting Alina again. Two days later, noticing Camilla wasn't at her heels as usual, she'd gone out into the courtyard to look for her. She found the spaniel, tail swishing so hard it wagged her behind, being made a fuss of by a movie star.

Janey rushed over, ducking between three enormous Greek pots and a water feature in the shape of a barrel. She caught one of the pots by the edge but thought mud on a film star's trousers was a bigger issue than saving an eighty-pound planter and ignored it. Luckily, after wobbling ominously for a few seconds, it rebalanced.

'I'm so sorry,' she said, as she grabbed at Camilla's collar to prevent the dog from jumping up.

Alina laughed. 'Oh honey, don't be, please. I love dogs and this one is a beauty.' She bent to ruffle Cam's silky ears. 'What's she called?'

'This is Camilla. The world's most spoiled spaniel. And a real dumb blonde. She belongs to Clare who owns this place, but she's on holiday so I'm looking after her.'

'You deserve to be spoiled, you gorgeous creature, you.' Straightening, she added, ruefully, 'I adore dogs, always had them as a child but my life's just too manic to have any kind of pet at the moment, let alone a dog. I'm on location so much it just wouldn't be fair.'

Camilla, sensing a new fan and therefore the possibility of a large number of treats, went to lean against Alina's legs, looking soulfully upwards.

It made Janey laugh. She shook her head. 'The biggest tart on the planet.'

'Who is?' Alina looked shocked.

'That dog,' Janey replied, enjoying the conversation. It was almost like talking to a normal person. 'If she even suspects you might be the source of biscuits, you've got a friend for life.' At the mention of biscuits, Cam snickered and pressed herself even harder against Alina's legs.

'Gone and done it now, haven't I? Mentioned the forbidden word.'

She looked at the film star, trying to make up her mind. Alina had said she'd love to talk films again. People didn't say things like that unless they meant them, did they? It had seemed sincere. Weird though it was, Janey felt a connection to her, thought they might be friends, or at the bare minimum, at least have a chat about films over a coffee.

'I'm due my break, I don't suppose you fancy a coffee?'

'I'd love one.' Alina looked genuinely pleased.

'We could go over to the café. They do a decent cup. Proper ground beans and things.'

Alina's face fell. 'It might be a bit awkward.' She gestured to her outfit. She was dressed down again, in jeans, a loose cheesecloth shirt and sunglasses. Her famous hair was mostly hidden by an enormous straw hat. 'I've come deliberately low-key but I might still get recognised and, to be honest, I don't feel up to doing the fame thing today.'

'Well then,' Janey said, rapidly coming to a decision, 'there's only one place for it,' and she led her to the office.

With Alina ensconced on the sofa with an ecstatic Camilla by her side, Janey made them both coffees.

'Can't promise it'll be anything like as good as the stuff Gwen serves but it's hot and wet.'

Again, Alina looked shocked and Janey made a mental note to watch her mouth. Perhaps movie stars weren't normal people after all? She reached onto a high shelf and found Camilla's chew. Giving it to her, she explained, 'That'll keep her busy and we can have some peace.' Passing Alina a coffee, making sure it was in one of the cleaner mugs, she toed out a chair and sat down opposite.

'Don't sit up there,' Alina reproved. 'Makes me feel like I'm about to be interviewed.' She patted the couch. 'Come and sit here.' She took off her hat and put a hand through her braids. They had beads strung through some of them and they chinked together melodiously.

To Janey, the actress exuded a hypnotic glamour and exoticism so she joined her on the sofa. With a contentedly chewing Camilla snuggled between them, she suddenly went shy. There was an awkward pause and her accidental slurp of coffee resounded around the silent office. 'Hot,' she said, embarrassed. To fill the gap in conversation, she added, 'So, what brings you over to Cheney House?'

Alina concentrated very hard on her mug. 'Becca gave me the three-line whip to get over here and discuss arrangements for the launch.'

'She's a bit heavy-handed, isn't she? Couldn't she have done that over the phone?' Bloody Becca, Janey added in her head.

'It's all good, I'm at a bit of a loose end at the moment.' Alina gave a tight smile and seemed to shrink into herself. She sipped her coffee and didn't quite hide the grimace at the taste. 'Besides.' She brightened, 'I really wanted another look around. I need a birthday present for my mum.'

'There'll be a load of stuff in the gift shop. Nice fancy-schmancy cashmere throws at a knock-down three hundred quid.' As Janey said it, the thought occurred that three hundred pounds was probably pocket money to a film star.

Alina smiled properly. A wide smile showing even, very white teeth. She really was stunning, Janey thought incoherently, caught in the wattage. For the first time ever, she became conscious of her untidy hair, which needed a wash, her clunky Dr Marten eight holes and her polyester uniform, which smelled stale. A glimmer of dissatisfaction at her lifestyle prickled. 'I'd like to look like you,' she breathed. 'I want to be you.'

'Sorry?'

Janey shook some sense into her head. 'I said the gift shop sells some nice things which might do for you.'

Alina smiled again. 'I think my ma would rather have a plant, maybe an indoor one, than something pretty-but-useless to sit on a shelf.'

Janey let a breath go. 'In that case, I can help you out. Got some fantastic areca palms just come in. Tall and elegant. I'll show you them after we've finished our coffee.'

'I'll hold you to that.'

There was a strange frisson in the air. Janey couldn't make sense of it. Why would a film star bother to visit a garden centre? Why would she tolerate mediocre coffee out of a not-very-clean Snoopy mug? And why would she want a humble gardener as company?

With a shudder, Alina abandoned her coffee and put it on the floor beside the sofa. She slid around to face Janey.

'So, girlfriend, tell me all about what films you're into. Come on, spill.'

With the merest of hesitations – the situation still seemed surreal – Janey launched into a conversation about her all-time favourite topic and the atmosphere lightened. The weird vibe disappeared and they became simply two friends gossiping over a favourite subject.

They were interrupted by Camilla raising her head and giving Will a snicker of welcome as he poked his head around the door. She flopped off the sofa and went to greet him.

'Ah, here you are, Janey. Becca's on the warpath,' he warned. 'Isn't your break over?'

Janey glanced at the ancient station clock hanging on the wall. Leaping up and making Camilla bark, she yelled, 'Oh glory. Is that the time? I was supposed to be back at work half an hour ago.'

Alina stood up too. 'Oh my gosh, I'm so sorry, Janey. I didn't mean to get you into trouble.' Glancing at Will she said, 'Look, I'll go and distract the delightful Becca. Come with me, Will, is it? Janey, go and pick one of those palm things for my mother and take it to my driver. He's parked up under the trees at the edge of the car park. It's a grey limo.' She rolled her eyes. 'You can't miss it. Put it on my account. I know I'll be back to buy more.'

'But we don't do accounts,' Janey began.

'I think we can make an exception for Alina,' Will suggested.

Alina retrieved her hat from where it had graced the computer. She went to join Will and then changed her mind. Rushing over to Janey, she gave the girl an enormous hug.

'It's so lovely to talk to a normal, everyday person.' Putting a hand to her mouth, she added, giggling, 'I didn't mean that to come out quite as it did. It's just great to chat with someone who doesn't treat me like a movie star, if you get what I mean. Let's do it again soon, honey.' Cramming her hat back on she took Will's arm. 'Lead on, gallant knight. Let us face the dragon Becca together.' Winking at Janey, she turned and left.

Janey stood in the whirling eddies of air left behind by Alina's departure. She was stunned. She had absolutely no idea why the star had befriended her. She was never all that popular at school, although people found her funny so she played the class clown a lot. At Cheney House it was more like a family most of the time. She rubbed along with most, everyone accepted one another's foibles and short-comings and they certainly tolerated her eccentricities. She didn't think of anyone being a friend as such; work colleagues, pub drinking mates, but not friends. She supposed Gwen came the closest and she was really more of a mother figure. This film star, this mega-famous actress, seemed to be actively seeking her out. Janey Trelawney: gardener extraordinaire, but otherwise humble and nondescript resident of Bereford, Devon. A surreptitious lapping brought her back down to earth. Camilla's wagging tail gave the game away; she was nose deep in Alina's abandoned mug and drinking the rejected coffee.

'Come on out, you,' Janey said, hauling the dog off and rescuing the mug. 'I really don't think Nisa's Finest Blend is good for dogs.' At Camilla's reproachful gaze, she added, 'Come on, you can help me choose a house plant for our resident film star.' Going starry-eyed and giggling at the thought, she gave another anxious glance at the time and rushed out.

Chapter 17

To everyone's astonishment, Alina became a regular visitor to the garden centre. She mostly strolled around the grounds, sitting quietly on a bench by the lake, sometimes watching Janey work in the nurseries. In a rare quiet moment, she insisted Janey take her to the shed and explain the snowdrop project, even borrowing Janey's precious volume, *The Galanthophiles: A Hundred and Sixty Years of Snowdrop Devotees*. If she was spotted, and the fans became too intrusive, she sought refuge in Janey's office where they gossiped and talked films. She took care to stop and chat only when she knew Janey had a break or when Becca was off site.

Once she brought her mother who gushed over Janey's choice of plant and proclaimed it perfect.

'I'll have to thank you properly for that,' Alina added. 'I've never given Mum such a successful present.' She promised to take her for lunch on her next day off.

When the day came, Janey had been in bits all morning. She had absolutely nothing to wear. She knew this was something women said all the time, but for her this was true. She was kicking herself for not asking what sort of place Alina was taking her to but assumed it wouldn't be the local pub. She'd asked Gwen's advice who had said smart casual covered most eventualities. Even if Janey knew what that really meant she was pretty sure her wardrobe did not possess a single item of clothing that fitted the description. She now had a pile of rejected clothes heaped up on the bed.

'I had no idea I only ever wore black or navy,' she muttered to an avidly curious Camilla. 'I must look like a bruise all the time. What did Nan used to say? "Pink makes the boys wink." Maybe I ought to branch out into colour.'

She picked out a t-shirt from the pile and held it up. It was one of her favourites and proclaimed: *Galanthophiles do it in Wellies.* Janey nosed the armpits and recoiled.

'Bugger. Possibly not.' Camilla whickered. 'It's all right for you, you have a permanent fur coat,' Janey addressed the dog. 'You don't have to go through all these dramas.' The spaniel gave a huge sigh and turned her back on proceedings. Janey sighed too. If only she had a pair of artfully distressed jeans and a casual muslin shirt like Alina often wore. Chance would be a fine thing. Most of her clothes came from the mega supermarket on the outskirts of Honiton. She imagined Alina's stuff was all designer. Little wonder it looked so good. Picking up her newest jeans and giving them the sniff test, she decided they'd have to do.

'Just the top to decide on then, Cam.' The only response was a throaty snore. The dog had long since given up being interested. Janey had some sympathy. It all seemed such a chore.

In desperation, she stuck her head in her wardrobe. She must have something else. Sitting crumpled up and long rejected in the farthest most corner was a glimmer of something dark red. Janey plucked it out.

'Perfect,' she breathed and, shoving the wardrobe shut, she held it against herself and gazed at her reflection in the mirrored door. It was a top Gwen had given her three years ago saying it was one of Elaine's rejects and did Janey want it? Janey had thanked her and had promptly shoved it to the back of the wardrobe. It was a long, Indian-style embroidered shirt made of some kind of very thin cotton. It was quite pretty. And horribly creased. Janey didn't possess an iron. 'Only one thing for it, Cam.' She put it on a hanger, hung it in the bathroom, turned the shower onto the hottest setting for maximum steam and hoped for the best. Wishing she had some shower gel more exciting than Radox, she hopped under the water.

She emerged, lobster-faced, and was mollified to see the worst of the creases in the shirt had dropped out. Time was running out; Alina was picking her up at twelve. Throwing some underwear on, she pulled on her jeans and boots, pulled the shirt over her head and took a sleepy and protesting Camilla out for a wee.

Once back and with the dog settled on the sofa, Janey went to hunt for her only handbag. She didn't use them as a rule, but Clare had given her a silky-soft crossover bag for her twenty-fifth birthday. It was on top of the wardrobe and needed a good dust. Trying it on with her outfit, and once again standing in front of the mirror, she saw, to her horror, that the Indian shirt, although pretty, was more or less transparent. And worse, was the glimpse it gave of her ancient and greying bra. It looked awful.

'No wonder Elaine rejected this,' Janey moaned. 'I can't go out with my seven-year-old Marks and Sparks t-shirt bra on show. It looks awful.' A swift hunt through her underwear drawer revealed her other two bras were in a similar, if not worse, condition. 'My black bra, that might not look as bad and it's at least a year newer. But what did I do with it? What did I do with my one and only black bra? Come on Camilla,' she complained, 'you're not helping one bit.' She hunted through her chest of drawers and then remembered. Running to the washing machine she retrieved it from the wash she'd put on three days ago and had forgotten about. The clock was ticking remorselessly towards twelve; there was no time to put it through the tumble dryer. 'Desperate measures,' she cried, and found her much-neglected hair dryer lurking under the bed. 'This had better work, Camilla my girl, or it'll be the snowdrop t-shirt.' Holding the bra with one hand she pressed the hair dryer as close as she dared without fear of singeing. 'Come on,' Janey moaned. 'I don't think it's the done thing to be late for a film star.' It was five to. 'It'll just have to do.' She put the bra on, wriggled into the shirt with difficulty as the bra straps were still damp, grabbed her handbag and tripped down the stairs from her flat, just in time to see the grey limo edge over the cobbles and into the old stable courtyard. She leaned against her rusty Fiesta and pretended nonchalance. It was only when she hitched up her bag and feeling it weigh suspiciously light that she realised she'd forgotten to put anything in it. Too late. Ime, Alina's enormous driver, who Janey had met when she'd delivered the plant and who she assumed doubled as bodyguard, uncoiled himself from the driver's seat and tipped his cap.

'Miss Janey.' His voice came from somewhere below his knees.

'Hello,' she said, trying to get her breath back. Glory, if it took this much effort to get ready, she wondered if she preferred staying at home. She had *Kiss Me Kate* to watch later.

Ime held open the back door and Janey obediently got into the car. It didn't feel right to argue with him somehow; he was at least six foot five.

'Janey!' Alina purred from somewhere in its depths. 'How lovely to see you again. Strap yourself in. Ime won't drive anywhere if we don't wear seatbelts. That's a pretty top. Champagne?'

Bewildered and uncomfortably aware of her damp bra, Janey accepted the flute offered.

'We're going to Samphyre in Exeter. It's supposed to be good for seafood and I adore seafood. Do you?'

'Don't know. Not really.' Janey ate mostly at the café at work and existed on takeaway pizzas at home. Seeing Alina's face fall, she added cheerfully, 'Willing to give it a go, though. Is it posh, this place?'

'Oh yes,' Alina answered blithely. Then she caught Janey's implication. 'But I've booked its private room. It's bound to be busy and I hate being gawped at while I'm off duty and trying to enjoy a delicious meal and good company.'

Janey felt her shoulders unknit themselves a little. 'Sounds good. Hope I wasn't late.' she gulped some champagne.

‘Not late at all. Right on time. I hope you didn’t rush?’

‘Not really.’ Emboldened by the alcohol, Janey began telling Alina the story of the bra.

When they’d stopped laughing, Alina choked out in between giggles, ‘Janey Trelawney, I don’t think I’ve ever met anyone quite like you.’

Chapter 18

After her second glass of champagne Janey admitted the handbag debacle explaining she had absolutely nothing with her. Alina laughed again and reassured that lunch was on her. Janey went on to say, if they were going all the way into Exeter, she was worried about leaving Camilla for so long. Alina passed her a mobile. The only number Janey could remember off by heart was Graham's, so she rang him. There was no answer, so thinking rapidly, she googled Cheney House's main number and got through to Will. After all, the spaniel belonged to his grandmother. He promised to pop by and take Camilla out. He sounded highly amused that Janey was lunching with Alina and more than a little intrigued.

'Lucky you. I've heard Samphyre is fantastic,' he said. 'Have a wonderful time.'

Janey explained where the spare key to her flat was and he went on to give her a mild telling off. 'Under a flowerpot? Janey, maybe you should rethink your security.'

'He seems a good friend,' Alina said, as Ime slid the huge car expertly into a space right outside the restaurant.

Janey was puzzled for a second. She clicked off the phone and handed it back.

'Friend? I suppose he is. But he's more of a boss really.' As she followed Alina into the restaurant, she pondered the words. Yes, technically Will was her boss, however temporary, but he'd never come across as one. So, she supposed he was definitely more in the friends' category.

The maitre d' ushered them, with almost painful obsequiousness, into a side room, where a table for two was set out. Janey fell in behind Alina and was aware of the silence that landed as they walked through. It was immediately followed by fervent whisperings of 'Did you see who that was?' and 'Was that really Alina Allen?' Her sympathy for the star grew. Having any kind of normal life must be nigh-on impossible.

They settled at the table, with Ime standing, legs planted and arms crossed, outside the door. No one would get past him.

Attended to by the maitre d' himself, Alina ordered the *fruits de mer* platter.

'Would you like to share it with me? I won't eat it all by myself.'

Janey hadn't a clue what to expect but agreed. When it came, on a tower which revolved so that they could each access the food, she was bemused.

'Looks like a plate of bones and skeletons,' she blurted out.

Alina laughed again. She showed Janey how to extract the succulent lobster meat with the special tool, how to squeeze lemon juice on an oyster and then tip her head back to slide it down. Janey had a go at everything, loved the meaty scallops, the lobster and the crab but decided she could probably live without eating another oyster. 'Scrummy,' she said, scooping up a smear of garlic mayonnaise with her finger and sucking it.

'You look like you enjoyed that,' Alina smiled.

'You bet I did. Beats anything the Star and Garter can put out.'

Alina looked puzzled.

'Local pub.'

'Oh.'

'It's okay but they don't do food like that. I love trying different stuff but don't have much chance to do it. I'm enjoying Tana's Thai grub that she does.'

'I love Thai food too. So delicately flavoured. Ah, here's your steak.'

'Oh glory.' Janey rubbed her hands together. 'Rare and bloody, just how I like it.'

Alina picked at her green salad. 'Constantly have to watch my weight,' she explained. 'As you can imagine.'

Janey couldn't imagine. Diets were unknown to her. In fact, if she didn't eat enough, she often found she was losing weight without meaning to.

She said as much to Alina who blinked enviously.

'I have to hit the gym every day without fail,' she said ruefully, 'otherwise I'm one big mass of blubber.'

Janey concentrated on her steak, remembering to pause before answering and not to speak with her mouth full. 'Lugging around eighty-litre bags of compost is a pretty good workout.'

'I'm sure it is. Tell me about yourself, Janey. Have you got a family?'

'Just my mum and dad. They decided to move to Spain last year after my nan died. Got fed up of the weather in the UK and the warmth helps my Mum's arthritis. Got a younger brother too, but he works in New York.'

'You must miss them all.'

'Yeah. We've got plans to get together this Christmas in Spain, but we'll see.' Janey closed the subject down. She didn't want to say that the thought of flying anywhere terrified her. Tackling a different language, trying to convert money, all the crowds at the airport, not to mention being stuck in a metal tube thirty thousand feet up in the air with a bunch of strangers. And there was the little matter of the departures board. All those numbers flashing unintelligibly away. She fought to disguise the shudder. 'Not much of a traveller, me,' she said gloomily, staring at her wine glass.

'And what about a boyfriend, girlfriend?'

'Not much of that going on either.' Janey put her knife and fork down, relieved the conversation had moved on. 'That was one of the best steaks I've ever eaten.'

'Good. So, there's no one special?'

Janey's tongue was loosened by the champagne and the red wine she'd drunk with her steak. 'Well, there is one person,' she admitted.

'The man on the phone? Will?'

'No!' Janey recoiled in horror.

Alina spluttered through her glass of water. 'Why is that thought so awful?'

'I just don't think of him that way.' As she said the words, Janey wondered if this was strictly true. A picture of Will's smile rose in her mind; he was very good-looking when he smiled. He'd been so nice to her, too. Much nicer than Graham ever was, to be honest. And what was that funny, squirmy feeling in her tummy all about when he looked at her through his specs? But she didn't fancy him. He was too much of a 'cross the ts and dot the is' sort of a bloke. She shook her head. No, she definitely didn't fancy him one little bit. 'Nope, it's someone else. But it's hopeless.'

'Why hasn't anything happened?' Alina spread her hands. 'You're hard-working, obviously intelligent and very attractive. What's stopping it?'

Janey's face heated at the thought of Alina saying she was attractive. No, scratch that, she'd said *very* attractive. She allowed herself a preen for a second and then remembered the hopelessness of the Graham–Becca situation.

'He just sees me as a friend. And he's interested in someone else,' Janey added repressively, and folded the stiff material of her napkin between clenched fingers. She felt Alina examining her closely.

'So, it's a he? I see. Well, maybe I can do something to help things along a bit. What about that?'

Chapter 19

ITALY

'That was utterly delicious.' Clare scrunched up her paper serviette and sat back on her wicker chair. She and Leo had dined at a little street café in Sorrento.

'However did you find this place? I haven't had seafood that good in years.' She took out a few more serviettes from the little metal dispenser on the table, wiped her fingers and then lifted her face to the hot Italian sun. It was at just the right angle to spear down through the narrow gap in the pastel-coloured buildings.

'Glad you liked it, *amore mio*. Sometimes it's worth finding out these family run places.'

'I so agree. One of the best meals I've ever eaten was in a tiny place in Rome. Right off the beaten track. A simply heavenly minestrone soup and huge chunks of bread. Gem absolutely adored it.'

'We do food well in this country,' Leo said, on a chuckle. 'The best.'

'The best!' Clare saluted the sentiment with her water glass. The elderly waiter came to clear their table. '*Grazie mille. Molto bene.*' Clare smiled up at him and he blinked slowly and performed a nod in response.

'*Parli italiano?*' Leo asked, looking pleased.

Clare gave a rueful grin. '*Grazie, prego, ciao.* That's about it, I'm afraid. Typical Brit abroad.'

Leo lifted his water glass as a return salute. 'But charming all the same.'

'Maybe I should learn some Thai? We have a new chef at the restaurant back at Cheney House. She's Thai. Does the most gorgeous *Tom Kha Kai*. Spicy chicken in coconut,' she added to Leo's bemused expression.

'*Capisco.* So it's no longer just a café anymore, eh? And this is part of the master plan to overhaul the garden centre?'

'I have to do something to keep up with the opposition. The plan is to develop the café into a restaurant and open it in the evenings. Maybe as one of these pop-up places? You know, let different caterers take it over for short sessions. Offer different types of cuisine. Spanish tapas, Chinese.' Clare flashed Leo a grin. 'Even Italian!' She disappeared into her thoughts for a second. 'I loved Gem with all my heart, and I love Cheney House too, but he wasn't exactly one for moving with the times. I had to battle to put in a computer system and he just couldn't see the point in selling non-garden related stuff. He always said folk came for plants not greetings cards.'

Leo lifted an eloquent brow. 'He probably had a point. But do you worry, that by updating, it will lose its unique appeal? Do you fear blending in with every other place out there?'

'Maybe.' Clare finished her San Pellegrino. 'I've been told by my manager that we have to have a unique selling point to make us competitive.' She stared into the bottom of her glass as if it might offer her the answer she was seeking. 'I've got to try something.'

'It's true. You have to stand out from everyone else. Something that customers want to come to you for, what others cannot offer.' Leo frowned. 'Although, with a Georgian house and beautiful gardens, I think you have that already.'

'I don't think our situation, stunning that it is, is enough. I have to find another revenue source. Several revenue sources. To be honest, Leo, we've been losing money.' She blew out a forceful breath. 'I've kept the worst from the staff. I felt I had to. There just wasn't the time to devote to the business while Gem was ill. His illness became a full-time occupation, with all the hospital appointments and everything that that entails. It dominated our lives even though we were determined that it shouldn't. Cheney House had to run itself for a while. And it suffered.' Clare's voice cracked and she took a moment to pull herself together. 'This is its last hurrah. I'm seventy soon.' She gave Leo a glance but he just shrugged. 'Time to retire?'

'And then what will you do?'

'Oh, I don't know. Sell the house, live in a bungalow and go to WI meetings?'

'The WI. What is this?'

'Women's Institute,' she explained.

'An institute?' Leo looked horrified.

It made her laugh. 'Leopoldo, you lived in England long enough to know exactly what the WI is.'

'No, no, no, not my Clare. No institute for you. You are still a vital, beautiful woman. You need to keep Cheney House on. For Gem.'

She sucked in a deep breath. 'For Gem. Of course. And for Alicia too.'

'From what you've said, your daughter doesn't want it.'

'No, she probably doesn't. But Will might.'

'Your grandson? Aw yes, the boy I spoke to on the phone. He took some persuading to give me your whereabouts. He is protective, eh? *Bene.*'

'He is. And far more business-minded than his mother. Almost too much so.' Clare smiled fondly. 'He could do with loosening up a little to be honest. He's rather,' she paused, trying to find the right word. 'Rigid.'

'He should come to Italy.' Leo pointed at the vibrant street scene in front of them. '*Italia*, she loosens people up.'

'You're right.' Clare followed his gesture. A stall opposite was selling fruit and vegetables, including the brightest coloured oranges Clare had ever seen. She could smell the sharp, intoxicating scent of lemons nestling in their glossy dark green leaves. Crowds milled along the narrow street. Tourists stopped to examine the leather sandals and the wooden inlay art on sale. Locals were buying vegetables and catching up on gossip in a way that was essentially Italian – demonstrating a love of life and talk, with much hand waving and loud voices. She watched them. 'I love it here,' she said on a happy sigh.

'You needed to get away, *amore mio.*'

'I did.' She met his concerned expression. 'Oh Leo, I desperately needed to get away.'

'And you have a good manager in place to run things for you while you are away?'

'I think so.' Clare visualised Becca's references displayed on her computer, blocking out the vivid Italian sun and the background of loud chatter and returning to her office in Cheney House. 'Her references were impeccable; she came highly recommended. I made sure I rang her previous employee as well as taking them.' She smiled. 'Gem taught me well. Everything seemed in order. I think she'll do an excellent job. And, if there are any problems, I can rely on Will to let me know.'

'A good boy.'

'A very good boy. He's the son I never had.'

'But too, what did you say, rigid?'

'Maybe I was being too harsh. Just a little buttoned-up. In lots of ways he reminds me of Gem. He liked his order and routine too; it was his security blanket. He was always so worried about anything new. With Will I think it stems from being on his own too much as a child. Alicia put him in a boarding school as soon as possible, and he came to me and Gem a lot. His parents, much as it pains me to say it, haven't spent nearly enough time with him. Too busy enjoying their ex-pat army lifestyle I suspect. Poor Will. He's always been serious.'

'Then he definitely needs Italy. Or a woman!' Leo added, mischievously.

Clare sniffed appreciatively at the tiny glass of limoncello the waiter had brought with the bill and then drank it in one. She giggled and put the glass down, catching a dribble with her finger and licking it.

'Or a woman. The trouble is, he rarely stops working long enough to find one.'

'Maybe he will find one in this Becca manager? Two business brains together, eh?'

'Possibly. Although I can't see it somehow. I'm not sure it's a good idea to date someone who is too similar. Gem and I were completely different and it worked so well for us. Will needs someone freer, someone eccentric, to shake him out of his ways.'

'Then he definitely needs an Italian woman,' Leo said warmly.

Clare laughed again. 'Maybe.' For some reason the image of Janey, in her denim dungarees and boots, complete with a smudge of soil on her cheek rose in her mind.

'And now we have eaten lunch, shall we take a stroll around to Piazza Tasso? Find a *gelateria?*'

Clare focussed back on Leo. He'd put down some notes to pay the bill, had risen from his chair and was gazing at her expectantly. 'I'd love that.' She smiled up at him. 'A stroll to walk off lunch sounds *perfetto*, but I'm not sure I have room for an ice-cream.'

'In Italy there is always room for ice-cream,' he replied gravely, and he came to her chair and took her hand as she rose. 'As it happens, I have another idea for your holiday.'

'What's that?'

'I will explain as we walk.'

'How very intriguing of you, Leo. Oh but first, I'd love to buy some of those luscious oranges.' She put her head onto one side, coquettishly. 'You wouldn't deny me my vitamin C.'

'I can deny you nothing, my love,' he said, and tucked her hand into his arm.

Chapter 20

'Have they put a colour in it?' Janey peered disbelievingly at her reflection in the salon mirror.

'No honey, that's your natural hair colour. They've just conditioned and straightened it. Makes the true colour come out.' Alina spun around in the next chair, holding her feet up with childish glee. She came to a halt facing Janey. 'I can hardly believe the transformation either. Franco has done an amazing job, girlfriend. And you are going to keep up the new skin regime, aren't you? It'll tone down the redness. A bit of make-up and a manicure next to complete the look. You look wonderful already though. The haircut really suits you. Layered bobs are easy to look after and you can tie it back for work if you need to.'

Janey scowled at the unrecognisable image of herself and swished her hair from side to side experimentally. True, it was astonishingly thick and smooth but she wasn't so sure about the change of style. 'Well, I don't know. I used to just plonk it in an elastic band.' She tugged a short layer nearest her ear.

Alina grimaced, suppressing a shudder. 'If you only knew what those things did to your hair. Promise me you'll only use a scrunchie from now on.'

'A what?'

Alina raised her eyes to the ceiling.

'Sorry, Alina.' Janey pulled a face. 'This transformation of earth-bound and earth-covered gardener into glossy seductress still needs work.'

'Honey, how have you made it to twenty-nine without knowing what a scrunchie is?'

'Never seemed important.' Janey stared into the mirror and lifted a strand of silky auburn fringe. 'Still doesn't if I'm honest. And, although I'm very grateful for all this pampering, Alina, I'm still not sure about this fringe.' She'd enjoyed the massages and had found them relaxing but had been completely bemused by the array of jars thrust into her hands at the end. They came with a bewildering list of complicated and time-consuming instructions. And this new haircut might be one step too far.

'It looks fabulous,' Alina went on. 'Brings out your eyes. And if you remember to condition and straighten it, it'll be so easy to do yourself. Besides, you know what Becca always says, you need to present a professional image to the customers.'

Janey bristled visibly. 'Can we leave her out of the equation? I'm trying to forget about her and work.'

'Okey-dokey, baby girl. From now on, hers is the name that will not be spoken.' Alina grinned, showing her perfect white teeth. She was obviously having a ball, in her element among all the potions and hair tongs, having the staff dance attendance on her every whim.

As promised, Alina had put project 'Let's Get Janey Her

Man' into action as soon as possible. She had whisked them both off, driven in the limo by the ever-patient Ime, to a health resort and spa in a hotel just along the coast in Poole. She insisted they both have the full range of treatments, beginning with a body massage and facial. These were followed up by a deep hair conditioning treatment and restyle for Janey.

'I won't mention her again,' Alina promised and then immediately broke it. 'But I can't wait to see her face when she gets to see the new you,' she said excitedly. 'And maybe even Graham will get the hot, hot, hots!'

Janey blushed. 'I'm not sure about that.' She'd filled Alina in on exactly who the object of her desire was in the car on the way to hotel. Alina had reacted with fevered elation at the idea of getting one over on Becca; at Janey stealing Graham away from her. 'Aw, Alina,' Janey now protested, 'I think it's hopeless. A new haircut isn't going to make any difference. He sees me as just a friend.'

'Not when I've finished with you, he won't,' Alina said stoutly. 'And when you've got a bit of mascara and lippy on, he won't look at anyone else, let alone Miss Bossy-Boots Becca. Just you wait and see.'

Janey's face fell. Anything girly was her worst nightmare, especially make-up.

'I don't have a clue about all that kind of stuff. I just shove a bit of Nivea on in the mornings. And a bit of Vaseline when it's really cold.'

Alina took in a deep breath and sucked her teeth. It was as if Janey had confessed to mass murder. 'Oh my gosh. You really do need help,' she said gravely. 'That's why you're having make-up lessons next.' She clapped her hands together. 'I haven't had this much fun in ages. What a ride!'

Janey wasn't having fun. She was grateful to Alina but nonplussed as to why the movie star was doing all this. And she was getting extremely irritated at having people poke and prod at her. Batting Franco away, as he attempted, for the millionth time to tweak her hair just-so, a thought occurred.

'Alina, are you doing a Pygmalion on me?'

'Come again?'

'You know. George Bernard Shaw. *Pygmalion.* The play, which was made into a black-and-white film with Wendy Hiller and Leslie Howard.'

'You've lost me.'

'It got made into the musical *My Fair Lady*. It's all based on the myth about Pygmalion falling in love with one of his statues, I think, and then she came to life as the perfect woman. Audrey Hepburn, it was, in *My Fair Lady*. And, to be honest,' Janey admitted, 'she was pretty perfect in that.'

'Oh yeah, I get you now.' Alina focussed. '*My Fair Lady*! What a film. And Audrey Hepburn, I love her. *Breakfast at Tiffany's*. Cool movie. The perfect woman, yeah I understand.' Alina became very busy staring into the mirror and tweaking her braids. 'Maybe.' She turned back to Janey and grinned. 'Maybe.'

'Well, you've got your work cut out with me,' Janey said, with feeling.

'You might have a point.' Alina stood up. 'Don't know about you but I'm ravenous. Shall we do lunch first? Then make-up and a mani-pedi.' She wiggled her fingers.

'A what?' Janey complained.

'I'll explain over lunch. Let's hope they do more than an egg-white omelette. Creating the perfect woman is hungry work.'

Janey got up and followed Alina out of the hair salon.

There was a lot about Alina that mystified her. Her enthusiasm for this make-over being one, her antipathy to Becca being another. Why was she agreeing to do the favour of opening the garden centre when she seemed to hate its manager so vehemently? And why hang around so much? Why not swan off somewhere more exotic than Bereford? Blowing hair out of her mouth, as it swished across her face in very unaccustomed fashion, Janey resigned herself to understanding Alina less the more she got to know her.

As they entered the restaurant, Janey became completely distracted by the superb view. The steel and glass exterior of the hotel had disappointed her; she'd hoped for a country pile with some history. This more than made up for it. The smooth beech flooring led through wide doors onto a terrace, which looked down upon Poole Harbour.

'How gorgeous,' she began to say, but had lost Alina. The woman had disappeared outside and was hugging a pale, reed-slender redhead.

As Janey approached them, she heard Alina squeal, 'Dora Bart!'

'Alina honeybun, how very wonderful to bump into you! You staying for lunch? Let's get them to lay up a table out here. It's warm enough. I've been treating my bestie, Millie; preggers and hasn't seen her toes for the last three months, so I've treated her to a pedicure and a bit of pampering.'

'This is Janey.' Alina turned and included her in the group. 'We've been having a little pamper all of our own.'

'Hi Janey,' Dora said with a wide grin. 'Nice to meet you.'

They were joined by a striking-looking dark-haired woman who was heavily pregnant. 'Had to pop to the loo. Curse of the pregnant woman.'

'This is Millie,' Dora explained unnecessarily. 'I don't know about pop to the loo, I think the poor love is about to pop full-stop.'

'I do apologise for my friend,' Millie said drily. 'I think the aromatherapy oils have gone to her head.'

'More like I'm food deprived,' Dora complained. 'I'm starving.'

Millie poked her friend in the ribs. 'That's not like you.'

'I know, can't think what's got into me.'

'Pregnant again,' Millie said smugly. 'Mark my words.'

Dora pointed an accusing finger. 'Don't even say the words!' she said, sounding horrified.

They stood for a couple of minutes as a waiter laid up the table nearest the glass balcony. It was out of the breeze and in the late May sun.

'Perfect.' Without waiting on ceremony, Millie collapsed onto a chair.

'Poor dear,' Dora said, with feeling. 'All sprogged out. Still, not long now.' She took the seat next to her.

'Just as well. I feel like an elephant. I'm sure the scan was wrong and I've got twins in here.'

Alina giggled as she and Janey sat down. 'Well, I think you look fabulous. What's the word? Fecund.'

'And Millie can't fecund wait for it to come out,' Dora laughed. 'We're rather hoping it will be a boy then, once he's thirty, we can marry him off to my Lily and we can wear big hats and gloat.'

'Of course,' Alina exclaimed. 'You had a baby too!'

'Not so much the baby. She's walking now.' Dora pulled a face. 'I know I always said I'd rather poke my eyes out with a sharp stick than be the sort of mother who showed off pictures of their offspring, but you have to admit she's gorgeous.' She got out her phone and showed a picture of a sturdy toddler with a mass of dark curls. 'Looks so much like her father,' she added, fondly. 'I am utterly besotted. My little Lily Love.'

'Beautiful.' Alina took a moment to admire the picture. 'And where's that luscious hunk of a man of yours?'

'Out with Millie's husband, Jed. With sprog and dog. Gone fishing.' Dora shuddered. 'Rather them than me. I had enough of the stink of fish when I was a kid.'

'We ate in your parents' restaurant the other day. Samphyre, is it? It was very good.'

Dora laughed. 'They've come a long way since the fish and chip shop. But thank you, I'll pass on the compliment. Might even try it if we get the chance. Mike and I decided to come down to the house in Berecombe for the summer. Before we have to get back to the Smoke. He's directing again in the autumn. The godmother here is supposed to be teaching Lil how to make sandcastles.'

Millie rubbed her bump. 'But there's not much chance of that with me in my current state. Even if I could get down on the sand, I sure as eggs wouldn't be able to get back up.'

The women laughed and Dora gave Millie a sympathetic hug.

'How do you and Dora know one another?' Millie asked Alina.

'I guest-starred in one ep. of *The English Woman,*' she answered, and looked around for the waiter. 'And we clicked, didn't we, Dora?'

'Then Alina's career went stratospheric and I came to Berecombe, met Mike and got all sprogged up,' Dora said, but without malice.

'And you came back to Berecombe, met Mikey again and you've never been happier,' Millie replied.

'This is very true. *Je ne regrette rien.*' The two friends smiled at one another warmly.

'Oh!' A lightbulb went on in Janey's head. 'You're Theodora Bart. I loved *The English Woman.* It was brilliant. About the only bit of TV I've ever watched. Properly, that is.'

'Janey is more the film buff,' Alina put in.

'I take the compliment even more so then, darling, seeing as you're a film person.' Dora raised her water glass at her. 'Is that how you know Alina? You in the bizz too?'

Janey snorted. 'Not really. I work at the garden centre in Bereford.'

'What Janey should say is that she's actually the head gardener. I'm cutting the ribbon on the grand reopening next month,' Alina added. She winked at Janey. 'And we've clicked too.'

'Alina seems to think I need an overhaul,' Janey said, so mournfully it made the others laugh. 'I'm being given the full works. No part of me has escaped untouched. I've been plucked and pummelled to within an inch of my life.'

Dora gave both a quizzical look. 'What fun, but you look fine to me. Love the hair. Is that your natural colour?'

Janey nodded.

'It's all in the course of true love,' Alina explained. 'I'm trying to get Janey buff enough to get her man.'

'How extremely intriguing,' Dora said, and gave them another penetrating glance. 'Alina, do you remember that hairstylist on *The English Woman?* Obsessed by straighteners.' She flicked a lock of her wavy red hair. 'Mine's in so much better condition since I escaped her.' She and Alina began an involved discussion about the hair and make-up on set.

Millie gave Janey a sympathetic look. 'Think we may have lost them for a moment. Dora doesn't have as much opportunity to talk showbiz as she'd like. This garden centre, it's Cheney House, isn't it?'

'Yes.'

'Oh it's lovely there. That beautiful red-brick house, and the lake and gorgeous gardens too. I've been several times. I loved my container plants when I lived in a flat. Jed and I have a proper garden now. We've moved into a cottage with the most glorious bit of land, I've really gone to town on planting it up. Or I did before I became pregnant,' she added, ruefully. 'Still love my bright geraniums in an old terracotta pot though.'

'So do I. Can't beat a geranium,' Janey said, on safer ground now the conversation was about gardening and not nail-varnish or hair styles. 'They stand up to a great deal of neglect and look wonderful. I like to clash the colours, you know, pink with a true red and a bright orange. The tattier the pot the better for a good look.'

'I'll have to try that. I've played safe so far and stuck to red.' Millie indicated her tummy. 'Might have to wait until next spring now. I'm going to be busy soon.'

Janey didn't really do babies. She thought most of them looked like Winston Churchill and hadn't seen what the fuss was all about when someone had brought her newborn into work.

'Oh right,' she said, although vaguely aware she was supposed to ask when the baby was due and if Millie hoped for a boy or a girl, along with a host of other questions.

Mille didn't seem to mind her evident lack of curiosity and went on to explain she was taking time out from her business. 'I've got Petra running the café and Amy is doing a fabulous job with the bookshop, so I'm making the most of my maternity leave. You'll have to pop into the bookshop. Amy's planning a film theme to go with the film festival the theatre is putting on. Think she's hoping to have a themed party too.' Millie laughed. 'We don't need much of an excuse to have a party at Millie Vanilla's. Although, with the weddings too, we've got our hands full.'

'I'll have to come down and have a look at the film books and I'll definitely check out the festival.' Janey took a menu from the waiter and laid it on the table. Millie's last sentence had intrigued her. 'The café is a wedding venue?'

Millie nodded enthusiastically. 'It's very popular, especially if the couple is after a relaxed beach affair.' She frowned. 'Although the main issue is we can't always guarantee the weather. We've just invested in a custom-made awning to protect the happy couple and guests from the worst of the elements and even then it's only do-able for part of the year.' She drank some water before carrying on. 'You know, I've always thought Cheney House would be a marvellous place to get married. With the house as a backdrop, the lake with swans gliding by. It could be an incredibly romantic setting. And a marquee would give you all-weather protection.'

Janey was struck by Millie's generosity in suggesting it. 'We've only got troublesome ducks at the moment. They leave feathers and stinky droppings all over the place.' She grinned. 'But I know what you mean.' She thought some more. 'You know, you could be on to something. Maybe I'll mention it.'

'What, to the owner?'

'Clare's away at the moment.' Janey sighed. 'I'll have to talk it over with the general manager, Becca Woods.'

'And she's not likely to be very receptive?' Millie asked gently. 'I can tell from your expression.'

Janey wrinkled her nose. 'You could say that. It's worth a go though, isn't it?'

'It would be another string to your bow. Always helps a business.'

'True. And weddings are quite lucrative, aren't they?'

'They can be. You know, it might be an idea for you to join WIBBLE. That's Women in Berecombe Business Local Events Group.' She caught Janey's look and they laughed. 'I know, it's a terrible acronym and a bit of a mouthful, but the actual group is very supportive. I'm a member and I've learned a lot since joining.'

Janey thought for a moment, wondering if Becca was already a member, and if so, why she hadn't mentioned for her to join too.

'I'll certainly consider it, thanks.'

There was a silence and then both women turned to find Alina and Dora staring at them, looking amused.

'I leave you alone for five minutes,' Dora accused, 'and you end up talking business.' She shook her head. 'You're a hopeless case, Emilia Henville. You're supposed to be on maternity leave! Look darlings, are we all ready to order? I'm absolutely—'

'Starving!' the other women chorused on a laugh.

'Yeah, babes, I think we guessed,' Alina said, and summoned the waiter.

Chapter 21

'Oh. Wow.' Will stopped dead at the entrance of the plant sales office. 'You look nice. Have you done something to your hair?'

Janey put a self-conscious hand through her newly acquired hairstyle.

'Just had it cut.'

Will peered closer. 'It looks great. In fact, you look great. There's something else that's different but I can't work out quite what.'

'Did you want me for something, Will?' Janey turned on her heel, embarrassed. Her hair slid down over her face and hid it in all its made-up glory. Only a touch of foundation, the merest slick of mascara and a hint of lip gloss, but it was enough to make her feel incredibly uncomfortable.

'No. Not really.' He seemed flustered. 'Oh yes, I did, but it was only this.' He held out a piece of paper. 'It's the details of the testing you can do for dyscalculia. I finally got hold of

Prakash. Turned out he was in Italy. Everyone seems to be in Italy.'

'Thanks.' She took it from him. 'Oh,' she said, disappointed. 'He went to somewhere in Bristol. That's a bit of a drive. Is Clare still having a good time?' she asked, changing the subject and stowing the information away in her pocket.

'Wonderful, apparently. She's bumped into an old friend and is living the high life on the Amalfi Coast and drinking her weight in limoncello.'

'No chance of her coming back any day soon?' Janey tried to keep the longing out of her voice.

Will shook his head. 'I don't think so. She should be back for the grand reopening though.'

'She'd better be.'

'Speaking of living it up, how did you get on at the spa the other day? Is that where the new hairstyle originates?'

Janey spun round. 'Will, it was fantastic. Not the messing about with my nails and hair stuff though. That drove me insane.' She rolled her eyes.

'It suits you; it really does. You know, I can't get over how different you look.' Will pushed his specs up to admire it again.

'Forget the hair,' Janey said impatiently. 'You'll never guess who we bumped into.'

'Let me see.' Will put a finger on his chin and pretended to think. 'Clark Gable? Tony Curtis?' He made his eyes go huge. 'Not Doris Day!'

'Idiot.' Janey thumped him playfully on the arm. 'No, but nearly as good. Turns out Alina knows Theodora Bart. I had lunch with not just one but *two* highly successful actors. Get me.'

'Get you. I'm genuinely impressed. I was glued to *The English Woman*. That was Theodora Bart, wasn't it? She's local, did you know? Comes from Berecombe.'

'Yes, she said. Told us about her parents running a fish and chip shop.'

'Still do, I believe. It's right on the front, near the harbour. They own that fancy place your tame movie star took you to as well.'

'Samphyre. That was lush. I had lobster and steak; did I tell you?'

'Get you. Again. You'll have to take me sometime.'

Janey stared at Will. He was joking, wasn't he?

'Yeah,' she said loftily. 'I may do, if I can fit you into my busy social schedule, that is.'

Will laughed. 'The way you're going, I'll have to book a slot sometime into next year.'

'Oh, and I met Millie. Millie Henville. She's got the café and bookshop on the sea front.'

'Not to mention the Henville family own the big hotel in town as well.'

'I thought the name was familiar. Well anyway, she was telling me all about how they host weddings at the beach café and how popular it is as a venue.'

'Yes, I can see it would be.'

'Millie got me thinking that we could do weddings here at Cheney House.'

Will thought for a minute. 'You know, that's not a bad idea. We'd have to look into licences and all the official stuff, of course.'

Janey deflated for a second. Then she brightened. 'There's always the church in the village. Folk could get married there and we could offer Cheney House as a reception venue. Think about it, Will, we've got a restaurant that seats a hundred covers, plus outdoor seating if the weather's good. We've got fantastic locations for photographs; the gardens and the lake and the house.'

'It's a bit of a crumbling old wreck of a place, Janey,' Will said, sounding cautious.

'Not as much as it was,' she defended stoutly. 'And some people like that. We could market it as, oh I don't know, what is it, tatty chic? No, shabby chic, that's it.'

Will laughed again. 'Bit old hat now.' Then he saw the look on her face and added, more kindly, 'You've really thought this through, haven't you?'

'We need to bring some money in, Will, and this might do it. I'd have to run it past Clare though.'

The unspoken lay between them.

'And Becca,' Janey added.

'Don't rush into anything,' Will warned. 'Let's think through how best to present the idea to her. Or we can wait until Gran returns. It won't be long now before she's back. Just don't rush headlong into it, Janey.' He went to go and changed his mind. 'If you want to thrash out any ideas with me, I'm happy to.'

'Thanks, Will.'

'Mind you, I'm no film star,' he added, without rancour. 'So, would I still do?' He pushed his specs up his nose again and pulled a face.

Janey laughed and flapped him out. Then she caught sight of Becca teetering across the courtyard, her stilettoes stabbing into the cobbles. 'Oops, better be seen to be doing some work. Don't want to give Madam another excuse to dish out a warning. I've already got a verbal.'

Will stopped in his tracks. He followed her look. 'Who's that with her? That bloke in the swanky suit and the Italian loafers?'

Janey peered through the smeared windows of the office to get a closer look. 'No idea. New rep from the garden furniture supplier? Becca made a big deal about some bloke she had coming. A rattan specialist.'

'He doesn't look like a rep, does he?' Will said thoughtfully. 'And she hasn't said anything to me.'

'What does a rep look like, then?' Janey asked, amused.

'Well you know, catalogue under the arm and an air of fevered desperation.'

Janey observed the man Becca was talking to. 'No air of desperation there. They look very friendly.'

'Almost intimate, I'd say.' He gave Janey a quizzical look. 'Very intimate.'

Janey felt a pang of concern for Graham. Then she remembered how he'd passed her first thing that morning and not even noticed her cherry-red lip gloss. All he'd done was moan that she'd forgotten to put the kettle on, and he needed a cuppa.

'Well, I'd best get on,' Will said, with a grimace. 'Or I'll be joining you on the verbal warning list.' He stopped again, this time with his hand on the door jamb. 'Oh, and if you want me to come with you to Bristol, I'd be happy to. That's if you want some moral support.'

'Thanks, Will. I appreciate that.' She smiled warmly at him and was puzzled to see some heat rise in his face. He blinked a few times, cleared his throat, seemed to be on the verge of saying something but then left.

Chapter 22

Becca had decided to do one of what she called her 'management walks.' Janey hated them and they seemed to happen with increasing regularity. Mostly it involved her boss hovering in the background, asking stupid questions and getting in the way. Today she was monitoring Janey more closely than usual. It made her feel harassed and on edge. Val, one of the till assistants in plant sales, had gone for her coffee break, so Janey had taken her place and rang through the sale herself. It was one of her regular customers, an eccentric and outspoken pensioner who was permanently tailed by her deaf assistance poodle.

'There you go, Biddy,' she said, as she entered the sale. 'That's a lovely pot you've got there, and the hosta you bought yesterday will go in it nicely. 'El Niño' is a super little plant and you'll have some flowers on it in no time. Just remember, with all this sunshine we're having, that it likes deep shade.'

Biddy beamed. 'Thank you, young Janey. Just wish I'd

thought to buy one when I was in yesterday, but when I got out the pot I planned to put it in, it only had a great big crack down the side, didn't it?'

'You should be okay with that one. It's frost-resistant. Just move it if you can, if we get a really hard winter.'

'Well, we don't often get bad weather down here, do we? Not that it stops my Arthur doom-glumbering every year that we're going to get snow. Used to get some rare old winters in Yorkshire, where I'm from. And they still call it God's own country!' Biddy shot a look at Becca standing to one side, clipboard in hand and scowl on her face. 'See you've got the management in town today.' She leaned closer and added loudly, 'You know what they say about folks who manage. Only one step down in the evolutionary scale from critics and too idle to do the job themselves.' She cackled.

Janey stifled a grin. It wouldn't do to side with Biddy, no matter how much she agreed. Besides, Becca wasn't idle exactly. More overbearing with a resolute sense of being right.

Biddy turned away, examining her credit card receipt. 'Let me know when you're getting in the autumn cyclamens, won't you? Arthur likes a pop of pink in the garden before it all shuts down for the winter. Oh—' she said and stopped dead. 'Think you've made a mistake here. How much did you say this pot was?'

Janey took the pot off her and checked the price tag. 'Nineteen pounds. It's new stock. Frost-resistant as I said. Will see you through the year. It's got a special glaze. Lovely pattern.'

'Yes, yes,' Biddy said impatiently. 'You said all that when I was choosing it. But, my girl, according to my credit card slip, you've charged me ninety-one pounds.'

'Biddy, I'm so sorry.' Janey blushed scarlet, aghast. 'Come back to the till and I'll sort it.' As she refunded the credit card the ninety-one pounds and put the correct amount through, she was only too aware of Becca's presence. The woman was almost breathing down her neck. By now thoroughly flustered, Janey made yet another mistake and had to ring through the amount a third time. 'I can't apologise enough, Biddy,' she repeated. 'Can't think what's wrong with me this morning.' She tried to lighten the mood. 'Probably haven't had enough coffee.' She didn't want to upset Biddy, who not only a regular and free-spending customer, was also uninhibited enough to say exactly what she thought and usually at volume.

'I know exactly what's wrong with you,' the pensioner boomed, as she took the correct credit card slip. 'You,' she clicked her fingers at Becca. 'Here, now.'

Janey's heart plummeted. Difficult though Biddy could be, she hadn't thought she'd bother to take the complaint to management. Straightening her shoulders, she prepared herself for Becca's wrath. 'Just don't say anything you'll regret,' she muttered to herself. 'Remember you need this job and you only have to hang on until Clare comes back.'

Becca approached them. 'It's Biddy isn't it?' she crooned. 'How may I help?' Then her attention was caught by Janey's snowdrop mug perched next to the till. Janey hadn't had time for a break that morning so had grabbed a quick coffee on the way to relieve Val. 'How many times have I told you not to bring hot beverages onto the shop floor?' Becca hissed. 'So unprofessional.' She swung round to Biddy, deliberately poking her elbow out as she did. The mug crashed to the floor, shattering. Luckily it was empty. 'Oops,' Becca said, barely registering what she'd done. 'Well you won't bring that mug out again, will you?'

She addressed Biddy, her voice taking on a silken quality. 'Can I first apologise most sincerely for that most unfortunate mistake. I can assure you nothing like it will ever happen again. Not if I can help it.'

Biddy had seen what Becca had done. Her eyes grew flinty and her lips thinned into a narrow line. 'No, it won't,' she began, 'and it's Mrs Roulestone to you. I can tell you why nothing like that will ever happen again.' The little black poodle whimpered at her tone and crept behind her legs. 'For one thing, if you have time to stand around doing nothing, then you're not doing your job properly. For another, I could see how nervous you were making this child, which is why she made the mistake.' Her voice rose and one or two other customers stopped to listen. 'If you think that's the way to get the most from your employees, my girl, I think you ought to go and look up a management training course. In fact, I know of several you might benefit from.'

Becca opened her mouth into a little scarlet 'o' but no sound emerged.

'And now, you'll hand over a nice little voucher for lunch at your caff to say sorry. Or better still,' at this the pensioner took the dumbstruck Becca's arm, 'you'll take me over there yourself. And while you're at it, you can carry this pot. It's getting heavy and I've got at least thirty years on you.' She handed it over to a stunned-looking Becca and pushed her in the direction of the exit. As they reached the door, Biddy turned and gave Janey an enormous wink.

Janey's shoulders resumed their normal position.

Temporarily. She was pretty sure, even though Biddy thought she had done her a favour, this wasn't the last she'd hear about it from Becca. It was just another nail in the coffin. Crouching, she picked up the remnants of the mug that Graham had given her. She put the parts back together but didn't think it could be mended. Blinking back tears, which were part anger and part sorrow, she bit down on her emotions.

'I won't let her get to me,' she muttered. 'I will not let her defeat me.' She put the mug fragments carefully by the till, annoyed her hands were shaking.

Val came back wearing a bemused expression. 'Was that Biddy Roulestone marching our beloved leader out of the store?'

Janey collapsed onto the stool behind the till; her legs had gone to jelly. She explained what had happened. 'I don't know how I could have made such a mistake. I'm usually so careful when I'm on the till. It's just with Becca right me behind me—'

'Oh, don't take on so,' Val said robustly. 'Happens to the best of us, especially when that woman's around. She puts the fear of God into me an' all. Go and get yourself something to eat and forget all about it. What's the worst she can do?'

As Janey slid off the stool, she knew exactly the worst Becca could do. Feeling the slip of paper with the dyscalculia details on it crackle in her pocket, she resolved to ring up for an appointment as soon as she could.

Chapter 23

ITALY

'This is glorious,' Clare said, as she lifted her face to the sea breeze that buffeted around her. 'I'm so glad I said yes, Leo.' She sat back on the glossy walnut bench at the aft of Leo's boat. Although to describe it as a mere boat was doing it a disservice; it was a large and very luxurious motor launch. She suspected detractors liked to call them gin palaces.

'Thought you might like it. She's good, eh? The *Chiara*.'

'She's yar.'

'What is this yar?'

'Oh, come on, Leo. Haven't you seen *The Philadelphia Story?* The yacht, the *True Love*. It was described as yar, meaning easy to handle, quick to the helm. Everything a boat should be.'

'A boat called the *True Love*. Now that I approve of.'

Clare wrinkled her nose trying to remember. 'Or was it in *High Society?* I'm probably making it all up. The prosecco has gone to my head. Or maybe it's all this delicious sea air. Janey would remember which film it was.'

'And who is Janey?'

'My head gardener.' Clare pushed her hair away from her face. 'She's a real film buff.'

Leo sipped from his glass. 'Work! Stop thinking about work,' he reproved. 'This is supposed to be your holiday. I refuse to allow you to think about England. Sit. Enjoy. Look at the view.'

And what a view. The *Chiara*'s crew had motored the boat along the Amalfi Coast, skirted around Capri and flirted with Vesuvius looming in the distance. They were headed for the north coast of Sicily.

'We will stop at Cefalu. I know it, you will find it interesting.'

'What if we can't moor up. Or tie up, or whatever you call it?'

Leo shrugged. 'You worry too much, *bella*. Leave it to me. I'll sort it.'

Clare looked at him from behind her sunglasses. She had been in control for so long. Had had to be the one in charge, the one making all the decisions. And it had continued long after Gem's death. The endless paperwork, the will, sorting a funeral that suited everyone, and her the least. Running the business. It was one reason she took Becca on so quickly; she couldn't wait to relinquish some of the workload, the strain. Holding onto the boat's rail as it hit a wave, she let herself live in the moment, enjoy the hot sun and the salt spray. And a man who said leave everything to him. She felt an exhilarating sense of freedom. Raising her glass to him, she decided she would indeed leave everything to Leo.

They moored up in a small marina to the east of the town from where Leo tried to arrange a taxi. From the animated conversation conducted in Italian, Clare could tell no taxis were forthcoming. The heat beat down and bounced off the hard rock. It made Clare feel very alive.

Leo came to her. 'Big wedding at the cathedral. No taxi but we can borrow something.'

'What?' Clare asked, expecting him to point to a tiny Fiat 500.

Leo gave her a naughty look. 'Are you up for an adventure, *amore mio?*' He took her hand and led her to a moped parked up alongside a dilapidated shed. Taking the helmet from where it dangled on the handlebars, he handed it to her.

Clare laughed in disbelief. 'We can't fit two of us on that thing!'

'But of course we can. I drive. You sit here, behind.' Leo pointed to the seat, a challenge in his eyes.

Clare laughed again. 'Why not. Let's have an adventure. You're a long time dead.'

'Tsk. A morbid thought but one I happen to agree with.'

From somewhere, the owner of the moped found another helmet, gave them brief instructions and they were off. Clare clung to Leo, feeling the heat of his body through his shirt and thanked the gods that she had decided to wear shorts; it would have been impossibly precarious riding pillion side-saddle.

It was less than a five-minute ride to the town itself, so Leo took them sightseeing. They admired the fisherman's houses, the walls of which fell straight to the sea, drove carefully through the crowds in the cathedral square and parked up just in time to catch the bride and groom and the wedding party come out to stand on the church steps. The bride was very beautiful in a gown and veil made from heavy cream lace and they watched for a while as photographs were taken and rose petals thrown. It was a happy scene to gladden the heart; a young couple embarking on the next stage of their lives. Afterwards, Clare refused to countenance the idea of climbing up the great *Rocca di Cefalu,* the enormous and overbearing lump of cliff that loomed over the town, and instead insisted Leo take them somewhere for lunch. Riding through the skinny lanes of the old town, she tapped him on the shoulder and yelled, 'Stop here.'

He parked up, helped her off and looked around him in astonishment. 'Here? But we could have a view, peace and quiet, relaxation.'

Clare surveyed the tiny café. 'It's perfect,' she breathed.

They sat outside at the only table, in a little vee at the join of two narrow roads. The town was quiet. The occasional moped, and the odd little three-wheeled vans that Leo explained were called Apes and were found all over Italy, passed them so close that it made the plastic tablecloth fly.

Clare peered inside. The interior was barely bigger than the outside and was dark and cool-looking. She could just make out a young man whose beauty, in a land where it was commonplace, took her breath away. She nodded to the elderly woman sitting outside on a rackety old chair pushed up against the wall. '*Buongiorno.*' Dressed in dusty black, with a wrinkled face burnished from long exposure to a Mediterranean climate, she grinned back a toothless smile. She's probably the same age as me, Clare wondered and smiled some more. The woman called inside for her son, or more likely grandson, to come out and wait.

The menu was limited. Risotto or cow's hoof. Clare, trying to keep her face straight, ordered risotto. When it came it was delicious and accompanied by a fresh salad of tomatoes and herbs and swimming in fragrant olive oil.

'How did you know the food would be so good here?' Leo asked, scraping his bowl with a hunk of bread.

'Oh, I don't know. Instinct. Besides, we're in Italy. The food is always good. The best.'

'The best.' Leo grinned. 'But, for this, you declined the *La Botte* and *Al Porticciolo*? They are the famous Cefalu restaurants.'

'It was the right decision though, wasn't it? Although I'm awfully glad they had risotto on the menu. Not too sure if I'm up to a cow's hoof.'

'Nor me,' Leo admitted, with a wink. 'Wait though, I thought I said leave everything to me, eh?'

'Oh yes. *Scusi*. It's a hard habit to break.'

He roared. 'For you, I forgive everything.' He got up. 'And now I must go and thank the chef.' He disappeared into the tiny interior, ducking to avoid several large hams and sausages hanging from the ceiling.

The woman shuffled over to the table. 'Good eh?' she asked, in heavily accented Italian.

'Oh, my darling. *Si si. Molto bene. Molto bene. Grazie mille*.'

The old woman's face broke into a delighted smile. She reached for Clare's hand and kissed it. 'Good. Good,' she repeated, and then she too disappeared into the café.

Clare put one arm on the rail that separated her from the

traffic scooting past. She was utterly relaxed. Full of good food and warmed from the Italian sunshine. For an instant, guilt overcame her; guilt that she was here and enjoying these simple pleasures and Gem never could again. She recalled one of their last conversations and Gem's order that she shouldn't feel guilty for living on when he hadn't, for enjoying something.

'I want you to live, my darling,' he'd instructed. 'And all that that entails.' Her eye was caught by a woman hanging out snowy-white shirts on a washing line on her balcony, high above. There was something about the action, humdrum and commonplace that it was, that soothed her. A serenity overcame her. She was content. Or as content as she ever would be without Gem. How he would have loved it here. That's if she'd ever been able to tear him away from his beloved Cheney House, she thought, on a slight giggle. Something shifted inside her. A fragment of the grief that she had carried with her for so long dislodged. It made way for, if not happiness, then the promise that at some point in the future she would be happy again. She felt almost ready to face England, Cheney House and all the challenges that lay ahead. And it was due, in no small part to Leo and the healing powers of Italy.

The man himself returned. He came bearing the inevitable glasses of limoncello but had a wrapped ham tucked under his arm too.

'How do they ever produce any food in that kitchen? It's a quarter of the size of the galley on the boat.' He sat down and put the ham on the chair beside him. Toasting Clare and seeing her raised eyebrows, he added, 'Maria insisted we have it. She was so impressed by your bad Italian. It charmed her, she said, the Italian spoken by the English lady.'

'Oh,' she said, crestfallen. 'How did they know I was English?'

'Clare, only a beautiful English woman would ask such a thing!'

Chapter 24

It was a peerless late spring day. In the cool of the dawn Janey had gone to stand underneath the chestnuts, leaning against the trunk of the fattest, to breathe in the heady scent of their newly unfurled greenery and feel the air against her skin. A slight wind got up and everything felt fresh and sappy. Susurration. That was the word to describe the whisper of a breeze through leaves. A beautiful word and a truly beautiful sensation. Some days, when she stood here, the trees raged and creaked with drama. But today all was soft. It filled her with a sense of optimism and new beginnings. Maybe, if she tried very hard, she could change things. With Graham and even with Becca. Even though reluctant to leave her trees, she made her way to work.

'Gray,' she asked, clutching a mug to her sweatshirt; this one was plain white and boring, but as such there was no danger of becoming fond of it and being distraught when it was broken by her vindictive boss. 'Have you noticed anything different about me lately?'

'Like what?' he replied, without looking away from the computer screen. They were in the office and they'd had a coffee together, a rare occurrence lately.

Janey came and rested a hip against the desk, dislodging a pile of paperwork as she did. It thumped to the floor but she ignored it. 'Oh I don't know. Do I look any different?' She swished her hair back and attempted a pout.

'Just as gorg as ever, Janey.' He still hadn't looked up.

Janey's optimism fled. Uttering profanities under her breath, she peered at the computer screen. 'What are you looking up?'

'The names of the rattan reps from Dallwings.'

'Why?' Although she could hazard a guess as to why he was checking up on the reps from their main furniture supplier.

'No reason, just want to see who that bloke is who's been hanging around.'

'The one who's been spending an awful lot of time with Becca, you mean?'

'That's the one.' Graham's reply was curt. His swear word was even more so. He straightened and clicked off Google. 'Can't find anyone on here who looks like him.'

'Maybe he's more senior? Becca's put in a huge order, hasn't she? Perhaps they sent out the big guns.'

'Yeah. Maybe,' he said, sounding morose. 'Hello, Will,' he added, as the man came in. 'What can we do for you?'

'I come bearing post.' Stepping carefully around the mess of paper on the floor, he bent and fussed Camilla who, as usual, scampered up to greet him, her tail wagging so furiously it made her fat bottom wiggle.

'We've already had the post,' Janey put in. 'It came at eight.'

'Ah, this is special. Hand delivered by Jed Henville.'

'Ooh, that's Millie's husband. What is it?'

'Have a look yourself.' Will handed over a thick cream envelope bearing her name written in beautiful copperplate.

Janey ripped it open, letting the envelope flutter down to join the discarded paperwork on the floor. 'Wow! I've been invited to the party at the bookshop to launch the film festival. I knew it was a special sort of a day. Something good was bound to happen. Oh,' she added, as her shoulders sagged. 'It's fancy dress.'

'What's wrong with fancy dress?' Will asked curiously.

'I just don't do it.'

'You can never bear to be parted from your overalls and Docs, can you, Janey?' Graham said, sniggering a little.

Janey felt her eyes smart. It had been a cruel jibe. 'I can never think of anything to wear, that's all,' she retorted. 'Unlike you, I don't have three wardrobes stuffed full of fancy clobber.'

'You've got some clues on this one,' Will said quietly. 'Read the invite properly. It's themed.'

Janey reread it. '*Some Like it Hot*?' Her eyes huge, she grinned at him.

'Thought that might cheer you up.'

'What's *Some Like it Hot*, when it's at home?' Graham grumbled.

'Well, you're just going to have to find out, my friend.' Will thrust two more envelopes at the man's chest, none too gently. 'As you and Becca are invited too. Give hers to her, will you?

That's if you can prize her away from the rattan chap.' He nodded in the direction of the courtyard. 'They were heading to the café the last I saw of them. The pair of them looked very cosy.'

Graham muttered something indistinguishable, grabbed the envelopes off Will, and ran out.

Janey stared at Will, trying to gauge his mood. 'Is she really with him again?' She giggled. 'She must've bought an awful lot of rattan.'

'No. Just couldn't resist. I don't like the way he treats you sometimes, Janey.'

'Who, Graham? Oh, it's just banter between mates. It's just the way he is.' She couldn't quite keep the longing out of her voice.

'Yes, well.' Will seemed lost for words. 'Look,' he began, 'obviously he and Becca will go to the party together, so how about if you and I – I don't mean as a date or anything – but I'm not all that keen on walking into parties on my own so you'd be doing me a favour. If you came with me, I mean. As friends.'

Janey wasn't sure if she was all that keen on walking into parties on her own either. Not that she'd been to that many. She certainly didn't want to be a Billy No Mates and be faced with the sight of Graham slobbering all over Becca.

'Not sure I'll be going.' She looked down and became very busy scuffing her boots together. 'It's not really my scene. I'm more of a pint in the pub sort of girl.'

'You've got to go. Millie's parties are legendary. Ah, come on, Janey. Come with me. As Gran's representative, it's expected that I go. And actually, I'd really like to but I'm not going on my own.'

‘As friends?’

‘Of course as friends.’

What could she lose? As long as she avoided the pain of seeing Graham and Becca together, she might even have fun. And it would make a change from a night in the Star. Recalling her optimism from earlier, she mustered some enthusiasm.

‘Yeah okay, then. No problem.’ Just as he was about to go, she added, ‘Have you heard from Clare?’

‘The last text I had said she was on a friend’s boat and they were cruising around Sicily for a few days. She promised to be back in time for the reopening though.’

‘Let’s hope so. I miss her.’

‘So do I, Janey, so do I.’

He began to head out but then turned back to her. ‘Is everything all right, Janey? I heard there was a problem the other day.’

To Janey’s shame, she felt her eyes go hot with sudden tears.

‘I made a mistake on the till.’ She scrubbed at her face with the heel of her hand, refusing to show emotion in front of Will. ‘Accidentally overcharged a customer.’

‘But it was noticed and put right?’

She nodded.

‘No harm done, then.’ Will came closer. He looked into her face. ‘Are you sure you’re all right?’

‘Becca was there,’ Janey blurted out, ridiculous tears spilling over. The image of the snowdrop mug smashed on the floor filled her vision. Any joy in the day gone at the memory of how Becca had been. She still hadn’t been called into the office for the inevitable and humiliating showdown.

‘Hey, hey, come here.’ Will came to her and folded her into

his arms. He murmured soothing, nonsensical words into her hair until she'd calmed, holding her tightly to him.

Through her distress radiated the simple joy of being held by him. It felt weirdly right that he should comfort her. Janey hadn't been held like this for a long time and never by a man as attractive and as kind as Will. Then she pushed him off, as anger flooded through her.

'She's going to sack me, Will. I know it. This place is all I've ever known. I've never worked anywhere else. I wouldn't know how to work anywhere else. I don't *want* to work anywhere else.' She rubbed furiously at where the button from his suit jacket had pressed into her cheek.

'She's not going to sack you.'

'How? How can you be sure?' Janey stamped her foot in frustration. 'How can you possibly know that?'

'Because I won't let her.' Will, a grim look on his pale face, turned on his heel and strode out.

Chapter 25

Will had rarely been as angry. Once back in his office, he fired off several emails to his grandmother, filling her in on what had been happening in her absence, and while not wanting to cut short her holiday, implored her to get back to Cheney House as soon as possible.

Once he'd done that, he poured himself a coffee and thought through how best to tackle Becca. Hearing her go into her office next door, he swallowed the remains of his espresso, straightened his tie and went to find her.

'Hi, Will,' she said, without bothering to look up. 'What can I do for you?' She gestured to a chair. 'Do sit down, won't you? I'll just be a second.'

'This won't wait, Becca. I'd like to talk to you about Janey.'

Becca took her time folding a piece of paper in half and setting it to one side. She steepled her fingers together and gave a grim smile.

'Really?'

'I think you're handling her all wrong.'

'Do you? How fascinating. Look, please sit down so we can discuss this properly.'

Will sat. Reluctantly. 'She needs more careful treatment to get the best out of her.'

Becca suppressed a laugh. 'That woman needs a firm hand and clear boundaries.'

'She's a valued member of the team.'

'She's a liability. Do you know I caught her overcharging a customer the other day? Seventy pounds too much, Will!'

'Yes, she told me about it.'

'And she put me in an extremely difficult position with an alarmingly demanding customer.'

'That's what you're paid for, Becca. To sort things like that out.' Will reined in his temper with difficulty.

'And if our dear Janey, of whom we all seem so fond, had not made this appalling error, I wouldn't have had to deal with a very rude and aggressive old woman. Although it was just as well I was there. I was the one who stopped it escalating. Think if it had hit the local papers! As it was, it cost the centre lunch on the house and twenty-five pounds in vouchers as a goodwill gesture. Now I'm wondering what else Janey has done that has gone unnoticed. I know she's frequently late, is totes a mess, spends far too much time talking to the customers and not selling them anything and I can never find her – she's always in that grotty little shack of hers, doing God knows what with snowdrops.' Becca raised a perfectly groomed eyebrow. 'And what a waste of time that is.'

Will felt hot blood rush into his brain. He clenched his jaw. He prided himself on his control. Emotion had no place in the workplace. Most problems could be solved by logic and common sense, but there was something about this woman that made his every nerve stand on end. And not in a good way.

'My grandmother herself sanctioned the snowdrop project. Have you any idea how much a rare or new variety of snowdrop could bring in?'

Becca blew out a tiny breath in frustration. 'I have absolutely no idea and even less interest.'

'Then perhaps you should. You are the manager of a garden centre, after all!'

Becca leaned back on her office chair. She observed him through heavily made-up, narrowed eyes.

'You're quite right. I am the general manager. And in overall control in the absence of your grandmother. What are you, Will? As far as I can see you're not even a permanent member of staff, just a family member helping out.' She gave a thin smile. 'Of course, we are all very grateful that you're here and for your obvious expertise,' she simpered. 'I don't know what we'll do without you and you'll be missed terribly when you go to the States.' She leaned forward and picked up a pen with a pink fluffy thing on the end. Scribbling something on the memo pad on her desk, she said, 'Thank you for reminding me. I must start drafting out the advertisement for a fully qualified, experienced senior accountant to join us. It may take some time to find the right person to suit me.' She replaced the pen on the desk carefully, placed one red-taloned hand over the other and said, with icy calm, 'Until then, please remember I am your senior, just as Clare wished it, grandson or not.'

Will shot up out of his chair.

'Well, Becca, as a non-paid up member of staff, who is doing his family run company a favour in his sabbatical, I think you'll find you have no hold over me whatsoever. And when my grandmother returns she'll find how you've been managing her business very interesting. Very interesting indeed. And one more thing, I think you've forgotten that Janey is one of her favourite employees. In fact, she's more like a member of the family. *My* family. So when Gran comes back to find Janey has been harassed unnecessarily, given verbal warnings and, quite frankly, *bullied*, it'll be another very interesting situation for you to de-escalate!' He'd gone too far. He'd lost his temper and walked right into the trap Becca had laid.

'I look forward to Clare's return, Will,' Becca said, her chin rising in defiance. 'And I am so looking forward to explaining how her grandson has completely lost it over an imbecilic and useless member of her staff. Maybe you should consider thinking with your head in future and not with the contents of your delightfully tailored trousers. Close the door on your way out.'

Will shut the door of Becca's office with elaborate care. He leaned against it. 'Now you've gone too far, Becca,' he whispered. 'Big mistake. A very big mistake. Huge.'

Chapter 26

(Not) The Galloping Galanthophile Blog: June

Strange happenings at Cheney House Garden Centre. Once a beloved establishment of Bereford residents and visitors alike, we customers can't help but notice changes afoot. And the changes haven't always been for the positive.

A favourite of the ladies, Graham, is no longer to be seen parading around the wooden planters, ready and willing to help with gradients of gravel and the best kind of bark chippings to use. Instead, he's misusing his gardening talents by staking out the ornamental lake and dishing out paddles for those in search of a cheap thrill on the punts.

Gwen in the café is serving Pad Thai instead of treacle tart and custard. And lovely though Thai food is, where's our old favourite Shepherd's Pie? I hear folk cry. Nine pounds seventy-five for a pot of coffee? Far too much for most people's pockets and certainly this person's, who would prefer a mug of instant like in the old days.

And what's become of our favourite gardener, Janey Trelawney? No longer greeting us with a ready smile, a witty riposte and freely given advice. Now she creeps around, dressed in unbecoming navy polyester, looking afraid of her own shadow.

Something else. Have you noticed the poor quality of the plants just lately? My begonias have already gone over and no amount of dead-heading is coaxing them into flowering again. And it's only June!

We, the loyal customers of Cheney House, demand answers! Maybe we'll get them at the grand reopening? I, for one, can't wait. Have you heard who is cutting the ribbon? Only the movie star Alina Allen herself! She's obviously taking some time out of filming those noisy Bond movies. I'm really looking forward to it, I'll have my autograph book at the ready. Giveaways are promised too, and to be honest, with the prices Cheney House have been charging lately, they can afford a few!

Happy gardening!

'You seen this?' Graham swivelled the computer screen towards Janey. They were in the office; for once their morning breaks coinciding.

When she'd read it, she blanched.

'You didn't write it?'

'Of course I didn't write it. I'm not stupid, Gray. Why would

I want to give Becca another excuse to fire me? Besides, she told me my blog was no longer needed now she was creating a new website. Gardening tips not necessary, apparently, on a garden centre website.' She laughed without humour.

'Who's behind it then?'

'Beats me. Could be anyone.' Janey scrutinised the screen more closely. 'It's a Word Press blog. Anyone can set one up. It's quite easy to do.'

'I'll take your word for it. Becca's going to do her nut when she sees it.'

'Becca does her nut about most things,' Janey said drily. She couldn't stand the woman but still worried about their manager's stress levels. Becca's anxiety attacks usually brought on a period of uber-busyness. And that meant she would be on the warpath over some invented misdemeanour. Usually Janey's. She brightened. 'Maybe she'll get so stressed out about it all she'll have to take some leave. Until, oh I don't know, just after Clare gets back. We can but hope.'

Graham was only half-listening but this got through. 'Aw Janey. Not like you to be so unkind. Making tea?'

She flicked the kettle on. 'Suppose. Although it wouldn't hurt for you to make a brew once in a while.'

'Go on Janey love, you always make it so much better than me.'

She fished out their mugs from the sink and gave them a cursory swill under the tap. Graham hadn't even bothered to wash them up. She sighed. Once, his excuses and wheedling ways would have charmed her into doing whatever he wanted. These days, she was getting sick of it.

'Who's your money on?'

Janey, her head in the fridge, muttered, 'On what?'

'Haven't you been listening? On who's behind this rogue blog. It's well-dodgy.'

'No idea.' She straightened and slammed the fridge door shut. 'And I don't really care. As long as everyone knows it's not me.'

'Could cause some real damage. We need to find out who it is and shut the bastards down. I really feel for Becca, having to deal with this on top of everything else.'

Janey eyed Graham. If only he was as protective of her.

'Don't think you can shut blogs down just like that. Think it's called freedom of speech. And anyway, don't they say any publicity is good publicity? You never know, it might get the punters coming in to see what all the fuss is about. Stranger things have been known to happen. You've forgotten to pick up some milk again. It'll have to be black coffee.'

'Yeah. Whatevs. I reckon it might be that crotchety old mare who ticked you off about overcharging her. Mind you, bet she wouldn't know one end of a computer from the other.'

'Biddy?' Janey snorted. 'She's no crotchety old mare. She'd soon sort you out if she heard you say that about her. You should have seen how she dealt with Becca.' She spooned coffee and watched as the granules liquidised and darkened in the wet mugs. Becca still hadn't asked her into the office to explain what had happened – or issued any further warnings, verbal or otherwise. Somehow it was worse having it hang over her. She almost wished Becca would come out with it and put her on a final warning or dismiss her. At least she'd know where she stood. Feeling thoroughly irritated, she slammed Graham's coffee down next to him. He didn't notice, he was still glued to the computer screen.

'Maybe if you had more practise at making tea and coffee

instead of getting everyone else to do it, you might make a better cuppa,' she snarled.

'Yeah. Cheers. Thanks Janey.'

Janey rolled her eyes to the ceiling and refrained from further comment.

Chapter 27

ITALY

Clare received the volley of emails from Will as she sat on the harbourside on the island of Lipari. Leo had persuaded her to stay with him and the *Chiara* while they motored around the volcanic islands off Sicily's northern coast. She was glad she hadn't missed out on this island; it was entrancing. Leo had demurred when she'd suggested they wander up to the archaeological museum, so she had left him on the quayside nursing a cold beer. She'd spent over an hour becoming fixated on the tiny terracotta carvings of Greek comedy and tragedy masks and then had wandered back. It was a sleepy part of the world and it was too hot to hurry. Finding Leo sitting at the same *trattoria* where she'd left him, she collapsed, perspiring and dusty, and demanded fresh, iced lemonade. Then her mobile had pinged several times in quick succession. Wi-fi had been patchy when on the boat and her phone had languished in silence. Now she looked at the messages firing through. Will had sent several over the last few days, each getting increasingly terse as he received no answer.

Seeing her knitted brows, Leo asked, in a concerned voice, 'Trouble?'

'You could say that. Trouble at mill.'

'Eh?'

'It turns out things aren't going well with the manager I put in place,' she explained. Clare gave a heavy sigh and reached for her glass of lemonade. 'I so wanted her to work out too. Thought she might be a breath of fresh air. A new start for us all.'

'And she's no good?'

'It's not that exactly. Lots of new ideas, but according to Will, isn't handling some of the staff in quite the right way.'

'Do you really have to cut your holiday short?'

'Will's terribly apologetic, says he's been trying to handle it, but Becca is now refusing to even discuss things with him. Charging ahead with some ambitious plans. Over-ordering stock, which is most worrying.'

Leo huffed. 'Is he a man or no?'

Clare smiled at his very Italian machismo. 'I'm afraid it's not quite that simple. Poor Will isn't there in any kind of official capacity. His role is ambiguous to say the least – and that is entirely my fault. He's only there as a favour to me before he goes to the States. He really hasn't any sway over Becca.'

'What is this *sway*?'

'Influence, authority,' Clare explained patiently. 'I put her in charge. Over Will. And now things are deteriorating. It seems my presence is required. Very much so.'

'So you do have to cut short your holiday?'

'It looks that way.' Clare gazed out at the turquoise waters, at the red and white checked tablecloths fluttering in the cooling breeze, at the tourists wandering around, hand in hand without a care in the world. 'I'm so sad to say goodbye to all this.'

'Italy will always be here,' Leo said simply. 'As will I.'

Clare's eyes glistened. A lump of emotion lodged in her throat. She reached out a hand to him. 'You have been marvellous. These few weeks have been marvellous. It's been just what I needed. Sun, wonderful scenery, good wine – and even better company. I can't thank you enough, Leopoldo. I've felt relaxed for the first time in years.' Her lips quirked in humour. 'And the food has been good too.'

'The best,' he cried.

'The very best!' She regarded him fondly. 'You've proved yourself a very fine friend.'

Leo turned her hand over in his and kissed it. '*Amore mio*. What I can do, I do.' He gave a tiny shrug.

'In which case, I have to ask you to take me back to the hotel so I can collect my things.' She pulled a face. 'And then I have to face the delights of Naples airport again.'

'Then so shall it be. But first we have lunch, eh?' He gestured to the harbour. 'I hear there is some very fine baby octopus coming in. You wouldn't want to miss those.'

Clare smiled at him. She supposed another hour or so wouldn't make any difference to the situation at Cheney House.

'I think lunch is a must. For one, I'm starving and for another, I can't wait to see you tackle baby octopus.'

Chapter 28

Will collected Janey, to take her to the *Some Like it Hot* party, at eight exactly. Somehow, she knew he'd be punctual so waited for him at the bottom of the flight of steps that led to her flat. He inched his sleek Jaguar carefully over the cobbles and came to a rest right by her. Getting out, he came to the passenger door and held it open.

'Your carriage, my lady.'

Janey snorted and pretended to look down her nose. 'I'll have you know I'm used to chauffeur driven limos.'

'It's the driver's night off.' Will made a face. 'What can I say? I do apologise for you having to slum it in my lease car.' He grinned. 'You're looking really good, Janey.'

'Thanks,' she said shyly, unused to receiving compliments. 'As I said, I don't do fancy dress. I don't even own a dress, so thought I'd go as Tony Curtis.'

'The blazer and cap suit you.'

'Could say the same to you. We're a matching pair. You didn't fancy dragging up then?' Will was dressed almost identically in dark trousers, a naval-inspired blazer and jaunty white cap. But, unlike her, he'd also found a silk cravat to complete the look of the pretend millionaire Tony Curtis played in the film.

'Really don't think the world is ready for my hairy legs.'

'You'd have to shave them,' Janey said sternly. 'That's what us women have to do. Apparently it's not acceptable to have hairy legs. At the spa I was threatened with being waxed everywhere nature designed to be hairy and *then* they wanted to stick on great big false eyelashes the size of tarantulas and draw in eyebrows that looked like caterpillars. Makes no sense.' She shrugged, mystified. 'What's wrong with hairy legs anyway? I quite like mine. Keep me warm. But maybe it's just as well I wear jeans all the time.'

She looked so irate, Will burst out laughing. 'Come on, get in. I know it's only a Jag but maybe you'll be gracious enough to put up with it tonight.'

It was a glorious evening, warm and still and soaked in the scent of newly greened-up countryside. Janey sat back against the leather seat, buzzed the window down and breathed it all in.

'Thanks for persuading me to go, Will. I think tonight is just what I need.'

They cruised around the little town of Berecombe until Will found a space made vacant by someone just leaving. He squeezed the car alongside the town's promenade and they strolled towards Millie Vanilla's café and bookshop. The sun was low over the sea and a mackerel-cloud sky was filled with vivid red and orange ripples. As Janey turned to Will, she saw he was suffused with a technicolour wash. 'Very *South Pacific*,' she murmured and took in a great breath of salt-laden air.

Even though she lived very near the sea she never seemed to get much of a chance to make the most of it. With the gently washing waves and the white lights twinkling along the sea front, it felt very romantic.

'This way, I think,' he said. 'The bookshop is just the other side of the café. I believe it used to be an old chapel before Millie converted it.' He held out his arm so she took it and moved closer; she could feel the heat emanating from his body. She gulped in another breath of sea air and got the scent of Will instead. He smelled gorgeous.

As they neared the bookshop, Janey exclaimed in delight. 'They've got a red carpet!'

And they had. The large terrace, which the café and bookshop shared and which overlooked Lyme Bay, had been cordoned off for partygoers only. A wide stripe of red carpet led to the entrance of the bookshop, the double doors of which had been flung open. On either side of the carpet was a fancy barrier made up of two lines of gilt-covered posts with chain links connecting them. Huge spotlights beamed down on the entrance and Janey was amused to see a photographer pretending to be paparazzi. It was only Andy Haywood from the *Berecombe News*, but it all added to the fun.

'It's magical,' she breathed.

'They've certainly gone to town,' Will said, sounding impressed. He held out his arm again. 'May I escort you in?'

'With pleasure.' She was always surprised, whenever she touched Will, at the hardness of his body. He was easily as well-muscled as Graham. 'You must work out a lot,' she said, testing a bicep.

'Well, those Bonsai trees take some pruning.'

They laughed and Andy caught it on camera. 'That'll be a nice snap,' he said. 'You two look just right together.'

Janey blushed and became very busy finding the invitations and handing them to a tall man at the door. He was dressed in full drag, in a twenties-inspired sequinned outfit, with a matching bandana in his blonde hair.

'Jed!' Will said and clasped his hand in a very manly handshake. 'Good to see you again. Looking ... erm ... very,' he struggled for the right word. 'Dapper? Or maybe that should be flapper?'

Jed roared. 'Had to make the effort seeing as Millie can't at the moment. She's absolutely fine but just getting more and more enormous by the day and really wasn't up to fancy dress. Alex, my big bro, dared me.' He raised a well-shaped brow. 'So I couldn't resist the challenge, could I? Wait 'til you get a look at what he's wearing. He's come as the full Marilyn.'

Will laughed. 'Can't wait to see him.' He turned to Janey. 'May I introduce Jed Henville? He's Millie's husband. Jed, this is Janey Trelawney, head gardener and all-round plant expert at Cheney House.'

This time it was Janey's turn for a handshake and then Jed came in for a double kiss. 'How very lovely to meet you. Millie said her gardening chat with you the other day was incredibly useful.' He pulled a rueful face. 'We're both complete garden novices, I'm afraid. And we desperately want to do justice to the place. The old couple who sold us the cottage kept it so beautifully but we haven't a clue.'

'I'd be happy to come and have a look,' Janey offered, a little nonplussed at being addressed by this astonishingly handsome man dressed in a flapper dress, complete with matching feathered boa.

'Would you? That would be marvellous. We need some advice on what plants might be poisonous to Trevor too.'

'Is that what you're going to call the baby?'

'Good Lord no.' Jed laughed again. 'That's our cockapoo. Although Millie does rather baby him.'

'Sounds as though you're going to have your hands full by the time the actual baby comes along,' Will put in.

'Wouldn't have it any other way.'

Janey decided she liked Jed. His love and protectiveness for Millie and his little family to come shone out. She could picture him and Millie walking along Berecombe promenade, pushing a pram containing a tiny baby, the faithful Trevor trotting beside. For the first time ever in her life, she could see the appeal of settling down with a man and making a family of her own. The pang that shot through her was half panic and half sadness, as she realised it was highly unlikely that the man would be Graham.

'Go on through,' Jed said. 'Millie is holding court from a chaise longue so go and say hi and grab a drink on your way through. Virgin Negronis on offer for the drivers.'

As they went into the bookshop proper, the noise hit them. Janey stood for a second, hardly able to take it all in. Massed nets of white lights were strung from the double height ceiling, making the place shimmer and sparkle. Waiters, naked apart from skimpy loincloths, their torsos gleaming with oil, moved around holding trays of drinks; flutes of champagne and cocktails in breast-shaped coupes. Most amazing of all were the partygoers themselves. Some had played it safe by wearing lounge suits or evening dress, but most had embraced the *Some Like it Hot* theme with abandon. There were numerous men in twenties-style gangster suits, complete with fedora hats. A tall lean man, who looked like an older version of Jed, stood in one corner talking to Biddy. He must be Alex, as he was dressed in a shimmering black dress barely held together by sequins and net and completed by a magnificent pair of fake breasts and a Marilyn Monroe wig. Biddy, herself, looked daunting in white satin. Janey had no idea who she was supposed to be but wasn't about to argue with her to find out. A willowy girl in sea-green chiffon floated past and joined them. Alex put his hand around her waist and drew her in for a kiss.

A voluptuous woman encased in a tight silver sheath dress, her blonde hair coiled into chic finger waves, came up to them and introduced herself.

'Hello! I'm Amy, the bookshop manager. Welcome. There's plenty on offer to drink, so please help yourself. And there'll be food later. Nico from the Icicle Works is providing ice-cream as pudding. But the main order of the night is to enjoy yourselves.' She collected a glass from a passing waiter and handed it to Janey, saying, 'See you later.'

They pushed their way through the crowds to find Millie, lying prone on a purple and gilt chaise.

'Janey! You've come. And this must be Will. Forgive me for not getting up, I'm not sure I can.' Millie beamed. 'I've come as a blue whale.' She indicated her navy maternity dress covering her enormous bump. 'But I've made a token effort with this.' She ran a hand through the two-foot-long sequinned feather she wore in her dark bob. 'You've met Dora, haven't you, Janey? Dora, I command you to find Will a drink. He seems to be empty-handed and that simply will not do at one of my parties. Are you driving?' she asked him. 'Yes?

Off you go, Dora, get him one of those delicious non-alcohol cocktails your gorgeous husband is drinking.'

Dora, wearing a pink fringed dress and a tall feather of her own, rolled her eyes. 'Hello honeybuns. I cannot believe this is my gentle, would-do-anything-for-anyone friend. She's turned into quite the monster.'

'Well, I am quite literally one at the moment,' Millie giggled. 'Go on, get the man a drink.'

Dora took a slightly starstruck-looking Will by the arm. 'Come along. I'm Dora, by the way. Come and meet some people.'

Millie beckoned Janey closer. 'He's gorgeous, your Will. Is he Superman or more Clark Kent? Actually, I always preferred Clark Kent; I've always had a bit of a thing for men in specs. And I love how much Clark loves Lois but never tells her.'

Janey looked to where Dora had dragged the man off and was introducing him to a David Essex in-his-prime lookalike. She supposed Will was gorgeous. Not obviously stunning like Jed or Graham, but he had his own quiet charm, and those dark eyes behind his glasses were really something. He was just like her snowdrops. Understated. Not showy but immensely charming once you got to know him. She smiled ruefully down at Millie.

'He's not my Will. We've just come together for a bit of mutual support. Neither of us are party animals, you see.'

Millie looked shocked but Janey couldn't tell if it was the fact that she and Will weren't an item or the revelation that they weren't the partying sort.

'I'm sorry, my lovely. Jed always tells me off for matchmaking but I can't help myself. I'm quite the expert. Worked with Dora and Mikey.' Millie nodded to where Alex was still deep in conversation with Biddy. 'And with Alex and Eleri. The gorgeous waif with the tumbling honey-brown locks and startling eyes is Eleri, my brother-in-law's girlfriend. Biddy tells me the sooner the baby comes, the better. As then I'll be too busy to meddle in other people's lives.' She wrinkled her nose. 'Miss being in the café I suppose. I like being rushed off my feet and maternity leave hasn't really suited me. Don't think I'm born to be idle. Shame you're not with Will though. I really thought you were a couple. You looked so right together.'

It was the second time that evening someone had said that. Janey couldn't see why. 'No, he's not the one I'm interested in,' she said, wondering if it was actually the truth any longer.

'So who is?'

Janey looked around. Through the crowds she could just about glimpse Becca talking to two older men. Graham stood slightly apart from them, looking thoroughly bored. He wasn't a party animal either; his idea of a night out was a pint in the pub and a packet of pork scratchings. For years she'd gone along with that, just to be with him. But actually, had it been her thing after all? She gazed around at the shiny glittery people, all having the time of their lives. Biddy had now led a few up to an improvised dance floor and into what might be a variant on the Black Bottom. It was difficult to tell; there was too much raucous laughter and falling about going on. What had she been missing out on all these years? It all looked to be such fun.

'He's over there,' she murmured, wondering if the man in question was over there at all. Or whether he was, in fact, currently talking to Dora and her husband, Mikey.

'You mean the bloke with the woman who is talking to

Dennis and Arthur?' Millie strained to see and then looked astonished. 'Not sure what film she's from.'

They both stared at Becca.

'Looks more Evita than Marilyn to me,' Millie said, at length.

Janey laughed. It was true. Becca had scraped her platinum hair back from her face in a severe style, so tight it looked as if it was pulling at her skin. Her face was made up in its usual over-the top way, with heavy dark brows and matte red lipstick. Dressed in an uncompromising and dull black dress, she hadn't bothered to adhere to the dress code at all.

'So it's him you were getting all dolled up for at the spa the other day?' Millie asked softly.

Janey nodded, miserably.

'But he's with another woman?'

She nodded again. 'That's Becca, my boss.'

'Ah,' Millie said. 'I see.'

Janey thought she could see everything. Even things that were becoming increasingly muddled in her own head.

'He doesn't look to be having a very good time,' Millie observed.

'He doesn't like parties much either.'

'Well, Arthur is a very lovely man – he's Biddy's husband, did you know? But Dennis, bless him, can go on a bit. He's a town councillor. Now chairing the whole caboodle, with a special interest in planning and the town's development plan.'

Janey looked again. The man Millie referred to as Dennis was deep in a serious-looking conversation with Becca.

'Wonder what they're talking about?'

'Who knows. If I were more mobile, I'd go and rescue your man. Hang on though, looks like Biddy is going to do it.'

They watched as Biddy, in true avenging-angel style, swooped upon her husband and dragged him and Dennis off to the dancefloor. Becca went white with rage. She turned to Graham and muttered something to him. Realising Janey was watching he put up his hand in greeting but was pulled away by Becca and they disappeared.

'How very fascinating,' Millie said. 'Ah, here's your Will back. I mean here's Will. Oh, my lovely, you've brought me a drink too. Is it one of those Virgin Negronis? Delish. Thank you. And I meant to say, Janey, message from Alina via Dora – she can't make it tonight. Now you two, at the risk of me sounding like an elderly dowager aunt, go and have some fun!'

Chapter 29

And amazingly, for two people who professed themselves not the party types, they did have fun.

Biddy, resplendent in her white satin flapper dress and matching elbow-length sleeves, had put herself into the role of master of ceremonies. She dragged people, willing and otherwise, onto the dance floor to dance to a variety of big band tunes and brooked no argument when Will and Janey at first refused. She even taught them some rudimentary Charleston steps and something she yelled out was the Texas Tommy.

Out of breath and hot, a giggling Janey led Will outside.

'Beats dancing under trees?' he asked.

'Nothing beats dancing under trees,' she defended, stoutly. 'You should try it some time.'

They joined the crowds of others who were also seeking respite from the heat and noise and joined a queue where food was being served from a stall with a striped awning. It was all cinema-themed with tiny hot dogs, mini burgers and what looked, at first glance, to be popcorn.

Janey bit into some. 'It's peanut chicken,' she cried, astonished. She ate some more. 'With a hint of sweet chilli. Oh we have to tell Tana to put this on the menu. It's yummy.'

Will, a little more cautiously, tried some. 'It is,' he agreed, 'as you say, yummy. And yet it looks just like popcorn. How clever.'

Janey, buoyed by one too many martinis, burst out laughing.

'What's wrong? What have I said?'

'Sometimes I believe you're even more wary of new stuff than me.'

Will began to protest and then admitted it. 'Yes, all right. I'm usually more of a steak and chips kind of a guy. Unlike some people I could name, I haven't got a movie star to wine and dine me.'

'Ha ha.' Janey swallowed the last of her drink and snaffled another from a passing waiter. 'Come on, let's go over to the edge of the terrace where it's less crowded. Aren't the lights fab? So pretty.' She led him to where there were fewer people and they could hear the shush of a gentle tide. 'Shame Alina couldn't make it. Think she'd have enjoyed it, especially the naked waiters.'

'They're dressed as the chap who banged the huge gong at the beginning of the old Rank films, apparently. Or so Dora told me.'

She saw him give her a measured look.

'I'm not sure they'd be Alina's cup of tea though,' he added.

'Oh come on, Will. They're all gorgeous bits of beefcake. She'd be lusting over them like all the women here are.'

'It was something that Dora said earlier. She met you and Alina at the spa, didn't she?'

Janey nodded. 'Yup. We all had lunch together, along with Millie.'

'She said Alina was looking at you as if she wanted to eat you up. As if you were on the menu along with the smashed avocado.'

'Don't you just love Millie? I really want her to be my best friend,' Janey continued, not registering what he was saying. She hiccoughed a little and looked cross-eyed at her fresh martini. 'Do you know I can drink pints of cider until the cows come home, but these cocktails have gone right to my head.' She re-focussed on Will. 'What did Dora say?'

'That, in film circles, there's a strong rumour that Alina is gay.' Janey choked on her drink. Will tapped her on the back and when she'd finished coughing, he added in an odd tone, 'Has she ever made a pass at you?'

'No!' Janey's eyes went huge with indignation. 'She's been a friend.'

'But she's taken you out to fancy restaurants, paid for all those spa treatments, keeps hanging around the garden centre—' Will let the sentence hang.

'I thought she liked me!'

'I think she does.'

'No, not in that way. As a friend.' Janey's eyes began to glisten.

'Well, she probably likes you that way too. I mean, why not? You're a very likeable person.' Will looked distinctly uncomfortable. 'I'm sorry, Janey. I didn't mean to upset you. You're not gay then? I've been so clumsy about this. I really shouldn't have said anything.'

'No, I'm not gay.' Janey said it too loudly and one or two curious faces turned to them. 'I thought she liked me,' she repeated in a whisper, 'that I was her friend,' she added, on the verge of tears.

Will sat her down on the low wall that separated the terrace from the beach. Sitting opposite, he took her hand in his. 'It must be an impossible situation for Alina to be in,' he began.

Janey nodded.

'It must be hard enough to have any kind of normal life if you're as famous as she's becoming, let alone make friends and meet people you might want to have a relationship with. Despite all her wealth and privilege, I feel really sorry for her. I've often thought she's come across as being lonely. You okay? You've gone very quiet.'

'Yeah. I'm okay. It's all a bit *Notting Hill*, isn't it? But with an extra dimension. And, jeez, what a dimension.'

'That's one way of looking at it. This must be a very real dilemma for the famous, in the public eye all the time, for them to find romance. And, possibly, it must be even more difficult if you're gay.'

There was a silence and then Janey broke it, her words tumbling over themselves.

'I'm a bit weirded-out to be honest. Not about her being gay,' she added, hastily. 'I've got no problem with that. It's just I've been wondering, these past few weeks, just why she was hanging out with me. I thought it was because she liked me, you know, as a person. Found me interesting. She made me feel good about myself. She thought I was clever, that I knew stuff about snowdrops. And, to be honest, I needed the ego-boost, what with Becca and everything.'

'You are clever. You do know stuff. Janey, you're a walking plant encyclopaedia. You must know that. Believe me, you'll do just as you are.'

'But all the time she just wanted to get into my pants.' Janey hiccoughed again. 'I just have to make some adjustments, that's all. Look at things differently. Actually, I feel sorry for her. As you say, it can't be easy.' She gulped back some cocktail and then placed the glass on the wall. She misjudged it and it wobbled on an uneven bit. Will rescued it, putting it somewhere safer. In the half-light, she couldn't see his face clearly.

'You asked me if I was a lesbian?' she asked suddenly. 'Is that what people think? Why do they think that?'

'I'm so sorry, Janey. I just blurted it out.' Will sounded mortified. 'I suppose I thought if you were gay it might be easier for Alina. And you.'

'What, do you think I'd be swept off my feet and taken off to live a life of luxury and decadence in Hollywood?' Janey snorted then reconsidered. 'Ooh, then again, I could see the Chinese Theatre and go on a studio tour. Maybe she would have taken me to the Oscars too? And, oh glory, think about that great Mediterranean climate. Good cacti out there.'

'Maybe.' Will laughed a little, sounding more relaxed. 'Trust you to focus on plants. Doubt if you would have been taken to the Oscars though.'

'No, you're right. It's still not that easy to be out and proud in the film industry.' Janey sighed. 'Now I really feel sorry for her. What a life!'

'Mmm,' Will said drily. 'I'm sure Alina's life has its compensations. And besides, we may have it all wrong. Dora did say it was only a rumour. She probably shouldn't have said anything, but I think she'd had one too many Negronis.'

'You still haven't answered my question. Why do people think I'm gay? Is it because I don't wear frilly stuff, don't cake my face in slap, don't bother with my hair?' she said hotly. 'Why are people so judgemental? Why shouldn't I wear what I want?'

'You *can* wear what you like, be who you want to be. Don't take any notice of what anyone says. And hey, look at me. Don't say I didn't get judged before people knew me better? The boss's grandson, boring accountant, stuffed shirt. Don't you think I've had my fair share of all that pre-judging nonsense?'

Janey met his eyes, inscrutable in the dark. She flushed; glad he wouldn't be able to see her colouring up. 'Guilty as charged.'

'Besides, it was me who asked you if you were gay, not people in general.'

'Well, I'm not. I'm in love with someone, for your information. A man.'

'Oh,' Will said, with a catch in his voice. 'Who might that be then?'

There was a pause, punctuated by the crash of a wave against the shore and the faint sounds of partying coming from the bookshop.

'Didn't you know? I thought everyone did. Except the man himself. It's Graham. I've been in love with Graham since the year dot.' Even as she said it, Janey wondered about the veracity of the statement, but she'd been saying the same thing for so long it had almost become a mantra, a habit. A route in life she had followed unquestioningly. She gave another, gusty sigh. 'I've been in love with Graham Carey since time immemorial. And there's nothing, not one damn thing I can do about it.'

Chapter 30

The day of the grand reopening dawned cool and clear, with a hint of summer heat to come. Chattering house martins flew from under the guttering of the old house, busy with fledglings homed in nests returned to year after year, and swallows swooped to scoop mud up from the lakeside. Out of the ancient and crumbling containers on either side of the porticoed front door tumbled fuchsias and petunias in a frenzy of pink and red, scenting the early morning air. Summer had arrived at Cheney House.

Becca had been in a micro-managing tizzy for days. She snapped and snarled and nothing was quite right. She'd upset Gwen and Tana, claiming the restaurant menu wasn't exactly as agreed, had had a shouting argument with the band leader about precisely where he was going to set up and his playlist and, of course, the hanging baskets and tubs that Janey had prepared to decorate around the marquee weren't up to scratch. Graham tagged behind Becca like an unhappy puppy and jumped every time she gave him an order. He looked so miserable Janey almost felt sorry for him. Almost.

Will cornered her in the plant sales centre as she was trying to rearrange a hanging basket. 'Not the right colour scheme for Miss Bossy Boots,' she explained.

'What did she want?'

'Red, white and blue.'

'But they are red, white and blue,' he pointed out equably.

'You can see red, white and blue. I planted up red, white and blue. Madam sees pink, purple and white.'

Will put his head on one side and viewed the offending plants again. 'Nope. Still see red, white and blue. Do you think she's colour blind? I'm not being funny,' he added hastily, 'but maybe she really is. They look fine to me.'

'Nope. Pretty sure that's not it. She just wants to make a last-minute panic for me.' Janey straightened and wiped her hands down her navy polo shirt. 'And to prove I can't follow the simplest of instructions.'

'So what are you doing about it?'

'Rearranging the same red, white and blue plants just in different combinations and in different pots.'

Will grinned. 'That should do it. Seen the latest blog? There's another penned by our mysterious guest blogger.'

'Haven't had time. I'll have a look later. Who do you think it is? And it's not me, if you're wondering.'

'No idea.' Will shook his head. 'Doubt if it's anyone directly to do with the garden centre. If they're caught it's a sackable offence. This one makes out how the new manager is spoiling the traditional feel of Cheney House. Lots of pointed references to stiletto heels, power suits and how corporate-speak and development plans from big business don't suit a niche organisation.'

'Ouch.'

'Precisely.'

Janey dug out a geranium from one basket, made a hole with her fingers in the compost of another and slid it in next to some trailing white bacopa. 'Sorted. Or at least as sorted as I'm prepared to do.' She brushed her hair back, leaving a trail of soil smeared across her forehead. 'Still no Clare? Thought she promised to be back for today?'

'I've just this minute had a text. She's on her way. Delayed though. Couldn't get out of Naples airport. Baggage handlers went on strike.'

'Oh no!' Janey was distraught. She couldn't wait for Clare to be back and for some normality to resume. And she'd hate for her to miss the reopening. 'How did she do it then?'

'A friend arranged a private plane apparently. Same friend whose yacht she's been on.'

'Nice friend.'

Will grinned. 'I thought so. He's coming back with her. Leopoldo. Old friend of my grandfather's I believe.'

'Oh it'll be so good to have her back, Will.' Janey could feel some of the tension leaving her shoulders already. 'It'll be so good to get back to how we used to do things.'

'Maybe.' Will looked unsure. 'There's one thing I'm concerned about.'

'Only the one thing?'

He blew out a breath. 'Point taken. I'm really worried about how much today is going to cost. The band doesn't come cheap, the marquee is ruddy enormous, there are extra lifeguards on the lake, all the food and drink is gratis and Becca's even arranged pony rides for children. She's donated a huge fee to a local animal rescue in return. It's all costing a fortune.'

'Didn't she agree the budget with you first?'

'Oh yes. And I've just found out she's exceeded that majorly.'

'Maybe she's colour blind when it comes to money too?'

Will gave a short laugh. 'Maybe. Have you seen Alina yet?'

Janey shook her head. 'No. Not looking forward to it either. I don't know how I'm going to react.'

'Just act normally. Just act as you have previously.'

'But how can I?' She kicked an empty compost bag under the potting bench and out of sight, and pulled a face.

'I don't know, Janey. Unrequited love is an awkward thing.' Will bit his lip, seeming to be on the verge of saying something else. He looked at his watch and blew out a frustrated breath. 'Look, I've got to go. Got to check on Gran's taxi from Exeter, otherwise, she might need a lift.' He came to her impulsively and enfolded her in a fierce hug.

'Get off me, you'll get your smart suit all covered in muck!' Janey pushed him away, although she wanted to stay held by him forever. The insight startled her.

Will stared into her eyes, an unreadable expression on his face.

'Funny thing is, I don't mind. Getting covered in muck, that is. Not when it's you. Look, you'll be fine with Alina. Just be honest.' And then he left, brushing a trail of compost off his suit as he went.

Janey stared after him, a tumult of emotion raging through her. The only thing she was certain of was a sudden and desperate need to feel his arms around her again.

Will hurried out and headed for his office. With his gaze locked on his phone, he missed Becca's imperious wave for him to join her in the marquee. He'd acted crassly at the party – fancy blurting out the question was Janey gay. What a fucking idiot! What must she think of him? His head reeled with everything that was going on but worse was the knowledge that Janey loved Graham. Taking the stairs in the main house two at a time, he slammed his office door shut. He hadn't anything against the chap but he was such an unworthy recipient of her feelings. Notwithstanding the fact that, for some bizarre reason, the man was besotted with Becca. How could he love Becca when Janey was in front of him every day? Had the man no brain?

He wasn't sure how it had happened, but he had fallen head over heels for Janey. A fact his rational brain found faintly ridiculous. He'd known, from the start, that she attracted him physically, but over the last few weeks he'd witnessed her bravery and fortitude, her delightfully off-kilter humour, the joy she took in life, or would if Becca wasn't around. Janey simply made life more fun. She was someone he wanted to be around. He cared about her deeply, he cared *for* her. He wanted desperately for her to succeed with her snowdrop project, to get the recognition she deserved. He even wanted her to get the man she deserved. Although, it didn't seem that it was going to be him. Relief at finding out she was into men had been swiftly followed by the painful realisation that she was in love with Graham. The pain that shot through him at the thought of them together – for surely Graham would eventually see her true worth – was visceral. He thumped the wall, alarmed to see he'd dented the plaster. He brushed at it, trying to cover the traces, and then gave up as his phone pinged. It was a text from Clare. The taxi he'd booked hadn't turned up – could he pick them up from the airport? Wrapping a handkerchief around his sore knuckles, he grabbed his car keys and hurried from the room, grim-faced and pre-occupied.

Chapter 31

It was turning into a gloriously hot June day, full of cobalt blue skies and cotton-wool ball clouds. Janey humped the last container full of the now rearranged flowers into place, shoved a mucky hand over her hot face, turned and came face to face with Alina. Typical. The one time she wanted to look her best, in control, or at least not red-faced and covered in compost, and she was discovered sweating buckets and decidedly grimy.

There was the slightest of awkward pauses and then she gathered herself together enough to say, ‘Hello Alina.’

‘Hi Janey. You look as if you’ve been busy.’

It might be her imagination but Alina looked nervous too. ‘Yeah. Last minute panic on. All sorted now though, I hope.’

‘Can we ... could we go somewhere to talk? Privately. Have you time?’

‘’Course. Come on over to the shed. I’ve got some homemade lemonade in a cool box.’

'That sounds wonderful.'

As they walked to the shed, accompanied by the ever-faithful Camilla who was sporting a sparkly pink collar bought especially for the day, Janey eyed Alina surreptitiously. She was looking stunning in a fifties-inspired sun dress covered in bright blue flowers. She had on her usual straw hat and over-sized sunglasses and carried an enormous semi-circular basketweave bag. Janey thought she'd never seen anyone who looked more like her idea of a movie star.

She unlocked the shed and brought out the cool box, setting it down between two ancient canvas deckchairs. 'Shade or sun?'

'Shade I think, don't you? It's very warm today. You must be boiling having to work.'

Janey slid herself onto a deckchair, choosing the most rickety and hoping the other wouldn't collapse when Alina sat down.

'I've been cooler,' she admitted and fished out two glasses, thanking her foresight for having given them a proper wash. 'This is Gwen's special homemade lemonade. She makes it really sharp.' She handed one glass to Alina.

'Just how I like it.'

For a moment they sat enjoying the tranquillity and the cool lemonade as it slaked their thirst. The shed, situated at the far end of the growing fields, was a long way from any customers and from the bustle of preparations.

'It's lovely here,' Alina sighed. 'So peaceful.'

Janey groaned. 'That'll be the calm before the storm. Make the most of it. Won't be very peaceful later on. I've heard we might get thousands.' She saluted her with her glass. 'The pulling power of a real star. You know I've always wondered why you agreed to do it, cut the ribbon I mean. The only connection you had with this place was Becca, and to be honest, she's never that nice to you. Then again, she's never that nice to any of us. Why are you doing it?'

Alina smiled slightly. She gave another sigh, more heartfelt this time.

'If I tell you, do you promise it goes no further?'

Janey nodded. 'Of course.'

'Becca has something on me. She made it quite clear what would happen if I didn't agree to do her this little favour, as she put it.' She shrugged. 'I didn't have a choice and besides, I was in the UK for a while anyway. So, I came along, said why not? Cutting a ribbon is hardly going to be onerous. Then I met everyone. Gwen and Will and heard about Clare and her husband and how much the garden centre means to you all. I learned how long the house had been in the Cheney family, how they struggled to keep it going and not sell it. I thought it was worth supporting, despite Becca. And then I met you.' Alina took off her sunglasses and turned her gaze onto Janey. 'I need to tell you something. Something difficult and I'm not sure where to start.'

'Maybe you don't have to.' Janey was panicking; she didn't want to have to handle this. Her head was reeling. What had Becca got on Alina? How could she negotiate this? She'd rarely been in this situation with a man let alone a woman and a movie star woman at that. Awkward didn't cover it. Forcing herself to act natural, she re-focussed. 'Alina you don't have to tell me anything.'

'Oh I think I do, baby girl. You see, I haven't been very honest with you.' She sucked in a deep breath. 'When I first met you I thought you were a breath of fresh air. You talked my language – films – even though we didn't have anything else in common. And then when I got to know you better, I saw how little you valued yourself. It frustrated the hell out of me. I could see all this potential in you of which you were oblivious. Not just the hair and make-up stuff.' Alina shifted irritably in her chair. 'Although that played a part. I mean how wasted your talents are. How much more you could offer. I couldn't understand the limitations you put on yourself. Your worry about flying somewhere foreign, the fact you fretted over driving anywhere new.' Alina laughed. 'And just when I'd put you in a little box labelled neurotic, you came out for lunch with me and tried everything on that seafood platter, even the oysters. You do know I hate the things, don't you? But how could I refuse them when you, who had never even seen one on a menu before, tried one so bravely?'

'I didn't like them much either, to be honest.'

Alina laughed. 'You are so full of contrariness, Janey. I wanted to get to know you better. I loved hanging out with you, hearing you talk plants, listening to your enthusiasm about a snowdrop of all things. I had never even really considered a snowdrop a proper flower before.' Seeing Janey's wince, she added hastily, 'I know all about them now. And think I love them nearly as much as you do.' She reached into her bag. 'Here's your book back, by the way.' She handed Janey the history of Galanthophiles book. 'I've never read anything quite like that before. I enjoyed it. It's bizarre how a flower can provoke such passion.'

'Thanks.' Janey leaned the book carefully against her deckchair, pushing Camilla's inquisitive nose away. It had been an expensive purchase and was one of her most treasured books; she didn't want the dog to chew it. She was glad Alina had read it but was even gladder to have it back. Pulling gently on the spaniel's ears to distract her, she was aware Alina was still talking.

'And, speaking of passion, I love how you itch to nurture a dead-looking cactus back to life, that you have the patience to sow seeds and then prick them out individually with tweezers. I love how delicate you are with tasks like that and how clumsy you can be at other times. I love how you have no idea how beautiful you are with that mane of wild hair and those gorgeous brown eyes. Janey—'

Janey half-rose in alarm. 'Don't say it. You don't have to say it.'

'I do have to say it. I want to say it. Janey, I love you. Not simply as a friend, although as that too. I love *you* Janey Trelawney. All that you are.'

'Oh.' Janey pulled a little too hard on Camilla's ears and the dog squeaked.

Alina flapped her hands. 'I know you probably don't feel like that towards me. And I know I've probably been selfish in telling you, but I leave for the States tomorrow and I couldn't leave without saying something. I still have the tiniest hope, babe, that you could feel the same way?' She sank back into her deckchair, looking exhausted.

Janey stared hard at the expanse of growing fields humming in the heat haze in front of them. Her work. The toil of the last thirteen years. She was a gardener. A humble plant grower. People liked her. Sought her out for advice on plants and gardens. Some thought her eccentric. Most tolerated her foibles. She found it astonishing that it should all come to this moment. That a film star was telling her she loved her.

'Tell me one thing.'

'What's that?'

'It's not just a ... sex thing. You like me as a friend as well.'

'Janey, honey, of course I love you as a friend too. Why do you think I've wanted to spend so much time with you?' Alina gave a little laugh, more relaxed now she'd said her piece.

Janey nodded, feeling more reassured. In fact she felt more than reassured, she felt on top of the world. Alina Allen, one of Hollywood's hottest tipped rising stars and incredibly beautiful to boot, had just proclaimed love for her. It was a hell of an ego boost. For a second she stayed silent, basking in the glow of it all. And then she remembered she had to let Alina down. Janey glanced at the star, reclining gracefully in the dilapidated deckchair. The dress was halter-neck and low cut. The shadow made by Alina's breasts dipped provocatively to promises lower down. Her skin was butter smooth and the colour of Janey's tea when made the way she liked it best. Alina's legs were long and toned, her feet elegant with narrow toes painted bright blue to match the flowers on her dress. She was a dream. A stunningly beautiful dream. Janey explored her reaction but the only one was of a warm gratitude that she had Alina as a friend. While she could objectively admire the woman's appeal, her attractiveness, she was left unstirred. For some strange reason, the effect that Will's hug had on her earlier, returned. She couldn't believe she was about to say it. 'Alina, I really like you as a—'

'Friend?' Alina laughed shortly. 'That's put me in my place, hasn't it?' She bit her lip and pushed her sunglasses further up her nose. 'I know you're into men. I just hoped I suppose that there was a chance that—'

'Trust me, if there was any chance of me fancying women

you'd be the one I'd pick,' Janey blurted out. She really didn't know how to phrase these things.

Alina laughed again but this time it sounded more genuine. 'Well I had to give it a go, I suppose.'

'God loves a trier, as my nan used to say.'

There was a pause, with the two women lost in their thoughts.

Then Alina began speaking again. 'For me it's not a case of whether it's a man or a woman, it's more the person themselves I fall for. I've been in love with a man before and women too, but I have to confess no one has quite got to me like you.'

'I'm really sorry, Alina, I wish I could return your feelings. I just don't. Not those feelings.'

'You have nothing to be sorry for. Don't be sorry. I've loved our time together.'

'Me too.' Janey slid herself round to face Alina. 'Oh me too.' There was another silence, filled only with the cheep of some high-flying house martins. 'So, are you bisexual then?' she asked, trying to sound grown-up and nonchalant.

'I try not to label myself. As I said, it's the person that matters not what sex they are.'

'Is that what Becca has got on you? Can't be easy being, well, you know, in Hollywood.'

Alina took in a shuddering breath. 'It isn't. Add being black, female and British into the equation and I'm amazed I ever got a part. The scene's gradually changing I suppose but it's taking too long. But no, that isn't what Becca blackmailed me about.'

'Blackmail. Glory, is it that serious?'

'It could be. She knew the re-launch here would be make

or break for Cheney House and for her as manager, so she's got a lot riding on it. Remember I said I was in love with a man once? He didn't treat me very well. He was a lot older; I was still in the sixth form in Yeovil with Becca. He dazzled me, I suppose; I'd never had that amount of attention before. My mum and dad were incredibly strict, quite controlling in a way, although it came from a place of love. They knew I was clever and wanted me kept on the straight and narrow, didn't want me to balls-up my exams. The irony is, I passed with straight A star grades and went to drama college, which they were dead set against. They wanted me to go to university.' She gave Janey a tight smile. 'I got a bit mixed up about that time. Went rebellious. Rebelled against everything. You name it, I was against it. The older boyfriend was part of it all.' She shook her head. 'My poor darling parents. They went through hell with me. I was awful to them.'

'But it turned out all right for you, didn't it? I mean, look at you now. Tipped to be one of the world's biggest stars.'

'Yes, it's turned out okay. More than okay. But none of us knew that at the time. You know what the unemployment rate is like for actors. Mum wanted me to put drama school off until after university. Have something to fall back on but I was adamant. Just after the results came through, and there was pressure on me from all sides – school, home, friends who were going down the academic route – I did something really stupid.' Alina faltered, her voice quavering. 'I let this man make a sex tape of us. I thought he destroyed it when we split up but it turns out Becca caught him on the rebound. Somehow she got hold of it.'

'And that's what she's got on you. Alina, how awful.' Janey

couldn't imagine anything much worse. Her own sexual experiences were limited and, to be honest, had been fairly fraught and short-lived. She couldn't imagine how much pain and embarrassment this had caused Alina. 'Oh my God,' she cried, as another thought occurred. 'What if it's leaked?'

'Exactly. That's my career down the pan and it's only just begun.'

'Is there nothing you can do about it?'

Alina shrugged. 'Once the money comes through from the next thing I'm making I intend to appoint the very best, most expensive attorney I can find. Until then, I'm at Becca's mercy.'

'Do you think she'll blackmail you more?'

'Possibly. Be warned, Janey, Becca is a ruthless woman. She stops at nothing to get what she wants.'

'And she's jealous of you,' Janey observed. 'I bet she always has been.'

'Maybe.'

'Were you close friends at school?'

'No, not particularly. I hung out with the academic crowd; she had her own friends from the estate where she lived.'

'Do you think you can stop this film ever seeing the light of day?'

'I'm going to give it a damn good try. You know, I'm not even sure she still has it, but I've never been confident enough to call her bluff.' Alina looked at her phone. 'Oh my gosh, better make a move. I'm due to do the deed in just over an hour and no doubt Becca will want to go through her very exact instructions with me first.'

'Alina, before you go, can I ask you something?'

'Sure honey. Anything.'

'Can we, do you think, could we manage to keep in touch?'

'Janey!' Alina reached out and took her hand. I'd love that.'

'Good.'

'Can I ask something in return?'

'Of course.'

'You didn't seem all that surprised when I professed my undying love for you.' Alina gave an embarrassed laugh.

Janey blushed a little. 'Ah, it's something Dora said.'

'Dora?'

'She said you looked at me as if you wanted to eat me up.'

Alina threw her head back and roared. Camilla sat up and gave a quick woof in shock.

'I hope that hasn't annoyed you?' Janey put a calming hand on the spaniel's back.

'No, it's the funniest and most accurate thing I've ever heard. Good old Dora. Never misses a trick. Actors, you see, trained to observe.' Alina winced and fiddled with the neckline of her dress. 'But I'm going to have to be more careful. Less transparent. Janey, about Graham.'

'What about him?' Janey was surprised at the swerve in conversation. She hadn't thought about Graham for hours. That surprised her too.

'It's just that I think you can do so much better.'

Janey huffed and got to her feet. 'Maybe.' The problem was Alina was right and Janey was rapidly coming to the same conclusion. How had this happened?

'I'm so sorry, honey, I didn't want to upset you. I just can't see you two together, that's all. Forgive me?'

'Done. You know I'd forgive you anything. But you can't always choose who you fall in love with.'

'Ain't that the truth?' Alina gazed up at Janey and smiled sadly. She held out her hand for a pull-up.

Janey smiled back, took Alina's hand and pulled her out of the deckchair. For a second the two women were face to face, close together. Janey could smell Alina's perfume; something floral and feminine, feel the heat off her skin. For the merest moment she regretted not returning her feelings. In some bizarre way it would make life simpler. And a whole load more complicated.

Alina reached forward and kissed Janey on the cheek.

'Baby girl, I'll always treasure you and this place. In a funny old way, you've given me peace. And strength to face the future, whatever that might bring. I haven't had either for a long time. And now, come on, work to do. Let me have Camilla's lead. Think she rather completes the image, don't you?'

Janey laughed, put a hand through Alina's arm and they turned back towards the marquee.

Chapter 32

An hour later Janey slipped through a flap in the back of the marquee and squeezed her way through the crowds to the side of the stage. She stood in between Graham and Will and kept Camilla on a tight lead at her side. It was stuffy and the smell of hot grass trapped under the groundsheet beneath her feet rose lushly and tickled her nostrils.

'You got here just in time,' Graham whispered. 'Where've you been? Becca's been looking all over for you.'

'Well, maybe she shouldn't have taken offence at my planting scheme then,' Janey retorted. 'I've been busy. Working.'

'Ssh.' Graham nodded, frowning, to the stage. 'Here they come now.'

On the other side of her, Janey was aware of Will.

'You okay?' he mouthed.

She nodded and was comforted when he put a light hand on her shoulder. He was always so considerate.

A swell of excited noise filled the marquee as Becca led Alina onto the centre of the stage. A barrage of rapid-fire flashlights went off from the ranks of photographers penned in at the front. Alina's name was yelled, with entreaties for her to 'look here, look there.' One of them was particularly aggressive; a bid to get the star's attention and get that perfect photo. Janey didn't know how Alina stood it. The noise and intrusion was horrible.

Becca came forward. She was wearing her Evita outfit again, and while spectacularly unsuitable for a hot summer's day, it had the effect of quelling even the most raucous of journalists. She said a few words, explained how the day would pan out, and then introduced Alina. Once again, the flashlights sparked and the catcalls rang out. Becca simpered a little and then, quite forcefully, pushed Alina centre stage.

There was a pause while Alina adjusted to the glare of light. She seemed nervous and cleared her throat but then began speaking and seemed to gain confidence the more she said. 'First of all, I'd like to say how delighted I am to be here,' she said. 'I've become very fond of Cheney House Garden Centre and was thrilled to be asked to cut the ribbon at its grand reopening.'

Janey was aware of something happening. Whereas Becca had had to glare and yell over the press core to get them to be quiet, Alina spoke softly. And where the stage had engulfed Becca, Alina seemed to fill it. Janey was in awe. She had the sense of watching a true star at work and, for the first time, could see why Alina commanded the millions of dollars she did.

'This is a very special place,' Alina continued. 'It's full of very special people.' At this she scanned the crowd. Janey waved and Alina smiled back. 'They are working incredibly hard to make it something even better. I've got to know the team here very well and I've witnessed just how committed they are.' She moved to the scarlet ribbon held in place by being tied to two ornamental box trees in tall Grecian pots. Janey had had her work cut out sourcing them, not to mention lugging them into position, but she had to admit they looked the part. It would have made more sense to do the ribbon cutting outside, but she'd chosen not to argue with Becca over it.

The flashes started up again, along with some violent jostling by the photographers eager to get the right angle. Becca handed Alina the scissors.

'I hereby proclaim Cheney House open,' Alina called, and cut the ribbon. She dutifully posed for yet more photographs and then Becca, with protection offered by Imo, escorted her off the stage to a press junket and it was all over. Everything seemed duller, the marquee far less sparkly. Janey was reminded of the scene in *Roman Holiday* where the princess met the press at the end of her adventure in the city. She loved that film, especially the lingering, poignant and tender moment between Audrey Hepburn as the princess and Gregory Peck's journalist. When they acknowledged their feelings but also the fact that their romance could never be.

'Suppose that makes me Gregory Peck,' she muttered on a laugh.

Will, overhearing, gave her an odd look. 'Are you sure you're all right?'

'Yes. Fine.' She replied sadly. 'It's just that I think something wonderful has come to an end.'

'Come on,' he said kindly, 'let's go and attack some food.'

They fought through the milling crowds over to the café. The band had started up and there were people everywhere. Ducking around the side of the building to avoid the queues, Will tapped on the window of the kitchen. An unusually harassed-looking Tana opened it. Greeting them, she offered crab cakes.

'Quite spicy,' she warned. 'I accidentally made them too hot and they're not popular. Looking over her shoulder for Gwen, she added, 'Go on, take the plateful.' She handed the plate through the window and disappeared for a second, only to return with a bottle of prosecco and two glasses. 'You'll need something to drink with them and we're packed to the rafters in here so don't bother coming in. Enjoy!'

'Thank you.' Will passed the plate of food to Janey so he could grab the glasses and bottle. 'Let's find a quiet spot, shall we?' He steered her to the far side of the lake and to a secluded bench. Camilla slunk under it, panting and grateful for the shade.

'Everyone's very dressed up,' Janey observed, watching a group of women in jewel-coloured dresses go past in the distance. She recognised one of them as Amy from the bookshop. Looking down at her garden centre uniform, she winced. The stains from earlier were still in evidence. Plucking her sweaty polo shirt away from clammy skin, she sighed, wishing she was in a flowery summer dress and sandals, like Alina had worn. 'Shame Clare missed the ribbon cutting.'

Will popped the cork on the prosecco and poured them both a glass. Handing one to her, he said, 'Wasn't it just? I dropped her at the flat after picking them up from the airport. She wanted to freshen up. It had been quite a fractious journey home, I gather. She's going to make an appearance later on, though. And she's really looking forward to the party. Cheers!' He clinked his glass to hers.

'Cheers,' Janey replied, still pre-occupied by Alina's confession. Dora, arm in arm with Millie, strolled past on the other side of the lake. They waved. They looked happy and carefree, two friends enjoying the summery weather and beautiful gardens. Janey waved her glass back at them and prosecco slopped out. She licked the alcohol off her hand, sighed again and drank the rest.

'There's an awful lot of sighing going on.'

She put her empty glass onto the grass where Camilla nosed it with interest. 'Sorry. Not like me. It's just that life has got a bit complicated.'

'Makes it more interesting, I suppose.'

'Suppose.'

'You could tell me if it would help.'

She shot him a grateful look. 'Thanks but I don't think it would.'

Will nodded, accepting she didn't want to confide. 'Alina did well,' he said, changing the subject. 'And she has certainly attracted the crowds. Becca, whatever her faults and I grant you, they are many, seems to know her stuff.'

'Yes.' Absentmindedly, Janey bit into a crab cake. A mini explosion enflamed her mouth. 'Ooh!' she spluttered. 'They are hot. Tana wasn't kidding.' She fanned herself frantically.

'Here.' Will passed over his mostly untouched glass of prosecco.

'Thank you.' Janey glugged it down in one and then wiped her hand across her mouth. 'You're a really good friend, Will.' She turned to him.

He gazed at her intently. Then he reached over and brushed a hand down her cheek. 'Am I?'

'Of course you are,' she breathed, hardly daring to move. His touch was featherlight but its effect was electric. She inched nearer. 'Kiss me,' she urged, silently. And shocked, wondered where the imperative had come from.

'What did you say?' Will frowned.

Oh glory, had she said it aloud? 'Filthy,' she said, backing away and scrubbing her hand over her face. She added, 'I must be filthy. Always get more compost on me than in any pot.'

'True. But you'll do as you are and always will, trust me. Promise me you'll never change?' Offering her the plate of crab cakes, he asked, 'Would you like another?' His tone was fractured and it didn't match the mundane question.

She shook her head and inched away. 'No thanks.' Disconcerted by his mood and the sudden yearning to kiss his face off, she pondered his last comment. What did he mean? What was that all about? Weird.

There was a charged silence and then Will cleared his throat. He took his glass off her and put it with the other.

'Janey,' he said, his voice a little more like his own. 'I've got something I've been meaning to tell you.'

'What's that?' She sat back on the bench, relieved that things between them were back to normal. She was also bitterly disappointed. An inch closer and she might have found out what Will's lips tasted like.

He shifted nervously. 'It's some news I've been meaning to—'

But he didn't get any further. Graham charged up to them. Taking in the impromptu picnic and looking from one to the other with narrowed and suspicious eyes, he said, 'Good thing I found you before Becca did. There's a problem in the marquee. She wants you in there now, Janey. Right now!'

Chapter 33

With a sinking heart, Janey trudged towards the marquee, a hot spaniel in tow. She really wasn't sure how much more of the woman she could stand. She normally considered herself a self-assured, positive sort of person, but Becca's attitude to her was a war of attrition; it was gradually wearing away any vestiges of confidence she had.

Arriving in the now empty tent, she encountered Becca standing over a wilted *Cordyline*. She had her hands on her hips and looked furious.

'Janey. About time. Are you responsible for this?'

Janey looked down at the urn. The plants had been potted up to complement the ones used at the ribbon cutting and would act as decoration for the dinner dance.

'It just needs a bit of water, that's all. It got very hot and steamy in here earlier on. It's funny though, I made sure the water reservoir was topped up after I put them all in place.' She bent and examined it more closely. 'Oh, I can see what's happened. Someone's obviously knocked it over and the water's emptied out. Look, the groundsheet is all soggy here.'

Becca lifted one stiletto heel and examined it grimly. 'I have one hundred and fifty of Berecombe district's finest society members arriving here in less than twenty-four hours. Including the mayor! They expect the best in a dining and entertainment experience. Not to have their shoes ruined by damp.'

'It's all right, Becca. I can remove the plant, or replace the reservoir, and the groundsheet will recover overnight. It's certainly warm enough to dry it out in no time.' Janey couldn't see why she was making such a fuss. 'I think I mentioned it was probably a mistake to put the plants out before the dinner dance anyway.' Too late, she realised pointing out Becca's error in judgement was not a good idea. In a weird kind of detached way, she observed how a vein began to pulse at the side of her manager's pale temple. A feeling of fatalism overcame her. If she was going to bow out of Cheney House, then she may as well go out in a blaze of glory. Straightening her shoulders for the onslaught, she remembered the apoplectic woman in front of her was the one who had been blackmailing Alina so cruelly.

'You!' Becca pointed an accusing finger. 'I cannot leave you to do the simplest of tasks. I should still be at the press call with Alina but instead I'm running around putting right your mistakes. Don't think I didn't notice what you did, or rather should I say, what you didn't do with those hanging baskets. Did you think I wouldn't check? And I saw you run off with Will and an entire plateful of canapés, not to mention a bottle of champagne. Can I remind you that you are still at work? You're not paid to fraternise with the family members and get drunk.' Becca took in a shuddering breath and began speaking again, this time on a hiss. 'I can see you, thinking this is all one big laugh.' She came closer and prodded Janey in the chest. Painfully. 'And look at you,' she snarled, 'hair a mess, not a scrap of make-up, your uniform a disgrace. I suppose you think by sleeping with Clare's grandson, your position is safe. Well, let me tell you young lady, your time at Cheney House is up. I give you your final warning. You're fired!'

A tiny spittle flecked at the corner of Becca's mouth. It made Janey want to laugh. Perhaps she was hysterical? Becca certainly was. Relieved that the showdown had finally happened and praying to hold on to her temper, she held her fingers up as she counted off the allegations. 'Firstly,' she began. 'If you had taken my advice and not had the ornamental plants put out until tomorrow night, this current problem, which I can't even believe you're making into a problem, wouldn't have arisen. Secondly, you wanted me to correct an issue this morning with no time to spare. I did what I felt was the best compromise and seriously suggest you have your eyesight checked. To me, and to everyone else I consulted, the colour scheme was exactly as you requested. Thirdly, I accepted Will's invitation to lunch. We had a plate of canapés, which no one else wanted, and precisely two glasses of prosecco. Hardly getting drunk, and may I remind you at that point I had been working solidly since six this morning and was long overdue a break. Fourthly, my uniform and my appearance are in this state as I have been run ragged trying to follow your stupid, inane and quite frankly *ridiculous* requests. And finally, if I have been fraternising with the family, as you so quaintly put it, it might be because ever since you came to work here,

Will is the only one who hates and detests you as much as I do.' Giving in to her temper, she tore off her name badge and threw it at Becca's feet. 'You can stuff your job.' Grinding the badge under the heel of her Dr Marten boot, she added, 'I fucking quit!' Camilla, excited by all the drama, began to bark furiously and shot out of the tent.

Janey turned to go, only half-hearing Becca's screams and profanities. Furious tears poured down her face and she scrubbed them away, mortified to show weakness in front of her enemy. A hand reached out and stayed her arm. Blindly, she shook it off. Now she had said her piece, the only thing she longed to do was get away.

'Janey, it's me. Wait.' It was Clare. 'Oh darling Cam, it's lovely to see you too but do get down a minute. Janey wait, child. Don't go, darling.'

Clare had a vice-like grip on her arm, so Janey had no choice but to allow her to lead her back to where Becca was still standing. She couldn't meet the eyes of either woman; she wasn't entirely sure she could be responsible for her actions.

'It seems one of my staff isn't at all happy,' Clare began, a note of steel evident in the cultured voice. 'And you're obviously not happy either, Becca, but I hardly think airing grievances in public is at all seemly. Please report to my office and I will speak to you there. Ah, here's Will,' she said, as he entered the marquee. 'If you can bear to fraternise with him a little more, Janey, would you let him take you for a calming walk? Then, if you would be so good, please also report to my office. And then perhaps we can sort this out, ladies.'

Chapter 34

Will took a still seething Janey by the arm and marched her away.

'I don't want to go for a calming walk,' she shrieked as she shook him off.

'Okay. Where do you want to go?'

'Don't patronise me!' She spread her hands as if to ward him off, obviously too angry to stay rational, and continued at a half jog.

Will took a deep breath and ran after her, rescuing his tie as it flew into his face.

'I'm not patronising you but I really think we need to go somewhere to talk this through and discuss strategies. Will you slow down!'

Janey stopped dead in her tracks and turned on him.

'Strategies? Strategies?' she screamed, making a couple wandering past stare. 'I'm out. I'm sacked. I've left, I mean. It's too late for strategies. Besides, I don't want strategies to deal with Becca. I want to bloody well kill her!'

Will took her arm again. He led her, pushing his way through the crowds, out to the shed. Leaving her to stew outside, he put the kettle on. When he deemed it safe he offered her a mug of tea. She was slumped in the deckchair, a mulish expression on her face, her arms crossed defensively. She ignored the tea so he placed it on the grass beside her, sat in the other deckchair and waited.

'That woman is the pits,' she said eventually.

'I agree.'

'I can't work for her anymore.'

'No.'

'In fact, I won't work for her anymore.'

'Indeed.'

She picked up her mug, slurped tea, then winced. 'Glory! Too hot. Burned my tongue. And I wish you'd stop being so bloody reasonable.'

Will refrained from comment. Looking at Janey while she cupped her mug between both hands and blew on it to cool the tea, he thought he'd never loved her more. The realisation came as a thunderbolt. Yes, he'd known she attracted him physically, had known that from the very first time he'd spotted her dancing under the trees. Had known he'd come to care for her. But the attraction now went deeper. Far deeper. He'd come to value their friendship. Had become increasingly fond of her eccentricities, admired her bank of knowledge. Enjoyed how she forced him out of his conservative shell and made his life more vivid, more fun. But love? It was completely irrational, wasn't logical. She was the exact opposite of what he wanted. But, as he looked at her now and observed her sulky mouth and the angry blush still staining her skin, maybe she was what he needed. An image of him and Janey thrust itself into his brain. Locked together, they were lost in a passionate, deep kiss. The longing to throw her into the shed and have her against the workbench shocked him to the core. He wanted desperately to yank that disgusting polyester polo shirt off, to run his hands over her breasts and feel the nipples peak under his urgent caress. He yearned to push his fingers through her mane of hair and bury his face in it. His entire being wanted to press himself against her, to be in her and pleasure her until she gasped. He shifted uncomfortably. There was no way he'd act upon such a reckless impulse, but for the merest second he imagined what bliss it would be.

'What's the matter?' Janey asked in a gruff voice.

He shook himself back to the present. To the reality that Janey was in danger of being sacked, that even if they got together she wouldn't remotely fit into his lifestyle and besides, she was in love with that idiot Graham. But overriding all this was the fact he was due to fly to the States in a few weeks and he hadn't even had the courage to tell her. It was hopeless. Even if he could persuade her to give up on the idea of Graham, how could they ever even begin to form a relationship when living so far apart? And that's what he wanted. He wanted a relationship with this woman, this annoying, eccentric, feisty woman. More than with anyone else he had ever met, he wanted … actually, he just wanted.

'Sorry. Just trying to think things through.'

'You'd got the most peculiar expression on your face.' She sipped tea and then tipped it away in disgust. 'And you can't make a cuppa to save your life.'

'Well, there's me trying to help.' He attempted focus.

'You can't help. I've lost my job. Walked out.'

'And you really think Gran will let you do that?'

'Don't think she'll have any choice.' Janey jerked her head towards the big house. 'I bet Becca is filling her in on what a lousy employee I've been right now.'

'And you think Gran will believe her? Come on, she's more savvy than that.'

'But that's just it, Will. I have made mistakes. I have argued against what Becca has been trying to do.' Janey's eyes were huge. 'If I were my boss, I think I'd fire me!'

It made Will laugh.

'Glad you think it's so funny,' she mumbled childishly.

'I don't, honestly I don't. I just have more faith in my grandmother's ability to see things fairly.'

'Well let's hope she does otherwise I really am out on my arse.'

'In which case, don't you think we'd better go over to Gran's office and find out?'

'Suppose.' Janey said, still sounding sulky.

'Come on then.' He reached a hand to her, in much the same way as she had to Alina. Had that only been a few hours before? It seemed like a lifetime. So much had happened. She risked a glance up to Will. How had she not noticed the cut of his cheekbones and the chiselled line of his jaw? His smooth skin and the way his dark hair formed a widow's peak before it swept heavily over to one side? She stared at the hand he offered and her insides went liquid at the sight. How had she never spotted what wonderfully long, capable fingers he had? What beautifully shaped nails? She swallowed. After the near kiss on the bench, she thought she'd never feel comfortable around him ever again. And she was right. She didn't feel at all comfortable. She felt the opposite. She was incredibly turned on. Honestly, falling for the boss's grandson was nearly as clichéd as falling for the boss's son. Is that what had happened? Had she fallen for Will? But he was her friend. Sitting on the bench, sharing the prosecco and those fiery canapés, that's what they had established between them. They were friends. And you didn't kiss friends. At least not in the way she wanted to kiss Will. An image sprang into her mind; one of Will and her pressed close together, his long naked leg pinning her to a bed of snowy-white linen, his tapered fingers running over her hot body and making it sing.

'What's the matter?' It was his turn to ask.

Janey felt heat pulse into her cheeks. 'Nothing,' she said quickly. Ignoring his hand, she grasped the arms of the deckchair and hoisted herself up that way instead.

He shrugged. 'I'll sit in on the meeting. Moral support.'

'If you want.' Janey couldn't shake off the awkwardness. She felt raw, stripped, as if every nerve and sinew was exposed. She also felt peculiarly quivery. Maybe she was coming down with the flu? No, she'd never had a day's illness in her life. Full of rude health, she was. She wasn't sure his presence at the meeting would help. She wasn't sure she could concentrate on what she needed to do in order to save her job, her career. Then again, she needed all the support she could muster in the face of that bitch Becca.

They walked slowly to the main house and reached Clare's office before Janey felt even vaguely ready or prepared.

Standing outside the door, Will paused before knocking. 'Ready?'

'No.'

He reached forward and kissed her on the top of the head. A friendly gesture she thought, no more. She straightened her shoulders and mustered a smile. 'Ready.'

He knocked, and at Clare's command they went in.

Chapter 35

Clare was sitting, not at her desk but on the small sofa she had in her office, with Camilla cuddled close. The dog's elegant face was pressed ecstatically into her owner's shoulder.

'Will, Janey, come in.' She nodded to the seats ranged in front of the sofa. At Janey's entrance, Camilla slid off Clare's lap and snuffled over. Janey sank onto a chair and felt the reassuring presence of a wet nose thrust into her hand.

'A sign she has been well and truly looked after in my absence,' Clare said, and smiled. 'Thank you for that, Janey. I knew my darling Cam would be in safe hands while I was away. Are you staying too, Will?' she enquired.

'If I may.'

'Of course.' Clare indicated the other chair.

Janey scanned the room. It was a cosy place, more sitting room than office, and with its pictures and cushions far more lived-in than Will's. His had all the hallmarks of a business-like but temporary residence. Janey recalled Clare's words from the staff meeting when he'd been introduced. That he was only going to be with them for a short while and she felt a little sick. Trying to concentrate on why she was here, she looked around for Becca but there was no sign of her. She was almost disappointed.

Realising who she was looking for Clare added, 'Becca has taken Leo, that's my friend from Italy, on a tour of the centre. Leo was desperate to stretch his legs and Becca needed to check up on one or two things so took him with her. I was rather keen to talk to you alone, Janey.'

Will stiffened. 'Would you rather I left, Gran?'

Clare glanced curiously from one to the other. 'Not if you'd rather stay.'

'Yes, I'd like to stay. I've an input here too.'

'Quite so. So, Janey, I've heard everything Becca has to say. I'd like to hear your side of things now please.'

As Janey listed, haltingly at first and then more confidently as she got into in her stride, the many problem areas between her and Becca, Clare listened. She didn't say anything until Janey had finished.

'It seems to me,' she began, after a reality TV length pause, that you and Becca have much in common. Far more in common than you know.'

'Gran, what are you on about? Janey and Becca are poles apart.'

'In personality that's true but I believe both have the centre's interests at heart.' She turned to Janey and smiled warmly. 'You're both perfectionists – in your different ways. You both eat, drink and sleep Cheney House. You're both committed to making it the best place it can be. You're both experts at the top of your field.' She smiled again and paused. 'It's just you have very different ways of going about things.'

'You can say that again,' Will put in. 'If you ask me, how Becca was treating Janey amounted to workplace bullying.'

Clare gave her grandson a sharp look. 'Yes, I asked her about that. It seems at Country Xteriors, where she was employed before, the system of warnings and reprimands was rigidly adhered to. That's what she was used to and so she applied the same here.'

Will raised his eyebrows. 'Really?'

'Yes really.' Clare clicked her fingers at Camilla and the spaniel jumped back onto the sofa beside her. 'I'll be very honest here, Janey. Becca offered her resignation,' she said it almost casually as scratched the dog under the chin.

Janey gasped. She hadn't anticipated that. She sucked in a breath.

'But I refused to accept it.'

Janey let her breath go. It had been too much to hope for.

'I need Becca to manage the place. It seems to me that she's actually doing rather an effective job.'

Will gave a harsh laugh. 'In terms of implementing change I agree with you, Gran, but in terms of managing people, she's a disaster.'

'That, I also agree with, Will. From what I can gather Becca is missing a vital ingredient in her management skills set and that is finding the key to getting the most out of her staff. You included, Janey. So, I am proposing this. I keep Becca on as manager, I keep you on as head gardener—' As Janey began to protest, she added, 'Yes, I refuse to accept your resignation too, Janey. I need you in the garden centre just as much as I need a manager. I've listened to your complaints and agree that Becca hasn't handled you at all well. If I'm reading the woman right, I suspect she knows that too but got herself entrenched into a position she couldn't back out of easily. She's an incredibly proud woman. Just as you are, Janey. I'm sending Becca on a Personnel Management course and I'm suggesting that, for the time being at least, you report directly to me. It might keep the heat out of the situation a little until things have settled down again.' Clare smiled. 'How does that sound? One more thing, I must ask you as I requested of Becca, if you have any grievances with each other, that you bring them to me first and not air them in public. That's one thing I must insist on.'

Janey didn't know how to react. Her thoughts tumbled anyhow. Relief that her job was safe was uppermost. Disappointment that she'd still have to negotiate Becca at work rankled. But what did she expect? She was the one who had run out on her job, so she was extremely lucky Clare had refused to let her leave. And had she really thought Becca would sail off into the sunset, never to be seen again? Even if Clare had accepted the woman's resignation, she would have had to work her notice. Janey gazed at Clare who was now clucking devotedly at Camilla. She wondered how much Becca had actually told her and what slant she had put on things. Something didn't add up.

'Clare, I can't thank you enough for keeping me on,' she began, 'and I'd very much like to continue working here. I also appreciate the suggestion that I report to you. I'll find that much easier. Can I just ask one thing?'

'Go ahead, darling.'

'Can I keep on with the snowdrop project? In my own time,' she added, hastily.

Clare looked up and blinked. 'But of course. My dear girl, why would you ever think you couldn't? You know Gerald gave you full backing, as do I. Please be reassured you can continue with it. I wouldn't dream of you not doing so.'

'That's great. I just wanted to check. Thanks Clare.'

'Good.' Clare got up and brushed dog hair off her white linen trousers. 'Well, now that's over we can all look forward to the dinner dance tomorrow, can't we? I can't wait. I think it's going to be fabulous.' Once again she glanced from Janey to Will and back again. 'Let's think of the last few month's problems as teething troubles, shall we? After all, it takes time for a new team to bed in. Let's hope we go on from this better and stronger. Off you go, Janey. I need to have a little catch up with Will now.'

Janey nodded. 'Yes Clare. And thank you again. For everything. I'm so relieved to have you back. I can't tell you how much.' She began to put up her hand to Will as a gesture of farewell, then felt foolish and shoved it back in her pocket.

She was almost back at the plant sales office when Will caught up with her. 'She's done a number on Gran, hasn't she?' he said without explanation.

Janey looked up at him. 'Oh yes. She's hoodwinked Clare good and proper.'

Will bit his lip and put his hands on his hips. 'Well at least we know she's definitely the enemy now.'

'Only just clocked that? She plays a good game, does Becca.'

Will stared at her, a smile playing about his mouth. 'Then we'll have to play an even better one, won't we?'

Chapter 36

The marquee was, once again, transformed. This time for the dinner dance. Janey got there early to check everything was in place. Becca had given her instructions a few weeks ago on exactly how she wanted it and Janey didn't want to give the woman any more ammunition to pick fault, even if Clare was back and mediating. Looking around with a critical eye, she didn't think anything more could be done to improve it. It was perfect. She had arranged yet more *Cordyline* and box trees in simple white containers and they looked elegant and understated; she was pleased with them. White chiffon curtains swathed the interior and snowy fairy lights hung in massed loops across the tented ceiling. Each table had a white gerbera, rose and gypsophila centrepiece. Janey's talents didn't extend to flower arranging, but she had supplied Gwen and Val with enough blooms to make luxurious looking arrangements. She'd also asked them to add in fragrant herbs for some contrasting green. It gave the flowers a subtle scent and an informal look. If Becca disagreed, she'd point out the trendy magazine she got the idea from. The catering company had set the tables with a green and white theme and it all looked fresh and beautiful – atmospheric in the evening dusky light and more than a little bridal. Seeing as the suggestion they might host weddings had gone down a storm with Clare, it might be a canny move.

Dress for tonight was strictly black tie and Janey had been dreading it. She had nothing in her wardrobe that fitted the requirements and was missing Alina's expertise like mad. She would have known exactly what to suggest and probably would have even loaned her something. But Alina had disappeared after the ribbon cutting and the press call. Now she had discharged her favour to Becca, she'd gone. Janey assumed she'd returned to work but had had no word. It was lucky, therefore, that Gwen had tipped her off about an evening dress spotted in a charity shop in Berecombe. After yesterday's events, all Janey had wanted was to go back to a flat now sadly empty of Camilla's soothing presence and curl up in front of a favourite film. She'd recently discovered the delight that was *Calamity Jane* and longed to lose herself in it again. There was lots in it that she related to. However, she'd forced herself into town to try on a dress she didn't want to buy and probably would only wear the once. Pride was forcing her to turn up for the party and, if she was attending, she was going to make damn sure she looked her best. Remembering the techniques learned at the spa, she'd applied some subtle make-up and had spent an age blow-drying her hair into submission. Now, standing in an empty marquee, she scraped one leg against the other – she'd shaved them for the first time ever and they were beginning to itch. She really didn't know why she'd bothered, her dress was long enough to cover her legs but it seemed it was what girls did before a big night out. She'd also picked up about pre-loading from Gwen's daughter and had had a quick cider in the pub before she'd arrived. The landlord had ribbed her mercilessly over her appearance, but the Dutch courage had been useful.

'Hi, Janey. Wow, you're looking good.' It was Graham.

'Could say the same about you.' She stared up at him, some of the old feelings trickling back. His muscles bulked out his brand-new dinner jacket in a very satisfactory fashion and he wore a black bow tie that was only slightly wonky. He looked incredibly handsome. 'Look good when you're all scrubbed up. Here, let me.' Reaching to his crooked bow tie, she straightened it, sniffing his neck as she did. 'You smell nice too.'

He looked embarrassed. 'Pressie from Becca.'

'Oh. Right. That's nice. Still going strong then?'

'Yeah. Yeah, think so.'

'Good.'

'Place looks fantastic, Janey. Didn't think you had it in you to do anything like this.'

Backhanded though the compliment was, Janey flushed with pleasure.

'Thank you. Know what table you're on?' The seating plan was Becca's responsibility; she'd insisted on it.

Graham nodded to a table near the stage. 'I'll be on that one with Bec and Clare and the others. Hope you have a good time tonight, my lovely.' He turned to go but changed his mind. 'And you really do look fab, you know. Hot!'

The other guests were slowly making their way in, so after consulting the seating plan and smiling wryly, Janey took her place at a table right at the back.

The food was good, the prosecco flowed and the speeches made by Clare and the mayor didn't go on too long. Janey sat in between a couple who ran a local packaging company and who were pleasant but dull. She was bored stiff. Discovering they didn't drink, she commandeered their bottle of fizz and drank at a steady rate to pass the evening. When it was announced that guests should make their way outside to watch the fireworks so the tables could be cleared and moved for dancing space, she stood up and wobbled.

'Whoops,' she said. 'Must be these high heels. Don't usually wear anything higher than two inches.'

Barbara, who had sat next to her all evening, looked on in concern.

'Perhaps you should get some fresh air, dear,' she suggested.

Janey nodded. 'Good idea.'

She staggered outside and sucked in a lungful of balmy summer evening air. If anything it made her even dizzier. Holding onto a marquee post, she balanced precariously and took off the strappy sandals she'd bought at the charity shop to go with the dress. They were the only vaguely suitable shoes they had and were too small and hurting. As she straightened and her eyes adjusted to the gloom, she saw in the distance over by the lake, Becca and Graham locked in a passionate clinch. 'Looks like it really is going well for you, Gray,' she murmured. The loss of him, the finality, hit her like a sledgehammer, its impact far more potent than any alcohol. She leaned against the tent post and silent tears ran down her face. Clutching her shoes to her chest, she made her decision. She'd find the bar.

It was after the fireworks, and just as ABBA was filling the dance floor, that Will found her. She was hanging off Ron, Gwen's husband.

'I really loved him, you know. And now all he can think about is her. And she's such a bitch,' she slurred as she gazed reproachfully up.

Ron was being remarkably tolerant. Trying to disentangle her arms from around his neck, where they clutched limpet-like, he answered, 'I know, my lovely. She don't deserve him.'

'She really is a cow, you know, Ron. And I've loved him for years and years and years. Long before she even clapped eyes on him.'

'Ah, Will,' he said, clearly relieved as he spotted the man pushing his way through the dancers. 'Maybe you could take Janey and find her some water? Think she's a bit over-tired.'

'Will do.' Will gave a tight smile and put his arm around Janey's waist. 'Come on, let's go outside and enjoy the evening. It's a lovely night.' As she fell against him, he looked down, seeming puzzled. 'Where are your shoes?'

'Oh.' Janey looked about her, confused. 'I've no idea. I took them off. Now I know why they're called killer heels. They killed my feet. Suppose it didn't help that they were a size too small.'

'Why were you wearing shoes that were too small?' Will put up his hand in surrender. 'Actually, you know what? Don't answer that.' He snagged a bottle of Perrier from a passing waiter, murmuring, 'I'm not sure if I want to kiss you or shake some sense into you.' Louder, he added, 'Will you be all right walking on the grass barefoot?'

'It'll be lovely.' Janey ran out of the marquee and onto the grass edging the lake and twirled. 'Feels all cool and silky.

Tickles!' She spun round again and then stopped abruptly, holding a hand to her head. 'Ooh.'

Will took her arm and led her to a bench. Sitting her down, he unscrewed the cap and handed her the bottle of water. 'Sip slowly,' he ordered, 'it's fizzy.'

They sat in silence while Janey glugged down the Perrier. After a while she burped. 'Sorry.' She giggled. 'You were right. It is fizzy. Nice though.' She drank some more and then lapsed into stillness, clutching the bottle to her and staring into the darkness that was the lake. There was a half-moon and it led a path of light to them over the gently rippling water. The only sound was the boom and thud of 'Waterloo' coming from the marquee in the distance.

In the silvered light, Will observed her. She had put up her hair into a loose ponytail, from which glossy curls escaped and kissed her ears and neck. Her midnight-blue dress clung to her curves like a second skin. One diamanté strap had fallen down and rested on her arm, the jewels gleaming in the moonlight. It exposed the lush swell of her breast. Will thought he'd never seen her look lovelier. He longed to slip the strap down further, his hand reaching down to cup, his mouth finding a nipple. The thought excited him beyond measure.

'I really did love Graham, you know.' Janey broke the silence between them. 'I fell for him as soon as he started here,' she added mournfully. She gave a huge, gusty sigh. 'But he only ever saw me as a friend. And tonight I realised that's how he would only ever see me, no matter how hard I try to convince him otherwise.' She hiccoughed a little and clutched the Perrier bottle even tighter.

Will didn't know how to respond. She was much drunker than he'd first thought. And it was clear she was still hung up on Graham. It was like a bucket of cold water to his arousal. Remaining silent, he let her talk.

'For a while I thought it was romantic. You know, the classic romcom material? Besties go from friends and find love in the end. *When Harry Met Sally*. All that crap. I watched him chase the girls. They didn't stick around too long but I heard all about them. How they were too demanding, had nothing to talk about, wanted him to pay for everything, weren't adventurous enough in bed. I listened. Long nights in the pub while he moaned on about Laura or Fliss or Katie. And all the time knowing I was perfect for him, if he only realised it.' She paused to drink some more water. 'I sympathised when he got fed up with his job. Helped him trawl online for others he could do. I even coached him through his driving test.' She laughed bitterly. 'He was hopeless at the theory, just couldn't get the info to stick in his head. I was his pal, his drinking buddy. But that was it. He never saw me as a girl. Even tonight when I was all gussied up, he just said I looked good. Sort of absentmindedly as if he really wanted to be somewhere else. Which I suppose he did. He wanted to be kissing Becca. Well, he did that all right. I saw them. Going at it hammer and tongs.' She laughed. 'Tongues is about right. Didn't think Becca had a passionate bone in her body. Got proved wrong on that front.'

Will stayed quiet, sensing this was something Janey had to get out of her system.

Suddenly, she threw the water bottle to the ground and reared up. 'I'm going to tell him. I'm going to flamin' well tell him how I feel and I'm going to scratch that bitch's eyes out. With a blunt trowel.' She wobbled. 'Yeah, that's what I'll do. How dare she swan into Cheney House, make my life a misery and have my man!' Swaying again, she flopped back onto the bench.

'Do you think that'll do any good? Telling him how you feel, I mean? He's with Becca now. It'll only make him embarrassed, make your friendship awkward.'

Janey lurched to her feet again. She loomed over him.

'It would make me feel better.' She prodded herself in the chest. 'And I would feel a lot better telling that cow-bitch-woman what I think of her.'

'But you've still got to work with her too,' Will pointed out reasonably. 'Even if Gran is acting as go-between, it's not going to help.'

Janey sat down again, abruptly, this time on the grass at his feet. She leaned her head against his knees and sighed. 'Since when did you become the relationship expert all of a sudden?'

He gave a short laugh. 'I'm not that, trust me.' His heart went out to her. 'I'm just sober and thinking clearly, that's all.' He reached out and stroked her hair and she sort of nuzzled into it, like a grateful puppy.

There was another long silence and then she said, 'You don't see me as a woman either.'

His hand stilled. He held his breath.

Scrabbling to her knees, she pressed herself against him. 'Look. You can kiss me.' She screwed her eyes shut, her lips slightly parted and glistening. 'Kiss me Will.'

Will froze. With every beating pulse in his body he wanted to grab her, throw her onto to the cool grass and take her there and then, in the silver shifting light and the soft, balmy air. He gazed at her. There was a sheen on her naked collarbone that he longed to lick, he wanted to bury his face between her breasts, in the exciting hollow that shadowed there. He wanted to mouth at the erect nipple he could glimpse under the thin fabric of her clinging dress. He wanted to fuck her, love her, until all thoughts of Graham were gone.

Graham. And that was it. She was still in love with Graham and she was still very, very drunk. Not once had he ever taken advantage of a drunk woman. And he wouldn't start now. Even if every fibre of his being longed to do so.

Summoning every vestige of self-control and forcing his voice to stay calm and even, he said, 'Maybe I should take you home. Get you a coffee.'

Janey's eyes opened and he couldn't bear the hurt and disappointment in them, the humiliation. 'You don't want me either. No one wants me. I'm not a proper girl. I wear clunky boots and don't own a skirt. I can't do make-up properly and I don't understand why I have to shave my legs. You all want the glamour girls. The ones drenched in hairspray and fake tan. The ones who paint on their eyebrows and wear fake nails and hair extensions. The cutesy types.'

Will reached a trembling hand to her and gently smoothed her shoulder strap back into place. Her skin was warm and silky smooth and he didn't want to take his fingers away.

'Janey,' he began hoarsely, 'you're a very beautiful, desirable woman. Trust me. Any man,' he took a deep calming breath, 'any man would be honoured to be with you.'

'But not you,' she whispered. 'Not you.'

He said the only thing he could think of and it sounded lame even to him. 'It's just not the right time.'

Janey got to her feet, pulling out her long skirt from where it had caught on a bare toe.

'No,' she sniffed, blinking back tears of humiliation, 'I can see. I'm not your sort. After all, what would a gardener and an accountant have in common, eh? A rich boy and a working girl. Things like that only happen in the movies, don't they? In *Pretty Woman*. And this is real life. Oh boy, is this real life.' She kicked the Perrier bottle. 'Ow,' she sobbed, 'and now I've stubbed my toe. Just to end a perfect evening.'

Will got up. He couldn't bear not to touch her any longer so enveloped her in an embrace, holding her close and feeling her quiver with unshed tears. They stood for a long time, taking comfort in one another. Will overwhelmed with guilt that he still hadn't told her he was leaving and battling his overwhelming desire for the contrary creature he held in his arms.

Eventually, after kissing the top of her head, he whispered, 'Let's get you home.'

Chapter 37

Clare rolled over in bed and turned the pillow onto the cool side. She wriggled with pleasure and felt her satin nightdress shift against her sun-tanned skin. Her Italian holiday had been a wonderful escape but there was nothing like your own bed in your own bedroom. She slid up and reached for her glass of water, trying not to notice how empty the king-sized bed felt. She'd never get used to waking up without Gem next to her.

Determined to stay positive, she wriggled her toes and looked through the gap in her muslin curtains. The sky was already a deafening shade of blue and it promised to be another hot day. Late June in England. What a glorious time of the year! She supposed she ought to get up and see to her guest, but Leo had promised he would be an easy man to have around. He'd told her he wouldn't get in her way but take himself off for walks in the countryside around Cheney House, or stroll through the grounds, or follow his latest obsession and drive to the newsagents in Berecombe to buy an English broadsheet. She pictured him sitting in a sunny spot in the house's private little garden, lost in a crossword, one of Gem's battered straw hats on his head and linen trousers rolled up to his ankles in impeccable Italian style. She wondered how long he would stay and then found she didn't care; his company was undemanding, which was more than she could say for her job. She hadn't been totally honest about Becca to Janey. Becca had been furious, beyond furious, and it had annoyed and appalled Clare in equal measure. Quite frankly, she couldn't see the problem Becca had with Janey. The gardener was hard-working, conscientious, knew her stuff and yes, was slightly eccentric, but if you learned to manage her she was fine and one of the most loyal members of staff. Clare had sought out Gwen's opinion, and Val and Meg's too. None of them liked Becca. That was unsurprising; she was implementing vast amounts of change to a staff who had cosied along very nicely indeed for far too long. And that had been Clare's fault. Her heart had left the business the same time Gem's had stopped beating and she'd taken her eye off the ball, which was why she had employed Becca. She'd thought it had been a good idea. It had certainly lifted the workload from her shoulders. Clare drained the rest of her water and sighed, the earlier sunny mood vanishing. Appointing Becca had seemed to create more problems. She half-wished she'd accepted Becca's offer of resignation but she couldn't let her leave now, halfway through a project. Besides, she'd have to work out her leave and Clare had never had full commitment from a staff member coasting their way to leaving. She wrinkled her nose. It was all most puzzling; why couldn't the women get on? Will had suggested the animosity centred on a man but Clare couldn't see that. Janey had, to her knowledge, never expressed a romantic interest in anyone and Becca looked too welded to her career. She swung her legs out of bed and headed for the shower. No, it was simply a clash of personalities. It must be. And at least now she was back she could keep a closer eye on things. Letting the water run to temperature, she bit her lip. For the good of Cheney House, she'd have to. With Will still determined to go stateside in the autumn, there was no chance she could do otherwise.

Having breakfasted and checked in on Leo, who proclaimed himself content to read in the garden, she caught up with Will and then ventured to the plant sales centre. Stopping to admire the wicker baskets overflowing with pink fuchsias and hanging along the entrance, she headed in to find Janey and express her appreciation. Camilla scampered ahead and Clare could hear Janey fussing her.

'Janey, they look gorgeous, darling. Those hanging baskets. I adore that pink!' She lifted her sunglasses to let her eyes adjust.

'Hi Clare. Yes, the baskets only came in this week. Thought I'd plant a few dozen up to give some planting ideas, and there's always a few folks after some instant colour.'

'Are you all right?' Clare peered more closely. 'You look rather wan.'

Janey blushed. 'Had a bit too much to drink last night. Bit of a hangover.' She fanned herself. 'And it's stuffy in here. Always is when the weather's good.'

'Oh isn't the weather glorious? And I sympathise about the head, darling. I'm feeling quite frail too. It was fun though, wasn't it? And achieved our aim?'

'Think so.' Janey nodded vigorously and then winced. 'The

journo from the *Berecombe News* said she was going to do a positive write up. And everyone seemed to enjoy themselves. Had one or two queries about wedding parties and a twenty-first.'

'Marvellous. That's a jolly good idea of yours, to use the marquee for parties and suchlike. We must discuss it in more detail.' Clare paused. 'Although I'm not too sure about those caterers we used. Will has just gone through the bill with me and they're rather eye-wateringly expensive.'

'A contact of Becca's apparently.' Janey hesitated. 'The food was good though.'

'Oh yes, it was excellent,' Clare said, appreciating the girl's attempt at bridge-building. Perhaps there was hope for a useful working relationship between her and Becca after all. 'But if we used them it would cut right into our profit margins. And there's a ceiling price people are willing to pay for a party in a tent, especially as we'd be a new venue. We're rather untested, aren't we?'

Janey put a completed basket to one side, ready to hang later. She wiped a hand across her clammy brow. 'True. I did have a suggestion for an alternative caterer but it would have to be agreed with the team. I wouldn't want to put anyone's nose out of joint.'

Bless her, Clare thought. She's really trying hard. Why on earth does anyone find her difficult to work with? 'Who would that be?' she asked.

'Millie Fudge, or rather she's Millie Henville now. She owns the café and bookshop in town. Caters for parties and events.'

'Millie! Of course!' Clare clapped her hands together delighted. 'She married the delectable Jed didn't she? Isn't she having a baby though?'

'Yes. Due soon. But she's got a manager in the café. Petra. Supposed to be great. And Millie would oversee everything, even on maternity leave. That's the sort of person she is. Likes being busy.'

'Excellent idea. Look into it, would you?' Clare turned to go. 'Actually, I've changed my mind. I'll look into it, if you don't mind. If it's me who broaches the subject at the next management meeting ... ' she tailed off but the implication was clear.

Janey nodded again. Then ran to her boss and flung her arms around her. 'It's so wonderful to have you back, Clare.'

Disentangling her, Clare smiled. She was really very fond of the girl. 'And it's very lovely to be back.'

Chapter 38

The Galloping Galanthophile: July

Hi and welcome back to the blog! Have you missed me? After a short break, the gardening blog is back to being a regular monthly feature.

July. Oh July. What a month to be in the garden! It's when you can allow yourself time to sit back and enjoy the labours of the year as your months of toil produce all those beautiful goodies. It's been a hot summer so far and looks likely to continue, so don't forget to water, especially if you've put in new plants, and try to use 'grey' water, that is, water from your washing machine or even your bath! For more advice on using grey water, come in and grab a leaflet. It's best to water early in the morning or late at night to avoid evaporation – and watering in the evening when all is peaceful can be a real joy and a time when the aromatic flowers like nicotiana are at their fragrant best. If you're worried about your water usage, we sell a range of drought resistant plants like lavender and verbena and our ever-popular geraniums. Watch out for pests in the warm weather too and feel free to come in and ask for specialised advice. Keep ponds clear of algae and regularly deadhead and you should have the perfect garden in which to relax. We've got a wonderful selection of outdoor furniture to tempt. Thinking ahead? Order your spring bulbs here at our Bulb Event next month. And, don't forget our new home delivery service, which is free to orders within ten miles and purchases over thirty pounds.

But, most of all, take the time to really enjoy your garden this month. As ever, happy gardening and don't forget your sun hat!

GG

BERECOMBE NEWS

MAJOR HOLLYWOOD STAR AT CHENEY HOUSE

Report by Keeley Sharma
Photography © Andy Haywood

Hollywood came to Berecombe last week when Cheney House Garden Centre was relaunched by film star Alina Allen. The megastar, who was taking a break before filming the next Bond film, cut the ribbon and announced the new-style centre open. Ms Allen (31) held a brief press conference where she answered questions about her upcoming role as Lila Martini in Deadgame before posing for photographs and signing autographs. She flew back to the States for filming shortly afterwards.

On Saturday evening a charity dinner dance was held in a specially erected marquee where members of Berecombe society enjoyed fine wines and good food, followed by fireworks by MagikSparkle and a disco courtesy of SpinToons. All proceeds went to Prostrate Care Cancer Trust and the RNLI. Cheney House owner, Clare Cheney, said she hoped this would be the start of a new phase for the garden centre and that she and her team had exciting plans in place for its future.

'And there's a great picture of us all underneath the one of Alina,' Graham said, after reading out the article in the local paper.

They were in the plant sales office a few days post-launch. Janey handed over a mug of coffee and took the paper from him. She studied the photographs. Alina looked her gorgeous best, with a Hollywood smile pinned to her face, sunglasses perched on her head. Underneath was a smaller one of the Cheney House team pictured with the house in the background, its red brick façade glowing in the late afternoon light. Janey had only a hazy memory of the photograph being taken. It had been sandwiched between the meeting with Clare and before rushing to the marquee to set it up. She examined it more closely. Clare stood at the centre, her arm around Will's waist and holding Camilla on a short lead. Will looked his normal good-looking self, in his tortoiseshell glasses and white shirt. He had his hands in his pockets and wore a slightly self-conscious expression as if uncomfortable being in the public eye. Flanked on Clare's other side, but slightly apart, was Becca. She stood, shoulders back, a wide smile on her face not entirely masking the underlying tension.

Graham was standing behind Gwen and Tana, his arms looped casually around their shoulders. He'd obviously just said something funny because both women were laughing. Janey looked at the picture of herself; hair mussed up as she'd just come from sorting a problem with the Portaloos they'd brought in for the extra numbers. Her trousers were rolled up over her eight-hole work boots and her t-shirt was only half-tucked in and had ripped across one shoulder. She flinched. She looked a mess. It was little wonder no man ever thought of her as sexy.

'Yeah. Great coverage,' she said dismissively. 'But it's only the local rag.'

'Becca said something about getting the publicity out nationwide.'

'What good will that do? Ninety percent of our customers come from a thirty-mile radius.'

'You're a little ray of sunshine this morning, aren't you?'

Janey ignored him and slurped coffee. Then she sat up and tried to drink it more politely. She ought to make more of an effort with her manners. The thought warred rebelliously with the idea that people really ought to take her as she was.

'Suppose it might improve our image,' she admitted.

''Course it will. And if you want to create a centre of excellence for snowdrops, people will be willing to travel.'

'Maybe.' Janey was cautious. The choice of plant for the centre of excellence status still hadn't been decided upon. Becca, even if she was willing to entertain the idea, would be certain to go for something with a wider customer base, like fuchsias or clematis. Snowdrops had a more niche appeal, the smaller number of followers compensated for with a sometimes rabid enthusiasm.

'You back to writing your blog again?' Graham said, interrupting her thoughts.

'Yup. Clare's given me the go ahead. She's said Becca can do a short piece on the new website about general things going on and I can still do a gardening blog. I've just written July's although it'll go out a bit late.'

'That's great, isn't it? Did you ever find out who the rogue blogger was?'

'No.' After a couple of controversial blogs, the mystery writer seemed to have gone back underground. Janey was hugely relieved. She couldn't help but think that people suspected her.

'And you and Will looked to be getting cosy at the party. Anything going on there that I should know about?'

Janey looked Graham straight in the eyes. 'Like you and Becca? Suppose it could be said you two were getting cosy too.' She shook her head. 'There is nothing going on between me and Will,' she said firmly. 'We're just friends that's all.'

'Like you and me.'

'Like you and me.'

'Well, he must be soft in the head then 'cos you looked gorg in that dress.' Graham laughed. 'If I wasn't already taken, you might even have tempted me.' He drank his coffee, making his Adam's apple work.

'Yep. Just goes to prove we can all scrub up okay, doesn't it? Even me. And now, if you'll excuse me, I've got work to do.' Slamming her mug down, she left Graham open-mouthed and puzzling over what he'd said.

Stomping over to the nursery site, Janey wondered just why she bothered with men at all.

Chapter 39

July slid into August and August eased into September. The weather stayed clear and sunny and visitor numbers stayed constant. The expected surge in footfall didn't materialise after the relaunch publicity, but Becca reassured Clare and the team that sometimes a publicity scheme took time to impact.

Janey, having done the Bulb Event, was busy selling pots planted up with autumn colour and the ever-popular cyclamens. On one particularly blustery morning, when a wind hinting at winter chill shivered through the chestnut trees, she went to stand underneath them. Gazing up at snatches of blue sky shifting through the wildly rustling leaves she had the distinct feeling that something major was about to happen. A sense of foreboding overcame her. It was still early and there was no one around, so she flung her head back, lifted her arms up to the sky, gave into temptation and danced. And then stopped. Somehow, the joy she had once found in dancing under the trees had evaporated. It was most peculiar. She couldn't shift this heavy weight of doom. Shivering, she wrapped her arms around herself. Maybe it was simply the change in season? It had been such a long, blissfully hot summer, melancholy that it was over made sense. And a slight ennui was traditional with autumn-mellowed leaves and dew at dawn. But it wasn't like her. She loved all seasons equally. She hurried back to the office and to the kettle.

Drinking her tea, she stared out at the courtyard. The wicker hanging baskets were now filled with violas and ivy instead of summer bedding plants but looked just as pretty. The selection of water features was still there. There were some compost bins and mulching boxes in one corner and an annoying free-standing display board, that Becca had insisted upon and which Janey kept knocking over, but otherwise the place remained the same. She thought back over the last few weeks. Life at Cheney House had quietened to a routine. Thankfully, she had had little to do with Becca and the senior management meetings had been overseen by Clare, which meant people were more guarded in what they said. Clare had given the go-ahead for the garden centre to become a centre of excellence for snowdrops, to which Becca had, astonishingly, agreed. If somewhat grudgingly. It had created more work for Janey, and she was liaising with a contact from the RHS, but was relishing the task. Becca had vetoed the suggestion they look into holding wedding receptions, declaring scornfully that they wouldn't be worth the effort. Clare had insisted they run one as an experiment and was working with Petra from Millie Vanilla's Café. The first was already booked. It was going to be a test event, at a special rate, for two of Millie's friends, Emma and Ollie and was going to be harvest-themed.

Janey found she cared less about Becca's relationship with Graham the longer it went on. These days she didn't even feel jealous. Surprisingly, she'd become good friends with Leopoldo, Clare's Italian friend. He was a knowledgeable fan of European films and they'd enjoyed an evening watching *Cinema Paradiso* together. It was Will who bothered her. He seemed to be avoiding her. Ever since their embarrassing drunken encounter at the party, things hadn't been the same. While he was perfectly friendly and courteous during meetings, he no longer sought her out for a casual coffee and gossipy chat or popped in with the excuse he was passing. He'd reverted to a work colleague, no more. She missed him. She missed his conversations, his kindness, even his insistence that things get done the proper way. Most of all she missed the interest he'd taken in her. She was dying to share the funny emails she'd begun to receive from Alina; he was the only person she trusted with the information they contained. Will was the only person she trusted? How had that come about?

She thought back a few weeks to when she'd had to drop something off to Clare and had come across Will in the old drawing room. The room wasn't used a great deal now, except to store extra stock, but it still housed the Cheney family grand piano. As Janey trod on the first stair to go up to Clare's flat, she heard a note being picked out. The door was ajar, so she tip-toed across the landing and peeked through. The piano was in the far corner and Will had his back to her. He was playing a tune slowly using just one finger. The other arm rested along the top of the instrument and his shoulders were slumped in abject despair. Janey watched, hardly daring to breathe. Everything about his demeanour screamed, 'I want to be alone.' Then she recognised the tune he was playing. It was 'Que Sera Sera'. Her heart went out to him, he seemed so desperately unhappy and she didn't know why. She itched to go in and hug him but the moment was broken by his mobile ringing. As he answered it, she'd slunk away, feeling like a voyeur.

She shook her head, trying to rid her mind of the image of a lost and lonely Will and finished her tea. Time to start work.

That afternoon, she'd just finished demonstrating a leaf blower to local councillor, Dennis, when Becca tottered past, deep in conversation with the man they all assumed was the rattan garden furniture rep. Janey thought it strange that he should visit in September, which wasn't traditionally the busiest time for selling outdoor furniture.

Dennis's wife sighed and said, 'Right Den, if that's really what you want for your birthday, I suppose I'll have to go and pay for it. Boys and their toys, eh?' She rolled her eyes at Janey who explained brand new boxed blowers could be found inside the plant sales centre next to the mowers, and the woman disappeared.

Dennis followed Janey's distracted gaze to where Becca and the mystery man stood.

'Heads very close together. Looking cosy,' he said.

'Don't they just? We're still puzzling over who he is.'

'I assumed they were both customers.'

'No. The woman is Becca. She's our general manager.'

'Is she now?' Dennis sounded intrigued. 'Ah yes, I remember her now. You know, she and I had a very interesting discussion at that party at the bookshop. Good do, that was.' He gave Janey a shrewd look. 'Wanted to know all about planning regulations for the area.'

Janey swung round on him. 'Planning regulations? For what?'

'A housing development.' He hesitated. 'Look, I might be speaking out of turn here, and I thought it odd at the time, but what with Clare being away and everything, I just thought this Becca person was talking on her behalf.'

'Talking about what?' Janey's sense of unease increased.

'Sorry. Not making myself clear. Becca was implying that Cheney House was on the market to be sold and the land used for a housing estate.' He puffed himself up a little. 'Would make a fortune. Nice little plot you've got here. Just about commutable for Exeter and the developer that did the executive housing development on the outskirts of Berecombe would jump at the chance. They'd probably get about a hundred four-bedders on here, retailing at about five hundred grand each. Well, you do the maths. You all right, my lovely? You've gone pale.'

Janey wasn't sure how she got to Clare's office, but on legs that felt like jelly, she found herself outside and hammering on the door. Without waiting for the command to enter, she burst in to find Clare and Leo sitting on the sofa having afternoon tea.

'You're selling up!' she blurted out. Pointing an accusatory finger and angry tears glistening, she repeated, 'You're selling us out to the highest bidder. And to build more bloody little boxes of houses. On this lovely land. All over the estate land. Killing the trees and my snowdrops and shovelling bricks all over the badger setts and the hedgehog trails!'

'Janey. Please stop shouting at me.' Clare replaced her teacup with a clink.

Leo went to get up. 'Would you like me to leave? This looks like business.'

'No, please stay, Leo. I'd like you to witness just what I'm being accused of. Janey get a chair, sit down, take some deep breaths and explain yourself,' she added tersely.

Janey blanched when she saw Clare's face. It was the first time she'd ever seen her properly angry. Dropping into an armchair she tried to calm herself down.

Clare passed her a bone-china cup. 'Some tea. Drink. And when you've collected your thoughts, please explain why you barged in here and accused me of selling Cheney House.'

Chapter 40

Janey drank the tea in one gulp, replaced the cup back onto its delicate saucer with shaking fingers and then, haltingly, told Clare everything that Dennis had said.

'Dannazione!' Leo exclaimed. 'How can this be true?'

'Because it isn't,' Clare retorted. 'There is no substance behind this Janey. I repeat, I have absolutely no plans to sell my house or land. And certainly not to build houses on it.' She gave a shudder. 'Although it does explain a very odd conversation I had with the chair of the East Devon Land Development Committee recently. He also seemed to be labouring under the assumption that the land was for sale and had a remarkably venal glint in his eye.' She frowned. 'Tell me again what Dennis said.'

Janey repeated it.

'And he was clear that it was Becca who was negotiating the sale?' Almost absentmindedly Clare offered Janey a sandwich.

Taking one, she replied, 'He said she was asking about

planning regulations and claiming the Cheney House land was up for sale.' She shoved the cucumber sandwich in whole and munched.

'And there was a developer interested?'

'He said Becca suggested there would be a housing estate built.' The tea and sandwiches were working. Janey was feeling a little less sick now. She trusted Clare implicitly, and if she said she had no plans to sell, then she believed her.

'Curiouser and curiouser. Ah, here's Will. Thank you for walking Camilla,' she added, as her grandson walked in. The spaniel bustled around the room, greeting everyone enthusiastically before flopping, exhausted, at her feet. 'Sit down. You need to hear this.'

Will looked around, picking up on the tense atmosphere. 'What's going on?' He perched on the edge of Clare's desk. 'You all look very serious.'

Clare poured him some tea while Janey, once again, repeated what Dennis had said.

'The bitch!' he slammed his cup down. 'The utter bloody cheek of the woman.' An angry flush bruised his pale complexion. Getting up, he strode about the room. 'I knew she was up to something. I just knew.' Camilla growled slightly at his agitation.

'Do sit down Will,' Clare said, 'you're making Cam nervous. And please mind my Royal Albert.'

Will glanced at the spaniel and flung himself onto Clare's desk chair. 'I beg your pardon, Camilla.' He adjusted his cup on its saucer. 'And sorry, Gran.'

'None of this makes any sense,' Janey interjected, puzzled. 'Becca can say anything she wants. But it's not her land to sell and, apart from making a lot of people confused and a bit excited, what's the point of it all?'

'That she creates enough speculation for someone to come clean with an offer?' Clare suggested. 'The chap from the EDLD was certainly keen.'

'But she'd be out of a job, along with the rest of us, if the garden centre closed. I still can't see what her motivation is.'

Leo, who had been silent up to this point, suddenly spoke. 'Permit me, if I may? I think I can see what has been going on. There would be much money to be made if the land was sold for houses, yes?'

Janey nodded. 'Megabucks according to Dennis.'

'So if *Signorina* Becca knew a developer ...'

'And is in cahoots,' Will put in.

'I do not know this *cahoots*.'

'She's working with him on the scheme to gain profit,' Clare explained patiently.

'*Po, po, po*. Exactly. He makes the money. She makes the money also.' Leo rubbed his thumb and forefinger together. 'In Italy we have this corruption too.'

'Will,' Janey said suddenly. 'The rattan furniture salesman. He's not a salesman at all!'

He looked at her, understanding dawning. 'Of course.'

'He was here today, when I was talking to Dennis. I thought it was strange, a garden furniture salesman touting for business in September. That's him. That must be the developer Becca is working with.'

'God, she's got it all worked out, hasn't she? Get the land sold and she pockets a share of the profits when it's built on.' Will thrust an angry hand through his hair.

'But hasn't she worked tirelessly to make Cheney House a success?' Clare asked. 'Why would she do that when her plans are to sell? Wouldn't it make more sense to run the place into the ground so the business isn't viable and I only have one option: to sell up.'

The group lapsed into silence while they digested what Clare had said.

'But has she made it a success?' Janey said, eventually. 'She's insisted we buy from an inferior plant wholesaler and that's caused me no end of problems. I can't tell you how many refunds I've had to dish out.'

'She spent an absolute fortune on that relaunch party,' Will put in. 'Far more than I was happy with or had budgeted for.'

'Not to mention the over investment in the lake project,' Clare added.

'And she was never happy about anything we suggested that might make some extra money, like the wedding venue idea,' Janey said.

'It would also explain why she had it in for you,' Will said, on a deep sigh. 'Getting rid of the head gardener would make a deep impact on profitability. No one wants to come to a garden centre where there's no expert advice available.'

'But, tell me, what have been the returns? Are you making more money?' Leo asked curiously.

Will answered. 'Not according to the latest monthly figures but Becca keeps insisting we have to look long term, that it takes time for a business to turn itself around. She keeps quoting the example of Country Xteriors where she worked before.'

'And this is true,' Leo agreed, with a shrug. 'But that was a much bigger organisation, was it not? It could soak up some initial losses. Here, it is a small independent enterprise. Some cautious investment is a good idea until you know how things are going.'

There was another silence as the implication sank in.

Clare broke it, her voice trembling with emotion. 'She's ruined the place, hasn't she? Or would have, had we not found her out.' A solitary tear ran down her cheek. 'And I trusted her. I trusted her absolutely. And then I ran off to Italy without giving the place a second thought.' She clasped her hands to her face. 'Oh, what a fool I've been. What would Gem think of me?'

Leo reached over to her and put an arm around her shoulders. 'My love be calm. How could you know? You took references. You checked her out.'

'You employed her in good faith, Gran,' Will said, in a hoarse voice. 'Don't blame yourself. If anything, blame me. I'm the ruddy accountant here. I should have stepped in and done something. I suspected something wasn't right but I ignored my instincts.' He glanced at Janey. 'I allowed myself to become distracted. I took my eye off the ball.'

'No good comes of all this blame,' Leo said equably. 'What we need to plan now is how to take revenge.'

Clare sniffed and moved away from him slightly. She found a tissue and blew her nose. 'This isn't Italy, Leo. We're English. We don't do revenge. We do very expensive court cases instead. I can't even sack the woman without grounds to do so. She'd take me for unfair dismissal.'

'Then we gather evidence,' Janey said, leaning forward eagerly. 'We catch her in the act of betraying us.'

Clare tutted. 'Betrayal. Revenge. Have I drifted into a television drama?'

'But this is what it is,' Leo said tenderly, and he took her hand and kissed it. 'The woman has betrayed you and must be dealt with.'

'And I say to you again, if we're not extremely careful in how we do it, we'll end up with an expensive court case on our hands. And that will ruin Cheney House just as much as any plan Becca has.' A sob tore into Clare's voice.

Will shifted on his chair. 'Don't get upset Gran please, I can't bear it. We'll think of something.' The group lapsed into silence yet again, the only sound Camilla's gentle snores. Then Will hit his forehead with the palm of his hand. 'I've got an idea. Janey, have you got a smart phone?'

She nodded. 'It's a bit ancient and the battery lasts about two minutes but yes.'

'Good.' Will smiled grimly. 'Leave it with us, Gran.'

Chapter 41

For once Janey was thoroughly looking forward to the management meeting. Gwen, Tana, Meg and Graham had been invited too; it was to be an extraordinary meeting of the wider management committee and held in the restaurant as it was a bigger space.

Gwen had put together four tables and arranged enough chairs for everyone. There were triangles of Tana's delicious prawn toasts, ginger cookies and an enormous Brown Betty teapot in the middle. Janey got there early and gazed at the food ruefully. She was certainly too nervous to eat and felt sure most of the others would be too.

Will appeared from behind the interactive whiteboard screen he was setting up. Ironically, it had been a recent – and very expensive – purchase Becca had insisted upon, saying she couldn't possibly chair meetings without one. He nodded curtly, looking preoccupied and on edge. Fiddling with the laptop connection, he said, 'There, that should do it,' and they sat down, side by side.

'Do you think this will work?' she asked.

He took her hand briefly and squeezed it. 'It had better do. I think, between us, we've managed to get enough evidence, but I've got the Skype connection set up just in case. As back up.'

'Let's hope we don't need it,' Janey whispered and reluctantly let go of his hand as the others filed in.

Clare, white-faced and tense, entered with Camilla trotting faithfully behind and Leo at her side. She took her seat at the head of the table. Graham, Meg, Tana and Gwen followed with Becca bringing up the rear.

Everyone shuffled around finding a seat, getting out pens and notebooks and chatting. Only Janey, Clare, Will and Leo sat in stony silence, waiting.

Clare called the meeting to order and Becca jumped in. 'May I ask why Leopoldo is present?' she asked abruptly.

Clare barely glanced at her. 'He is my friend and advisor and, as this is an extraordinary meeting, I deemed it appropriate that he should attend.'

'It's hardly regular, Clare,' Becca protested.

'And this will hardly be a regular meeting, Becca,' Clare replied frostily. 'As you will see. Is the technology ready, Will?'

He nodded in response.

'Then I will begin. First picture please.'

Will pressed the keypad on the computer and a picture of Becca and the mystery man flashed up.

Clare took a deep breath. 'Can you tell me who this is please, Becca? He's not a sales representative, is he?'

Janey saw Becca stiffen as she glanced from the screen to the faces in front of her and back again.

'He's Ian Yates,' she answered, eventually. 'He runs the

antique and collectables centre in Taunton. We've been having meetings to discuss the possibility of running a franchise of his business as part of the craft centre. He thinks it would do well. As do I.'

Glory, she was smooth, Janey observed. The lies dripped off her tongue like honey.

'And yet you felt unable to mention this man, or your plans, to any of us during any of our management meetings?' Clare asked.

'I hardly thought it necessary until plans were more definite.' Becca looked around. At Clare and Will's grim expressions, at Gwen and Graham's confused ones. 'What is this? An inquisition?' She tried to laugh but it came out hollow.

'What you forget to mention is that Ian Yates is the son of Alan Yates who owns Pellow-Yates Construction and that he runs the company on behalf of his father.'

'Well, yes,' Becca began to bluster. 'He does help his father out on occasion but his real interest is in antiques and—'

'Collectables yes,' Clare finished for her. 'So we gathered. He rather seems to have collected you, doesn't he, Becca?'

'What do you mean, Clare?' Graham demanded. 'What's all this about?'

Another picture came up. One of Becca and Ian Yates in a passionate clinch.

Graham gasped.

'I'm sorry to tell you this, Graham,' Clare said gently, 'I gather you've been seeing Becca. However, your girlfriend and Ian Yates are in a relationship and have been for some time. Isn't that correct, Becca?'

'I fail to see what my private life has to do with anything.' Becca's answer was confident but a muscle began to tick in her neck.

Clare leaned forward. 'Oh, it has to do with everything. Do you deny having a conversation with Dennis Hall about Cheney House being sold?'

Graham and Gwen gasped. Becca remained silent.

'I'll repeat the question as you seem to be having difficulty in understanding it. Have you suggested to Dennis Hall that Cheney House is on the market?'

'I may have asked about planning. I'm interested in such things. It's not against the law,' Becca huffed.

Clare remained icily calm. 'No, it is not. However, spreading rumours that I am about to sell Cheney House could be construed as grounds for dismissal. Colluding with a known developer to do so is certainly not working in the best interests of the centre.'

Becca went white. 'Prove it,' she snarled. 'And are you saying having a few speculative conversations about building land is grounds to sack me?' She laughed, mirthlessly. 'You're deluded.'

'Next picture please, Will.'

A shot of Becca and Ian came up on the screen. Ian had his arm around Becca's shoulders and was nuzzling her neck. They were sitting on a bench in a secluded part of the lake. Janey remembered the thrill she'd got when she'd taken the photograph and alerted Will. He'd sneaked behind the tree the bench was under and had recorded their conversation. It had taken them days of stalking Becca but they'd finally struck gold.

Will pressed play on his phone. After a slight pause, a man's voice could be heard. The recording was crackly and a nearby duck nearly ruined it but you could hear what was being said.

'And the old dear doesn't suspect a thing?'

'Nah. She's too busy making with the googly eyes at her Latin lover. She doesn't care about the business. Can't see what's happening right under her snotty nose. These people, they make me sick. Born into all this and couldn't organise a piss up in a brewery. I've been bleeding it dry since I got here.'

'But doesn't the accountant bloke notice?'

Becca gave a hard laugh. 'He trusts me. I give him the monthly figures and he takes them at face value. I tell him I've paid a supplier cash and, oopsie, silly me, I've forgotten to get a receipt. Some bean counter he is. He's fucking useless. They're all the same. Too up their own arses to do a proper day's work and check the figures out properly. Not to mention he's always dribbling over that lesbo bitch, Janey. I've been syphoning off funds ever since I started here and no one has a clue.'

'And you've got it safe?'

'Yeah babe. It's all safe. And when the old fart realises her business is losing money hand over fist, the only option she'll have left is to sell up and swan off into the sunset with her Iti lover boy. You'll get the land at a snip.'

'You've got it all worked out, haven't you?' Ian panted. 'God you make me hard when you're like this. Baby girl ...'

The recording ended abruptly. Janey couldn't look at Graham or Will. She couldn't bear to look at anyone. Instead she concentrated on pleating and unpleating her hated polyester sweatshirt.

There was an awful, leaden silence.

Chapter 42

'Have you anything to say for yourself, Becca?'

Janey had never heard Clare sound so hurt. Furious on her behalf, she forced herself to look up.

Becca sat back on her chair and laughed for a long time but there was a shrill note of hysteria in it. 'You had no right to record my private conversations. Get off on it, did you?'

Leo shot to his feet. 'Have some respect when you speak to Clare,' he roared. '*Baldracca!*' He flicked his thumb nail off his teeth in a gesture that Janey could only assume was the greatest of insults.

'Sit down, Leo,' Clare said, still resolutely calm. 'Let's hear what Becca has to say.'

'I could sue you,' the woman said insolently. 'For invasion of privacy. For defamation of character.'

'You could,' Clare replied, 'except, as an individual and a nonemployee of the business, Will is perfectly within his legal rights to record anything on land I own. Will, you were recording the ducks quacking, weren't you? You have a new interest in ornithology. And you just happened to include Becca and Ian's most fascinating conversation, didn't you?'

'That's right, Gran,' Will replied. He was ashen.

'Of course, Becca, you could risk a court case claiming otherwise, but I think you'll find we have rather damning evidence that money laundering and blackmail has been something you've been expert at for quite some time.'

'Blackmail?' Becca whistled through her teeth. 'Now you really are clutching at straws. I haven't blackmailed anyone here.'

'Not here as such but you might find this message from someone who has become a good friend to Cheney House rather interesting. I think we need our next bit of evidence, Will, if you would be so kind.'

Will fiddled with the laptop and, via the Skype connection, Alina's face appeared on the interactive whiteboard.

'Hi guys.' She gave a wave. 'Hope I'm coming through okay. I've had an early morning filming, so I hope I make sense.'

'Hello Alina,' Clare replied, 'you and I haven't met in person, but I'm extremely grateful to you for this. Over to you for this part, Janey.'

Janey got up and crouched next to Will so she could be seen by the laptop's camera. She waved back to Alina. 'Hi Alina. We need you to say your piece. Our friend here isn't very convinced about how we all feel about her.'

'Ah. Okay. I sort of guessed that might be the case.' Alina gave a tense smile. 'Hello everyone at Cheney House, I miss you guys. I loved my time with you and felt as if you'd sort of become family.' She took in a deep breath. 'Well, here goes. This is my piece. I'd like you to know that Becca has been blackmailing me over something stupid and ill-advised I did when I was a mixed-up kid. She's never let me forget it. She blackmailed me into coming to your relaunch but, as it turned out, once I'd got to know you all, I would have done it anyway. It was my pleasure to be part of your rebranding.' She wrinkled her nose. 'You know, I kind of wondered why Becca got me involved, especially as I really didn't think she had the best interests of Cheney House at heart. I decided she couldn't resist one more go at making me remember what I'd come from.' She paused and her voice cracked. 'Well, Becca, that was the last time. I've just appointed the best litigation attorney in LA. If you ever, *ever* attempt to blackmail me again, I'm coming for you. And one more thing, whatever wrong you've done those good people at Cheney House, undo it. Otherwise, the same applies. 'Cos you know, girlfriend, however much you hate the fact, I'm making good money out here, I can make sure you go down. No question.' Her tone changed. 'Is that what you wanted, Janey?'

'I think that will do fine,' Janey answered, risking a glance at Becca's livid face.

'Speak soon, then honey.'

Will clicked the laptop and Alina disappeared.

Janey stood up. It was her time. It was her chance. If she didn't say it now, she never would. And she was bursting to say the words. They were storming around her insides. She'd waited too long.

'Becca,' she began. 'I've no idea why you hate me so much. Why you made my life so difficult. Why you ground any self-confidence I had under your elegantly shod foot. I have no idea why you deliberately stole the man I loved. I don't even know why you thought I deserved all those warnings.' Becca went to speak but Janey shushed her. 'No, this is my turn. It's your time to be silent and listen. I've been talking a lot to Alina. You see, even though she's on the other side of the world and working really hard, we've stayed friends. Good friends. You didn't have many friends at school, did you? Alina's been filling me in. You were a bit of a loner. You were jealous of her, weren't you? Couldn't stand how effortlessly popular she was. Still is. I was a loner at school too. I used to get into trouble and get kicked out. Never had the chance to make many friends as I was never in any one school long enough. It wasn't until Clare took a chance on me that my life really began. You see, Becca, Clare believed in me. She saw past the sulky teenager, the girl who lashed out with her voice and occasionally with her fists. Clare saw I had talent. A real talent. Not for acting like Alina has. Or for cooking like Gwen has, or for kindness like Leo.' She shot a look at Will. 'Or for numbers like Will has. Clare saw I knew instinctively what to do with plants. How to nurture them, make them thrive, get them to produce the most beautiful flowers or the best fruit. And Clare took me in to this wonderful place and I found a home. A family of sorts. Something that I think you may not have had. Not properly. And I wasn't about to let that home, that family, be destroyed. You might think you'd ruined me and my career – you certainly had a good go – but I wasn't about to let you kill Cheney House. So I suggest, very strongly, that you do as Alina says and pay back every penny you've stolen from Cheney House, from Clare, from *us*, and get the hell out of our lives.'

Applause rippled around the little group, accompanied by some 'well dones.' Janey was shaking. But it was triumph, not fear or anger. She'd done it. She'd stood up to her bullying, unfair manager. She was a juror in *Twelve Angry Men*, *Love Actually*'s sexy prime minister outwitting the president, she was Atticus Finch! On wobbly legs, she flopped back onto her seat and tried to breathe normally.

'Get out, Becca,' Clare said, on a whisper. 'Get out of my sight. Get off my land. And be assured, if one penny of what you owe is not repaid, my lawyer will be in touch.'

Becca surged to her feet so suddenly that her chair crashed with an awful echoing slam onto the floor. For one second she pointed a wavering finger at Clare. Everyone stared, not daring to breathe. Then she turned and left, her stilettoes tapping furiously over the hard, wooden floor.

Clare, looking pinch-faced with exhaustion and leaning heavily on Leo's arm, murmured goodbye and left in her wake.

Graham had his head in his hands. He was moaning. As Janey put her arms around him, whispering meaningless words of comfort, she didn't notice Will packing up the laptop and leaving. Those remaining gathered around Graham, offering sympathy, advice, and eventually they all got to the drinking tea and nibbling biscuits stage.

Gwen made a fresh pot while they digested what had just happened. 'Can't believe what that woman was up to. Wait until I tell my Ron. And I'm sorry, Graham,' she said. 'I know you was keen on her but I never liked her myself.' She jabbed a biscuit in his direction. 'That was no way to find out she'd been doing the dirty on you, though.'

'Had no idea Clare knew about us,' he sniffed in response. He looked around at everyone in panic. 'And I swear I didn't know anything about what Becca had planned. I swear! She didn't tell me anything.'

'We believe you, my lovely.' Gwen sipped tea and lapsed into a thoughtful silence.

'I'm so sorry, Graham,' Janey said, putting a reassuring hand on his shoulder.

He looked at her with reddened eyes. 'You'd got her measure right from the start. Should have listened to you, Janey. Should have taken notice of my old pals. She screwed Cheney House over and me too.' He scrubbed a hand over his face. God, it feels so bad. Feels like actual pain,' he added, in surprise.

Janey took his hand and squeezed it. He was as self-absorbed as ever. Her comment to Becca that she had stolen the man she loved seemed to have passed him by.

'It'll take time,' Gwen put in, wise as ever. 'But you'll get over her, my lad. Trust me.'

'You will, you know.' Janey squeezed his hand again.

'Oh Janey,' Graham put a sorrowful head on her shoulder and sighed. 'Whatever would I do without you?'

This was it. This was the moment she could convince Graham that she was the woman he needed, even if it meant she'd be rebound girl. The very least she could do was to offer a sympathetic ear. But instead of feeling exaltation, Janey was swamped by conflicting emotions. Sadness that Graham had been betrayed in such an awful way warred with a deep uneasiness. She hugged the man closer to her. How did she feel about him? How did she *really* feel about him? Did she still feel the tsunami of desire? Did he still make her pulse race? Panic overwhelmed her. Now that she might have a chance with him, she suspected she no longer wanted it. Carefully disentangling him from her, she looked around. Gwen was chatting to Meg but she noticed, for the first time, that everyone else had left. Outside, an autumn dusk was falling, clouded by a light, mizzly rain. Chairs were empty and left at angles although someone had righted the one Becca had overthrown. The plates now only contained crumbs, ring marks from mugs of tea the only evidence of the drama. The laptop and whiteboard had been tidied away. And there was no sign of Will.

Chapter 43

Janey took the stairs two at a time. She had a very bad feeling about this. Bursting into Will's office she came to an abrupt, horrified halt. He was standing at his desk packing stuff into a cardboard box.

'Will, what are you doing?'

'What does it look like I'm doing?'

'You're packing? You're leaving?' Even to Janey's ears, her voice sounded shrill and hysterical. Taking some deep breaths, she forced herself to calm down. 'But we did it, we got rid of Becca!'

Will allowed himself a small smile. 'We did. I doubt very much if she'll dare to darken our doors again. And let's hope she pays back all the money she's pilfered.'

'She'll do that, all right. Alina has her running scared.' Janey watched as Will walked over to the bookshelf and picked up the Bonsai tree. Her heart thumped painfully. '*Are* you leaving?'

He paused, seeming unable to meet her eyes. Placing the Bonsai carefully on the corner of his desk, he said, 'I was only ever here temporarily. To help out.' He gave a strangled laugh. 'And a fine job I did of it too.'

'But you did. You have.' He did meet her eyes then and she was shocked by what she saw. His expression was a far cry from Graham's mournful, slightly self-pityingly red eyes. Will's face was taut with pain, his sharp cheekbones even more pronounced with misery. Behind his glasses the dark eyes were tortured and stormy.

'I'm glad you think so. I'm more of the opinion that I've made a complete cock-up, as you would so quaintly put it. I failed to keep a close enough eye on Becca, I let her get away with things that should have been easy to spot. My negligence allowed her to take money from my grandmother's business. I even let her convince me that all the overspending was a good strategy. That it would pay off.' He gave another, hard laugh. 'What did she say about me? "Too up my own arse to do a proper day's work."' Taking off his glasses, he closed his eyes in pain and rubbed at his temples with thumb and forefinger.

'But that was just Becca lashing out. She was saying any old thing just to get back at us.'

'It had a modicum of truth though, didn't it?' He gazed at her and she realised what truly beautiful eyes he had. Warm, chocolate-brown and fringed by luxurious, dark lashes. Only, at the moment, they held a heart-breakingly bleak expression. Shaking his head, he replaced his glasses and then shoved his hands into his trouser pockets. He stared at his feet. 'I was here to help Gran out and all I've done is make matters worse.'

'That's simply not true,' Janey said hotly. 'You've done

a fantastic job. I could never wrangle all those numbers. I wouldn't have a clue.'

'But I'm supposed to be the trained accountant, the hotshot number-crunching guy. I'm supposed to know how to wrangle the numbers, as you put it. Instead I let myself get distracted. I failed to see through Becca, even though the woman was as subtle as a brick most of the time. I'll never forgive myself.'

'Don't be so hard on yourself, please. I can't bear it. Becca was a player. None of us really knew just how vile she was.'

'You did.'

It was the second time someone had said as much. Janey let it go. There were more urgent issues to discuss than Becca Woods.

'So, where will you go?' she asked, thinking he'd probably head back to London. At least that wasn't too far away. She might see him again. For Will, she'd be willing to risk a South Western train to Waterloo, even though the thought made her queasy. All those timings and numbers to get right. How would she cope?

Will became very busy placing immaculately sharpened pencils into the box. 'Boston,' he answered, eventually.

Boston. Janey wracked her brain. Geography anywhere north of Bristol wasn't her forte. Actually, geography wasn't her forte full stop. It involved numbers and a sense of direction. Boston though? Somewhere near the east coast? Not too bad. Train to Birmingham and a connection, she guessed hazily. Shuddering at the thought of having to read one of those enormous departure boards with the flashing orange numbers, she said, 'Why are you going to Boston?'

'It's where my next job is. I was only here until my sabbatical ran out and the position in the States became vacant. And now it is, so I'll be on my way. Shouldn't think anyone here will miss me. Leo can help Gran out with stuff until she appoints a proper accountant. One who will do the job that I failed so spectacularly at.' His bitterness hung in the air like a bad smell.

'I didn't know Leo had a business background. Should have guessed though. But Boston, isn't it a bit flat there? Won't you miss the rolling Devon countryside?' Janey was finding it hard to focus. Something about this situation was seriously awry.

Will gave her an odd look. 'It's Boston Massachusetts, Janey. I'm going to America to work.'

'But you can't go there. You have to fly,' she blurted out. Had she heard right? Was Will really disappearing off to the States?

'That's the general idea.' Will shoved a folder into the box.

Janey staggered back to the door. She felt behind her and hung onto the handle, needing something fixed to centre on. Her thoughts were whirling.

'You can't!'

'I'm so sorry, Janey. I know we've become friends.' He flicked her a look and sighed heavily. 'Good friends. I kept trying to find a time to tell you but things kept getting in the way. And then Gran came back and all this Becca nonsense started up and we were busy doing the espionage stuff ...' he tailed off. 'There never seemed the right time.'

'I didn't know,' she gasped.

'But you must have known I was only here for a while.

Until Gran returned from Italy and she and Becca had got things going.' He winced at the last sentence.

'I don't know. I suppose. Maybe.' Janey tried to think, tried to steer her thoughts into a more cohesive heap. It was no good, her brain was fried. Had she known Will was only at Cheney House temporarily? Possibly. But when she'd learned that, it hadn't mattered as much. *He* hadn't mattered as much. And now she found that he mattered very much indeed. 'You didn't tell me you were going to the States!' she accused, randomly.

Will bit his lip, seemingly on the verge of saying something. There was a long pause.

'I'm sorry, Janey,' he repeated, eventually. 'I'm really sorry. I just didn't know how to tell you. Or when, as I said. The right moment never came along.'

'I'm sure.' Janey was filled with a sudden, glorious surge of pure white-hot temper. 'After all, we've hardly spent any time together at all. Haven't hung out at parties, crept around in bushes for a week trying to entrap Becca, shared umpteen cups of tea in my office, sat in meetings together. No, we haven't spent any time together at all!'

Will hung his head. 'I know. I know. Add coward to my list of failings. It just got too difficult to bring it up.'

'Why? Why did it get difficult? What possible reason could you have for not telling me?' She stamped her foot.

Will lifted the box. He faced her square on, the box in his arms as a defence. 'It just did, Janey,' he said wearily. 'It just did. And now, if you'll excuse me, I have to go.'

Opening the door, she stood to one side. 'Be my guest,' she spat.

Janey stared into the void he'd left. It was only then that three things cannonballed into her. Frustratingly, he still hadn't explained what it was that had distracted him from monitoring Becca more closely. Secondly, he had left his precious Bonsai on the desk. Thirdly and most importantly of all, that she loved him. She loved the very bones of the man.

And she'd let him walk out of her life without telling him.

Chapter 44

The Galloping Galanthophile: October

October brings us the sense that everything is leaving. Leaves droop and drop, then fester on the ground making enormous piles to gather up, roses shrivel on the bush, the days shorten and become cold so there's less time to spend outdoors. It's definitely better to curl up inside with a good gardening book. We have lots in stock so come and browse.

Tips for this month: don't forget to move tender plants into the greenhouse. Plant up your spring cabbages. Divide your established rhubarb crowns to create new plants. Cut back foliage and tie up climbers in preparation for harsh winter weather. Lots of trips to the tip anticipated. Far better to create your own mulch in a compost bin. They're on offer at twenty-five percent off at the moment. Stocks limited.

As ever, happy gardening.

GG

‘Oh dear, Janey, this is a miserable read,’ Clare muttered to herself, as she read the latest blog offering. She wrapped her pashmina a little tighter; it wasn’t warm in her office. With its high ceilings and original Georgian bricks, the old house was a nightmare to heat. She closed down her laptop screen with a resounding click. The blog hadn’t hit the right note at all. Instead of the usual chatty, occasionally informative tone it was positively downbeat. She sighed. The girl hadn’t been the same lately. She’d hoped, now Becca had gone, that everyone would snap back into how they used to be – and most had. Gwen was her usual bustling, inquisitive self, Meg and Val seemed back on form in plant sales and even Graham had a new spring in his step, which was astonishing considering the emotional trauma Becca had put him through. It was just Janey who was limp and hollowed out. She was working hard, perhaps too hard. Yesterday Clare had witnessed her humping great bags of pea gravel around for hours on end, without stopping. It was almost as if the girl was punishing herself but Clare couldn’t think what for. And while Janey could be, on occasion, a little socially awkward, she was usually cheerful and outgoing in her own unique way. Not at the moment. She was going through the motions, zombie-like. Well, whatever the matter was, it would have to wait. Clare glanced at the clock. In just under thirty minutes, eighty guests would crowd into the newly decorated marquee for Cheney House’s very first wedding reception. It had been an awful lot of work to get everything organised in such a short timeframe but the team had pulled together. Two friends of Millie’s had offered to be guinea-pigs. Emma and her fiancé Oliver were saving hard for their first home together, so had jumped at the chance at a cut-price wedding reception on the understanding that they would very much be an experiment.

Clare went through things in her head. Borrowed heaters to warm the marquee and switched on well before the event, Graham on hand for car park duty, decorations in place, enough prosecco to greet guests on arrival at the restaurant, a warming menu to feed them, and a disco and fireworks set up for the late evening party. She wracked her brain but couldn't think of anything she'd not considered.

'Time to say goodbye, Cam.' Clare clicked her tongue at the spaniel. 'I'd better get myself down there.' She bent to straighten the dogs specially bought sparkly bandana. 'You look so pretty, Cami. Perfectly attired for a wedding. Perhaps you can come and meet the bride later? And don't worry my darling, you and I will be tucked up in bed well before those pesky fireworks start. I know you're not a fan.'

As Clare walked across the courtyard she thought it couldn't be a more gloriously romantic day for a wedding. True, it was cold but the sky was a clear crisp blue and the trees were burnished with golden autumn colour. It was a perfect setting for a bride like Emma who was possessed of a fiery, earthy beauty.

Janey greeted her as she entered the marquee and Clare was relieved to see she was dressed smartly in today's agreed uniform of a black shirt and skirt or trousers. Janey, of course, wore trousers but at least they were pressed and unusually clean. Looking down, Clare tried to suppress a grin. The clumpy boots were still in evidence. Well, it wouldn't be Janey without a little quirkiness and at least she'd polished them.

'Janey, it looks beautiful in here. You've all worked so hard.

I couldn't be prouder.' Clare looked around, taking in the hollowed-out pumpkins, some containing tealights, others abundant with arrangements of sunflowers, orange and red roses, sheaves of corn and apples. Looking up, Clare saw that to complement the lush autumn feel, orange and red sparkly bunting was strung across the ceiling and interspersed with soft golden lighting. 'The bunting is superb, who did it?'

'Biddy. She's a brilliant sewer amongst her other talents.'

Clare pulled a face. 'Ah yes. And I heard her other talents include holding Viagra parties for pensioners. Am I correct?' In the past, it would have been the sort of comment that had Janey hooting with laughter until tears ran down her face.

'Yeah. Apparently.'

Clare gazed at Janey's pinched expression. She would have to tackle this but now wasn't the time. She pulled her wrap even tighter. The heaters were blasting out warmth but it wasn't quite enough to dispel the chill in the tent, most of which was emanating from the woman in front of her.

'Well, as I said, you and the team have done an amazing job,' she said in another attempt to bring cheer to the girl. All Janey did was nod back. Clare felt a twinge of alarm. She really needed everyone to be on top form for today. A lot was riding on it. If this was a success, then it might lead to other bookings. Weddings were lucrative, and heaven knows, another income stream would be very welcome.

'Best foot forward, darling.' Impulsively, she reached out and gave Janey a hug. 'And, as a good friend of mine who delighted in the amateur stage used to say, "Remember teeth and tits, teeth and tits."' Her attempt at humour backfired. She was disconcerted to see tears start. This simply wasn't like

Janey. She tried another tack. 'Bright smiles and shoulders back, darling girl, no matter how awful we feel inside. Right then,' she added, bracingly, to stem the emotion that threatened, 'let's get this show on the road.'

The happy couple walked back down the aisle, beaming. Clare didn't think she'd seen a more naturally beautiful bride. Emma's glorious red hair and exuberant personality was perfectly set off by a coronet of orange and deep-red roses, a flowing georgette gown in deep cream and a fake fur cape sparkling with diamanté. She held a bouquet made of more roses and dotted with sunflowers and corn sheaves. It was a riot of colour. On her arm, new husband, Oliver, looked handsome, if a little overwhelmed, in a smart grey lounge suit.

It had been the happiest of ceremonies. Emma and Oliver had been legally married in the registrar's office in Honiton the day before, but had chosen to have a blessing in the marquee, with poems and readings read out by friends and family and accompanied by much affectionate laughter.

As they all came out of the marquee they were met by mellow October sunshine, a cerulean blue sky and a cordon of Oliver's fellow lifeboat volunteers holding up an arch made of standard RNLI-issue yellow wellington boots. The guests threw confetti punched out of autumn-hued leaves, which had taken ages with the team up most of the night trying to make enough. A teenage boy, Emma's brother Clare assumed, threw a handful so accurately it landed right on Emma's décolletage and settled between her cleavage.

'Score!' he yelled and retreated from his sister's wrath to stand next to Clare.

'Good shot, young man.' She couldn't help but giggle.

'Yeah.' He nodded to the RNLI volunteers. 'See them. That's what I want to do when I'm older.'

Clare was about to ask him more when she saw the pockets of his ill-fitting blazer wriggle. 'What have you got in there?' she asked, taking a step back.

'Todger and Snog. The guinea pigs.' He opened the pocket nearest to her to reveal a small, potato-shaped brown and white rodent. 'Couldn't have them miss out on all the fun, and Em refused to let them be bridesmaids. Thought they might eat the decorations.'

'She might have a point.' Clare beckoned Janey over from where she was directing guests to the restaurant. 'Don't you think they might be happier in a cosy box for the rest of the day? We sell pet food and supplies, so Janey here can sort you out. On the house. Think of it as a sort of pet creche. I'm sure we can find them a couple of juicy carrots too.' Seeing he was about to argue, she added, 'After all, you'll want to concentrate on your meal, won't you? It's roast beef with the most marvellous red wine gravy. And Yorkshire puddings too, of course. I hear our cook Gwen has also made some of her extra special apple and caramel ice-cream cheesecake. You can't eat that when worrying about,' she paused, 'what did you call them?'

'Todger and Snog.'

'Quite. Ah Janey, could you take this young man and his, erm, guinea pig companions and find them somewhere warm and safe for the duration of the wedding breakfast?' Janey grinned in response. She had been looking, if not brimming over with joy, then at least professional during the ceremony. However, Clare suspected she'd far rather deal with a teenage boy and his pets than wedding guests. 'And perhaps you could both pop in to check on Camilla? She's been on her own in the flat for a while.'

'Camilla?' The boy screwed up his face in disbelief. 'What, as in—'

'As in Clare's very gorgeous spaniel,' Janey explained.

He brightened. 'I love dogs. She won't eat the guineas will she?'

Janey laughed. 'She's more likely to lick them to death. Come on. Let's get you sorted and back before the photographs happen. You won't want to miss those. We can collect Cam and she can join in the party.' She put a hand on his shoulder and steered him away. Clare heard her ask, 'What sort of guinea pigs are they then?' and saw her peek into a pocket before saying, 'Cute!'

Clare watched as they walked away, deep in conversation. She was exceedingly fond of Janey and it grieved her to see her so unhappy. She turned and stopped Millie and Jed who were coming out of the marquee. 'Oh I just have to admire this little one,' she said, and gazed at the tiny infant held in a papoose on Jed's chest. Her parents' faces, although rimed with exhaustion, shone with pride.

'Four months old today,' Millie whispered. 'Come meet Edie Henville.'

'So precious. Utterly gorgeous.' Clare touched a feather-light finger to the downy head. The baby yawned and uncurled a tiny, perfect jewel of a hand. 'Hello young lady. You were so good during the ceremony. I didn't hear you make a peep.'

'Makes a change.' Jed grinned. 'Kept us up most of last night.'

'Ah, I remember those times only too well. How is it going?'

'All a bit of a blur at the moment,' Millie admitted. 'But we wouldn't have it any other way.' Sending a look of pure love to her husband, she rested her head on his broad shoulder.

'So much good luck with her.' Clare dropped the lightest of kisses on one teeny finger. 'Go and get yourselves in the warm. And if you want a break from her, I'm sure Gwen will take over for baby snuggles in an instant.'

'Thanks, Clare.'

She watched the little family go and a wave of nostalgia overcame her. A fierce longing for when Alicia was tiny enough to only need feeds and cuddles shot through her. She had been a contented baby; it had been mystifying to see her grow into such a complicated and aloof adult. As a much-wanted baby Alicia had brought such joy. Being a grandparent to Will had brought even greater. A quiet baby, he'd been born with a headful of dark springy hair and an expression in his alert eyes that he was prepared to take on the world immediately. She wondered if he was ready to settle down, start a family of his own. But that would make her a great-grandmother. Good heavens, was she really ready for that? Surely she couldn't be that old? How terribly vexing. Forcing herself to concentrate back on Will, she pondered his last phone call. He had seemed so unhappy. He'd taken the Becca business to heart. She knew he felt he'd failed them all and Will didn't take failure well. He had little experience of it. The image of him practising a piano piece came into her head. Age nine, he'd spent much of his summer vac hunched over the baby grand in the old drawing room, relentlessly playing 'Für Elise' until it was perfect. Such a driven child. She wondered if there was more to his current mood, though. A flare of selfish hope had her wishing the Boston job wasn't working out and he would come home to Cheney. Janey's miserable face came into her mind again. Was it possible Will and Janey's unhappiness were connected? They'd certainly forged a close friendship but surely Will would have told her if a relationship had begun? She knew Janey was keen on Graham, but even though Becca was now out of the equation, they seemed to be continuing as just friends. And pleasant though Graham was, she rather thought Janey could do a little better. Could Will have fallen for Janey? The more she thought about it, the more it made sense. He'd certainly championed her against Becca and kooky Janey was just the sort of woman to bring him out of his rather infuriatingly self-contained state. Vowing to get to the bottom of it all she narrowed her eyes in determination and watched as a crimson leaf skittered across the cobbles.

'A wonderful wedding.' It was Leo. He kissed her on the cheek. 'Congratulations, *amore mio*. It's going splendidly.'

She took his arm and sank into him gratefully, suddenly exhausted. 'It's been a long day.'

'What is the matter?'

'Oh Leo, you can always read me so easily.' Smiling up at him she added, 'Let's walk for a while.'

His face creased in concern. 'Are you all right?'

'I'm perfectly fine. Just tired and feeling rather old.'

'*Po, po, po*. Nonsense.' He took her hand and kissed it. 'You will never be old to me.'

'You're so good for me, Leo.'

'I hope to be always.'

'Such a good friend.' It came out on a long wistful sigh.

They'd reached the chestnut trees and paused to contemplate the red-brick house glowing in the late afternoon sunshine. Broad shards of shadow yawned across the grounds beyond, deepening the valleys and blurring the horizon in the soft autumn light. A breeze whispered through the leaves above and a conker fell at their feet, glossy and fat.

Leo picked it up. 'For you.' With an old-fashioned bow, he handed it to her. 'It shines like a jewel.'

Clare took it and smiled. 'Not a jewel but a jewel all the same.' The wind whipped her hair into her eyes and she put a hand through it to shake it back.

Seeing her shiver with cold, he took off his jacket and placed it tenderly around her shoulders. 'I would be happy to give you rubies and pearls.'

'I don't need them, Leo.'

'Every woman needs jewels.'

'Not this one. I have my family and friends, my house, my business, which astonishingly, despite all that has happened, isn't faring *too* badly.'

'And love?'

'I'm surrounded by love.' But even as she said the words, she knew it wasn't strictly true. Alicia was on the other side of the world enjoying her ex-pat army life to the full and Will was in Boston and far away too. Tears prickled in her eyes and she blamed the sudden melancholy on the high emotion of a wedding day. Part of her longed for a tiny baby to hold, like Edie. For a huge family like the one she'd just seen celebrate so noisily and chaotically. Even if it came with a truculent teenager with guinea pigs stowed in his pockets. Part of her mourned her youth, the things she hadn't had chance to do and now probably wouldn't.

Leo came to her. He put his arms around her waist and pulled her into an embrace. 'There. Now you are surrounded by love.'

Clare rested her head against his solid chest breathing in his unique aroma; a mixture of the lemons from his homeland, the occasional cigar he indulged in and the faint tang of his spicy aftershave.

'You're a good man, Leo,' she murmured. 'I don't know what I would have done without you these past few months.'

'Then don't do without me.' He loosened his hold, and taking her by the shoulders, gazed into her eyes. 'Be with me, *amore mio*. Clare, my love.' He looked suddenly and disconcertingly unsure. 'I love you. I have always loved you. I loved you when I knew you were Gem's. I love you now, so very much. It has always been you.' He kissed her, tenderly at first and then deepening it as her passion answered his own. He released her, and after whispering something passionate in Italian, he added, 'I am yours forever.' Then he took her hands in his and kissed each of her fingers in turn.

Clare stared at him, astonished. 'You love me? You've always loved me? Even when I married Gem? Why have you never said anything?'

Leo looked at her in reproach. 'How could I?' He shrugged. 'You and Gem, you were so much in love. Who was I to get in the way? What good would it have done to tell you of my love?'

'So you kept away? It hurt Gem, you know, that you weren't

around more.' She reached up and touched a tender finger to his cheek.

He turned his head and his warm mouth found her hand and kissed it again. 'It is my shame. But to see you together made my heart break. I had to go away, heal my heart. Try to love again. Try to find someone of my own to love.' He shook his head. 'It did not work. I never forgot you. I never stopped loving you. My Clare, my Chiara.'

'That's the name of your boat.' Clare's eyes widened. 'You named your yacht after me?'

Leo shrugged again and pursed his lips. 'Chiara, Italian and Clare, English. This is true. What can I say? I would rather she was called the *True Love*. She has been with me when you could not.' He gave an impish grin. 'She outlasted my marriage. As did my love for you.'

'Oh Leo.'

He gave a gentle laugh. 'Perhaps it was that which made Carla unhappy. She had not only another woman as rival, but a yacht too. The guilt, it stays with me. How could I marry when my heart belonged to another? To my Clare.' He smoothed her hair away from her face. 'My love. *Amore mio*.'

'I don't know what to say.' Clare's mind was racing, her emotions running from confusion to certainty and back to confusion again. She couldn't deny the physical reactions she'd had to his kiss, couldn't deny the longing for more. Little flares of excitement were shooting through her body, awakening after a long sleep. 'But Leo, we're old. You live in Italy; I have my life here. I don't know, it's all so sudden. How would it all work?'

'Not for me. Not so sudden.' He kissed her again, as if

unable to resist and then abruptly stopped. 'But I see that for you it is too soon.' His expression sobered. 'For you it is too near Gem's death. I will wait. After all, I have waited all this time. I can wait a little while longer. I do not want to rush you.' He dropped contact and moved away.

Clare immediately felt the chill of his departure, the loneliness of standing on her own and without a man who loved her holding her tenderly. What a fool she was being. One of the last things Gem had said to her was a command to be happy, to not grieve too long, to find love again. Had he known about his best friend's feelings for her? Probably. Would he bless any relationship she had with Leo? Certainly. The one thing Gem loved in life was love itself. Confusion fused into clarity. She wanted this man. She wanted him at her side through the next phase of her life. Reaching out, she took Leo's hand.

'I don't want to wait, Leo.' She smiled. 'After all, I'm seventy next year. I may not have much time left.' She tugged him to her and kissed him passionately. 'We can work this out, can't we? A few months here, a few in Italy. The best of both worlds.'

'My darling Chiara.' Leo's voice was hoarse. 'Of course, I will do anything to make this happen. And yes we take this slow, we take our time. The pace is up to you but yes, we will make this work.'

Clare, long-forgotten lust heating her mind and body, said daringly, 'You know, maybe I don't want to take this slowly, Leo.' She laughed at his surprise. 'Actually, I don't want to take this slowly at all. I happen to know there is a very fine bottle of champagne in my flat.' She nuzzled into his neck. 'Perhaps we should share it. I have a plan to seduce you.'

'*Po, po, po*,' he exclaimed, his Italian machismo momentarily affronted. 'It is I who seduces.'

Clare took him by the hand and began leading him to the main house. 'Do you know, I don't care who seduces who just as long as it happens.' Laughing at him from over her shoulder, she blew him a flirtatious kiss.

Leo, catching on to her humour shook his head and smiled. 'In that case, my darling Clare, it seems I have no choice. From somewhere I will find the strength for this ordeal. Lead on, my wicked tease. My Chiara. My love.'

Chapter 45

The Galloping Galanthophile: November

November is all about loss, remembrance and fallen leaves. It's a sad time of year, made damp with tears. However much you rake, more leaves seem to take their place. Back-breaking work but it has to be done. It's the ideal time to get your compost pile begun, but no matter how tidy a garden you like, remember to leave the odd pile of material for hibernating animals. Hedgehogs in particular can be vulnerable. You might see one or two at dusk. They're feeding up before hibernation and soon they'll be looking for somewhere cosy to hole up in for the winter. They love heaps of wood and piles of leaves, so make sure you check thoroughly before lighting any bonfires. Better still, buy one of our specially made hedgehog houses to home your prickly guest. Food can be in scarce supply for birds too. Come in and stock up on your winter feeding supplies – we have birdseed, peanuts, fat balls and mealworms on offer at the moment. Wrap up tender plants with our special fleeces against any early frosts or chill winds – you don't want to lose them. And, speaking of remembrance, we'll be selling poppies for the poppy appeal right up to the 11th, so please give generously.

As ever, happy gardening.

GG

If Janey had been in pain over Graham, it was nothing as to how she was feeling over Will. She couldn't believe she had only recognised how much she was in love with him when it was too late. When he'd walked through the door and out of her life. How could she have been so stupid? She hung onto Clare's occasional mentions of his name and asked questions without being too obvious about it, taking the snippets of news home to analyse and go over in her head, again and again.

To make matters worse, Graham rebounded fast, extremely fast. And onto her. It was an impossible situation. Clare had discovered, to add to her crimes, Becca hadn't bothered to take out proper public liability insurance on the punting business on the lake. She had had no option but to close it down until something was sorted. It looked likely that part of the business wouldn't be up and running until the better weather in the spring in any case. With no lake and punts to oversee, Graham returned to the plant sales centre and took over garden furniture, fencing and hard core again. He was much happier back doing what he was expert in. He was also under Janey's feet. And lovesick. She tried to be kind. She also tried to be distant and fob him off gently. It was hard hearing all the things that once she would have been desperate for him to say. They were the right words. It was just that he was the wrong man. Janey didn't miss the irony. She had no one to talk it over with. Alina was on location, working twenty-hour days and with dodgy Wi-Fi, she didn't think Gwen would understand and anyway, was in full wedding prep mode for her daughter, and there was no one else. She'd always discussed most things with Graham, as he had with her. Their current relationship was too fraught with misunderstandings for heart to hearts. Besides, she could hardly talk through her feelings about Will with the man who was now professing undying affection for her.

Instead, she threw herself into work, spending hours in the shed coaxing snowdrop seedlings into premature flower in the search for that holy grail – a new variety.

Her parents took her refusal to fly over and spend Christmas in Spain with them badly. Janey felt awful at letting them down but simply couldn't face the horrors that an airport and a flight in a metal tube thirty thousand feet up held for her. These days she was so morose it was all she could do to get in her car and drive the short distance to work each day. Everyone was too gung-ho after the departure of Becca to notice her misery. Clare seemed increasingly besotted with Leo. Millie and Jed were in ecstasies over baby Edie. Graham hung around gawping at her with puppy eyes, and hot on the tail of the recent wedding reception in the marquee, Gwen was obsessed with bridal magazines. It seemed to Janey that everyone had found their happy ending. Except her. Thank goodness for Camilla. If Janey hadn't the spaniel to talk to and bury her teary eyes into the dog's soft fur, she thought she'd go mad.

The appointment for the dyscalculia test was the final straw. It came in the post along with the passport that she'd applied for, thinking she'd need it in December. Will had encouraged her to apply for an appointment promising to take her and offer moral support. A rebellious tear ran down her cheek as she remembered him laughing and saying he'd treat them to a slap-up lunch on the way back. Opening the official-looking envelope and seeing its stark contents took her straight back to feeling like the hopeless adolescent who had suffered her way through school. With her arch enemy no longer blighting her life, Janey felt she should be back to her loud, bouncy self. The truth was, everything seemed meaningless since Will had left. Throwing the letter onto the kitchen table, she slumped down on a chair and burst into loud and very untidy tears. She drove into work, eyes still swollen and red-rimmed.

Clare found her hunched over a display of discounted African violets. She was half-heartedly picking off the brown leaves to make them look more attractive.

'Oh my goodness,' Clare exclaimed. 'They look rather tragic.'

'Last batch of plants from the wholesaler Becca used.' Janey straightened and added, on a gloomy sigh, 'I'm doing my best but it'll be a job to shift them. Nothing sadder than a plant no one wants. I'll have to discount them to practically nothing, give them away. That usually does the trick.' She turned to give Camilla a cuddle. 'What can I do for you, Clare?'

'Speaking of sad,' Clare peered anxiously into Janey's face, 'whatever has happened? I know we're still clearing up Becca's mess and being a man down couldn't happen at a worse time, what with the utter madness that is Christmas in a garden centre, but she's out of our lives forever. In fact,

I've some rather wonderful news. It seems Becca and her young man have taken themselves off to France, opening an import-export antique and curios business, it would seem. With any luck, she'll never darken the doors of Cheney House again. What's more, every penny she stole has now been paid back. That's good news, isn't it?' As Janey made no reply, she repeated, 'Isn't it, Janey?'

Janey scuffed her boots together. 'Suppose.'

'Oh my.' Clare made a decision. 'Come on, coffee and biccies time in my office. Gwen is trying out a *biscotti* recipe Leo gave her. Between you and me,' she added, as they walked towards the main house, 'I'm not terribly keen but haven't the heart to tell her.' She grimaced. 'They're rather hard. Cam enjoys them but I've sneaked in a packet of Tesco double-choc cookies. If you don't tell Gwen, I won't.'

Clare settled Janey on the sofa and a sympathetic Camilla jumped up and snuggled next to her. 'If I'm really honest, darling girl, I've been worried about you for ages. You simply haven't been yourself. At first I put it down to shock and the after-effects of our esteemed manager leaving.' She put a mug of coffee into Janey's hands. 'I think we were all rather emotionally frail for a time but I look around and see people bouncing back. Everyone except you.' She eyed Janey shrewdly. 'And, if I may say, the last two gardening blogs, as well as being rather brief, were, how can I put it, a little morose?'

Janey stared into her coffee. 'Sorry.'

'So, assuming it's not Becca who is making you so very miserable, may I ask what is? Or is it a who?'

Janey put her untouched coffee down with a jolt and some slopped out onto the coaster Clare had prudently provided.

She hugged Camilla a little more tightly. How could she tell Clare she was in love with her grandson? And that grandson wanted nothing to do with her and, in order to escape, had disappeared not only to another country but another continent.

'It's Will isn't it?'

Janey second glanced Clare in shock. 'I ... well ...' she tailed off.

'He's in love with you.' Clare stated it as fact. She sank down onto the chair opposite. 'Oh dear, he didn't make you feel awkward did he? My grandson is a lovely boy but he's sometimes not terribly good at the social graces.'

'Makes two of us,' Janey said glumly.

'Yes, I suppose you have that in common. Otherwise you are as chalk and cheese, as the saying goes.'

'No, Clare, he's not in love with me. He made that very clear. Doesn't see me as girlfriend material.'

'But why ever not?'

'Can I refer you to the chalk and cheese?'

'I rather think you'd be good for him. He's such a hard-worker I sometimes think he forgets to have any fun. And you have always been able to see the more frivolous side of life. Until recently.'

'Until recently.' Janey bit her lip to stop the tears that threatened and stared very hard at Clare's oriental rug. Obviously old and probably once very expensive, it was liberally endowed with Camilla's hair.

'So, what is the problem, Janey? Is it still Becca? I know she treated you appallingly but that's all in the past now. We've a marvellous opportunity to rebuild Cheney House exactly as we want it. I'd really like you to be part of our renaissance but I need you on top form.'

'No.' Janey shook her head miserably. 'It's not Becca. Things at work have been much better.'

'Then what on earth is it, darling?'

Janey sucked in an enormous breath. She knew Clare well enough to know she wouldn't be fobbed off. And, after all her boss had done for her, she owed her the truth. Besides, Clare was right; she really wasn't able to give Cheney House her best when so miserable. Only that morning, she'd had to rescue several trays of heather she'd potted up in the wrong type of compost. 'You're right in a way. It is to do with Will.'

Clare nodded sagely. 'I thought as much.' She sighed. 'I wondered why he'd high-tailed it off to Boston in such glums.'

'Except it isn't like that at all. It's not that Will is in love with me, it's that I'm in love with him.' The dam burst and tears poured down Janey's face. 'Clare, I love him so much and I don't know what to do about it!'

Chapter 46

Janey wasn't sure how it happened. Once Clare had decided on the plan, she steam-rollered Janey into submission. She helped her pack, booked her ticket, assured her that the flight time wasn't *too* long and had bid her farewell at security after steering her through the steel and chrome bewilderment that was Heathrow. She'd had to prise Janey's fingers off hers before reassuring the girl it was all going to be fine. And now, here she was, about to fly for the first time and it might be the most important flight she ever made.

After she'd told Clare the whole sorry tale of how she'd fallen for Will, Clare had thought for a minute and then declared that Janey should go to see him and talk things through.

'But he's in Boston,' Janey said stupidly.

'And there are ways of getting there, my darling. It's not the end of the world. You have lots of holiday owing, why don't you go over and see him? It would be the ideal time to go before things here get too impossibly manic in the Christmas rush.'

Janey had felt Clare's puzzled eyes on her. Could see it from her point of view. Here was a woman contemplating flying regularly to Italy to maintain a relationship with Leo. How would she ever understand why a short flight to the USA could hold such terrors?

So, Janey had slowly and haltingly explained the problem.

'You don't see numbers properly?' Clare said, obviously not really understanding at all.

Janey sighed. It would have to do. It was too complicated to go into detail. Even she didn't really fully understand it. Maybe she should take up the dyscalculia appointment after all.

'And this was behind that mistake you made at the till with Biddy?' Clare added.

Janey nodded.

'And Will has been helping you? Trying to find you an educational consultant?'

Janey nodded again.

'Hardly the action of an indifferent man, Janey darling.'

'He's never been indifferent. He's a friend.'

'But you'd like more. Obviously. Well, the only way to find out,' Clare said briskly, 'is to tackle him about it and a conversation such as that can hardly be done over the phone. Terribly unsatisfactory. Let me have a think.'

Clare had had a think and had sprung into action. She booked a First Class return to Logan International, promised Janey she would be met by private taxi and taken to the hotel where Will was staying and that all would be well. Not only that but she refused to take any payment. Just before they said goodbye at the airport, Janey had tried to pay Clare back.

'Janey, Will told me the truth about who really saved darling Camilla from drowning.' The older woman took Janey's hands in hers, eyes glistening with grateful tears. 'I confess, I've been so pre-occupied with that horrid Becca business, wrapped up in Leo and organising Emma's wedding that I haven't got around to thanking you. And you're such a funny miss about feelings that I wasn't sure how you'd take it. Take this as my thank you. If I can make you and Will happy then it will make me happy too.'

Janey, going through to the departure lounge and clutching her precious passport was in such a dazed state, she hardly noticed the member of airport staff approaching her.

'Hi, my name's Ewan and I'm your special assistance escort. I'm here to look after you until I hand you over to cabin crew.' He smiled and showed immaculately capped white teeth.

Janey waved the instructions Clare had painstakingly written out for her. She was beginning to feel proud of herself for getting this far. 'I think I might be okay. I've got this.'

Ewan took the piece of paper from her, scanned it, nodded and said, 'Very comprehensive.' Handing it back to her, he added, 'If you'd like to come this way, I'll show you to the First Class Lounge. If you want me, I'll be there. If you want to sleep, then just tell me to go away.'

Ewan proved good company and Janey didn't tell him to go away. It turned out he was a huge Tarantino fan. They chatted about films, she ate some delicious food and sipped champagne and the time waiting for the flight disappeared. She tried to avoid looking at the departure board; all those orange blinking numbers made her nauseous. When the time came, Ewan took her through the boarding tunnel and handed her over to the equally charming Nancy. Janey didn't know if it was the fizz or nervous exhaustion, but after the excitement of take-off, she plugged into a film and slept through *Jojo Rabbit*. Nancy handed her over to Logan Airport's equivalent of Ewan and he steered her through the manic confusion of the luggage carousel and immigration. And then she found herself standing outside in the blessed relief of Boston's chilly night air and responding to Enzio, who relieved her of her suitcase and opened the rear door of a limousine.

'We'll have you in your hotel just as soon as we can, Miss Janey.'

His distinct Boston accent filtered through Janey's dazed and exhausted state and a thrill of achievement shot through her. She was in the USA. She'd made it! Resting her head on the seat, she watched as car lights blurred past. What time was it? The flight was seven hours, Boston was five hours behind the UK. It might possibly be the early hours of the morning. She gave up trying to work it out.

Her hotel was a grand old building right next to a large park.

'And Boston Common's right over there,' Enzio explained proudly as he escorted her to check in.

Janey took one look at the vast bed in her hotel room, took off her travel-stained clothes and fell into it. Will would have to wait.

Chapter 47

BOSTON

When she woke, daylight was edging its way around the blind. Sitting up, she groaned. Her head was thick and fuzzy, her skin felt papery and her teeth were disgusting. After drinking a bottle of water and taking a long hot shower, she felt slightly better. Pulling up the blind, she gasped. Her room looked directly onto the park she'd spotted the night before. It spread out before her, its neatly cut lawns interspersed with tidy paths and bordered with trees in riotous autumn colours. Beyond the profusion of fiery trees, she could glimpse water glinting in the sunshine. It was beautiful. Too beautiful to miss. And, after all, she didn't know how long she'd be in the city.

Navigating the crossing over a busy road by following the crowds, she went through some impressive gates and into the park. The air was bracing after her over-heated hotel room but not as cold as she'd thought it would be. The trees glowed a vivid orange against a dazzlingly blue sky and the fresh chill stung at her cheeks. It was good to be back out in the open air after hours of airports and planes.

The sun was high in the sky and office workers teemed into the park, mixing with the tourists and finding a bench to eat lunch. She strolled over the bridge spanning a lake and paused to watch the squirrels scamper about, audaciously stealing crumbs of sandwiches. For someone like her, unused to built-up areas, it was like finding a living, breathing lung at the very heart of the city. Crossing a second road she found herself in another part of the park; it was more open and not as cultivated. She wondered if this was the Boston Common Enzio referred to. The aroma of bread dough and hot cheese assailed her nostrils so, suddenly ravenous, she bought a slice of pizza off a vendor. She ate it sitting on a bench, ear-wigging a conversation between two office workers sharing boyfriend problems. She'd binge watched some classic *Ally McBeal* recently and it all felt very familiar. Giggling, she couldn't quite believe she was here. Glancing up to where the land rose on a gentle slope, she took a photo of an impressive building with a dome, which blazed golden in the bright light. Then a group of spectacular trees shimmering in a quieter corner attracted her attention so she wandered over. It was all so impossibly glamorous and American; she felt as if she was starring in her very own movie. Feeling giddy, she eyed the trees. They were red maples, of course, grouped together like the three bears, two bigger and a baby. She couldn't resist. To the music of a nearby busker, she danced. Easing the travel ache out of her shoulders and the chasing the fug from her brain, she pirouetted and leaped, spun and twisted. Lifting her face to the brilliant sun and the wintry air, it felt utterly right.

'Janey? Janey!'

She slid to a stop, panting, and whirled to face the man who was shouting her name.

Will!

He was standing at the edge of the path, some distance from her. He wore a suit and dark overcoat and looked edible.

He came closer. Thin and pinched, his nose was pink with cold. 'It *is* you. How the hell are you here? I saw you from the other side of the Common but I wasn't sure. But it had to be you dancing under trees. Who else could it be?'

Janey said the first thing that came into her head. 'Hello Will. I've looked after your Bonsai.'

'Thank you, I guess.' He looked bewildered. 'Janey, why are you in Boston? You hate the idea of flying.' He thought for a second. 'You surely didn't come by ship?'

'No, I flew. Got in last night.' Her nose wrinkled. 'Or possibly early this morning. The time change has confused me. Clare organised people to look after me. Or it might have been Leo; he seems to know about stuff like that.' She beamed. 'And I did it! It was amazing. Will, you should have seen my seat. First Class. I had one all to myself and could lie down if I wanted to. I kept getting offered champagne and there were all these goodies, snacks and skincare stuff. It was amazing. I felt like a film star. I felt like Alina!'

He laughed; his shoulders visibly relaxing. 'Sounds like First Class suited you.'

'And the film was *Jojo Rabbit* but I fell asleep and missed it. Quite cross, actually. It's not on anywhere near us at home yet.'

'Too much fizz?' he teased gently.

'Gwen gave me some travel sickness pills before I left. Said they send you sleepy. She was right, they did. I sort of floated my way through Heathrow.'

'Good old Gwen.' He came to her and took her hands. 'I still can't believe you're here.'

'I know. I'm pretty proud of myself.'

'So you should be.' He led her to a bench in the sun. 'It's the most amazing coincidence that I found you. I walk through here most days at lunchtime. Clears the head.'

Janey shrugged. 'Not so much of a coincidence. I'm staying at the same hotel as you. Clare organised that too.'

Will looked nonplussed. 'Handy.' He frowned. 'So are you here on behalf of Clare? Cheney House business?'

Janey inhaled, the cold air making her nostrils sting. It was now or never. And hadn't she just managed to cross the Atlantic in a metal tube? After doing that, telling the man in front of her that she loved him would be easy-peasy-lemon-squeezy as her nan used to say.

'I'm not here on business,' she began, and faltered.

'How's things at home?'

Disconcerted, she stuttered out an answer. 'Okay. The wedding went well. We've already got three enquiries for next year.'

'No one missing Becca then?' His smile was grim.

'Hardly. She's gone off to France apparently.'

Will winced. 'Lucky France.'

'Yes but what I was about to say was—'

'And is Gran all right? I'm worried she seems to be rushing into this thing with Leo. I want her to be happy, of course, but it all seems so sudden. She disappears off to Italy and comes back with him. They're old friends, I get that, but it's a bit of a leap from friends to a relationship, especially at her age. I mean, I've talked it over with her on the phone and she seems really happy—'

'Will!'

He stopped talking, recoiling at her forceful tone.

'Much as I love Clare and, like you, wish her all the happiness in the world with Leo, that's not why I came to Boston.'

'Then why did you?'

'That's what I've been trying to tell you!'

He ran a nervous finger around the collar of his snowy white shirt. 'Fire away then.'

'Oh!' Janey leaped up, her hands balled in fists, which she waved at the sky. 'I don't know how to put it into words.' She stopped, on the verge of frustrated tears. 'I've come all this way. Conquered you don't know how many fears and silly phobias.' She shook off a crimson leaf that had fallen and landed on her arm.

'Your phobias aren't silly, Janey.'

'You're right. They're not silly. They're very real and very painful and it took me all my courage to get into that plane and fly to see you.'

'You came to see *me*?'

'Don't look so surprised. Of course I came to see you.'

'And why did you do that, Janey?' Will's voice was hoarse, his eyes brilliant behind his tortoiseshell specs.

Janey turned and met his siren gaze. 'Because I love you, you daft bugger. That's why.' And she went to him, sank onto the bench next to him and kissed him until they were both breathless.

Chapter 48

'Well, I think that sealed the deal.' Will ran a satisfied hand over Janey's naked side and cupped her breast. He nuzzled into her neck.

She wriggled her back against him, sleepy and replete. Never had sex been this good. 'Won't they miss you at the office?' she giggled.

'Tough. I've been working practically twenty-four-seven since I got here. They can do without me for a few hours on a Friday afternoon.'

Janey rolled onto her back for his kiss. They'd been making love, napping and waking to make love again for hours. She didn't even know whose hotel room they were in. She hazarded a guess at hers. 'I had no idea it would be like this.'

'Like what?' He scraped his bristled chin over her tenderised lips until she squealed.

'Sex. With you. It's right what they say in *Bridget Jones*.'

'And what do they say?'

'Nice boys aren't supposed to kiss that well.'

He quirked a dark brow. He looked different without his glasses, more approachable, more vulnerable and easier to read. 'Am I a nice boy? Suppose I am. And I'm pretty sure that's a misquote. Call yourself a film buff?' He slid down her body. 'Miss Trelawney, I think that calls for a spot of punishment.'

Janey shrieked and tried to push him off. Then reared up as his tongue found her. Her back arched as the waves of hot pleasure began. 'Oh Will,' she sighed, her eyes glazing over. 'Have I said I love you?'

Later, much later, when they were too exhausted for anything other than conversation, Will said, 'I love you too. Did I say?'

Janey found his hand and held it. Her heart swelled with love for him. 'Not until now. I didn't know, you know.'

Will propped himself up on an elbow and gazed down at her. 'I thought you were hung up on Graham. How could I launch in and blurt out how I felt? Even though, Lord knows, I was tempted.'

She feathered a hand wonderingly down his finely sculptured cheekbone. 'I was. Hung up on Graham, I mean. For so long. And then it was you. All I could see was you. But I only realised it when you announced you were coming here. I've been so unhappy since you left, Will. I missed you so much. Clare made me confess everything and forced me onto the flight. Once she went into action, I didn't have much choice.' She pouted. 'But for you, I was prepared to do it.'

He laughed and kissed her softly. 'Sounds like Gran. But why did you never tell me how you felt?'

'How could I?' Janey retorted. 'You made it very clear you only saw me as a friend. That night of the party, when I practically offered myself to you on a plate, you rejected me. I was mortified. Could hardly look you in the eyes afterwards.'

'Oh Janey, Janey. You were drunk. Completely bladdered. You were saying all sorts of wild things. And I thought you still loved Graham at that moment.' He looked mildly affronted. 'Besides which, I could never take advantage of a drunk woman. That wouldn't do at all.'

'No,' she gazed back lovingly, 'my Atticus Finch. You wouldn't do that. Far too much of a gentleman. But there's one thing I don't understand. Why did you run off here, when you knew you loved me?'

Will gave an exhausted laugh and flopped back. 'Where do I start? For one, I was contractually obliged. Two, I was under the misapprehension that you were besotted with Graham and didn't want to stand in your way when Becca had so helpfully scarpered.' He sobered and blew out a breath. 'And three, I'd failed everyone. I felt thoroughly ashamed of myself. I was the one who should have sussed what Becca was up to. Should have done my job properly. And I'm not good at failure.'

'You said that before but didn't explain. What was stopping you? Doing your job properly, I mean?'

'You still haven't guessed? Darling Janey. It was you. All I could think about was you. All I could think about was how much I loved you. How much I wanted to love you. But I knew – thought – that you loved Graham and I didn't stand an earthly. And, when Becca went, I knew there could be no obstacle between you and Graham. I couldn't torture myself seeing you two get together and be deliriously happy. I had to get the hell out. It's the first time I've been in unrequited love and, I won't lie, it was awful. Made it impossible to concentrate on anything else.'

'Oh.'

'Is that it? Oh?'

'It's a lot to take in.' She rolled onto her side. 'But I know all about unrequited love. And it is awful. Oh Will, we've wasted so much time, haven't we? If only we'd been honest with one another, maybe we wouldn't have ended up living on either side of the Atlantic?'

'True. But maybe we had to go through all this to fully realise how much we love each other?'

'Pollyanna!' she accused, laughing. Then she stopped, her eyes huge. 'We're in the exact same situation as Annie and Sam. *Sleepless in Seattle*. Trying to find one another across the width of the United States. Not to mention Leo and Clare, trying to conduct a love affair on two continents.'

He tugged her earlobe, teasing. 'Not for the first time do I have to worry about your lack of geographical knowledge.'

'Whatcha mean?' Janey sat up indignantly.

'The last time I checked, Italy and the UK were on the same continent.'

'Pedant.' She flicked the edge of the sheet at him. 'You know what I mean.'

'Ouch!' In revenge, he lifted her on top of him. 'Is that what you want, a love affair? It's a delightfully old-fashioned way of putting it.'

She bent down and trailed her hair over his chest. 'I'm a delightfully old-fashioned sort of a girl.'

Will snorted. 'I'd call you lots of things, Janey, but old-fashioned isn't one of them.'

'Do you think it's going to work?' she asked, going rigid with sudden fear at his words. 'Do you think we're too different? We are, aren't we? Clare said we're chalk and cheese. I'll drive you crazy, won't I?'

'And I you.' He reached up to kiss her. 'Yes, we'll drive each other crazy but I'll risk it. Think of the fun we'll have.' Lying back again, he added, 'But in all seriousness, Janey, I want more than a casual fling with you. It's not my style. Even if we're living in different parts of the world, I want a proper relationship with you.'

'It's not my style either.' She kissed his nose, blithely ignoring the fact that this was uncharted territory for her. She frowned. 'Trouble is, I won't be able to fly over to see you all that often.'

He tucked a strand of hair behind her ear tenderly. 'Why, because of your dyscalculia?'

She bit her lip. 'Well, there is that. Also the fact that I don't have the money spare to buy transatlantic flights. Clare subbed me this one as a present,' she added, embarrassed.

'Then I'll just have to come to you. It won't be a hardship. Trust me.'

They kissed yet again then Janey broke off. 'Will, don't hate me for what I'm about to say.'

'What?' he answered sleepily.

'I'm absolutely, completely, utterly starving.'

He rolled over and reached for the telephone. Handing it to her, he said, 'That's the beauty of hotels. Order whatever you like and it arrives. Room service is a truly wonderful thing.'

'A burger. I want a burger. A really big one. Double. With loads of cheese and pickled gherkins and one of those skewer things holding it all together. And chips, I mean fries, real American fries. Then chocolate ice cream, which I intend to trickle all over you, so I can lick it off and have you for pudding.'

Will roared. 'I think that can be arranged.'

Chapter 49

Janey's return flight wasn't until Monday evening.

'We have a whole weekend together,' she declared with relish, over breakfast the following morning in a nearby diner. 'Bacon and maple syrup. Oh glory!' She rolled her eyes as she forked up a mouthful. 'I thought it was only a thing in movies. What are we going to do with ourselves? This weekend, I mean.'

Will waggled his eyebrows suggestively. 'Well, we could spend it in bed, or we could sightsee?'

She pulled a face. 'Tough choice. I mean, really tough choice. Could we do a bit of both, do you think? After all, I might never be in Boston again.'

Will reached for her hand and kissed it. 'Your fingers are all delicious and sticky,' he said, licking them.

'That would be the maple syrup.' She giggled. 'And there's me thinking you'd be too fastidious to lick food off me.'

'May I refer you to the chocolate ice cream incident?' Will huffed in mock indignation.

'Yes.' Janey giggled again and blushed crimson. 'The ice cream. Delicious!' She thought of what they'd got up to last night and her eyes widened. 'You're turning into a very surprising man, Will Cheney-Mortimer. But really,' she added, more seriously, 'would you mind if we did a bit of sightseeing? I'd love to see more of the city.'

'I think we can do that.' He leaned back on the banquette and grinned. 'And to be honest, I've been working so hard I've barely seen anything either.' Glancing outside he said, 'And the weather's perfect. A beautifully clear fall day.'

'Fall,' Janey rolled the word around her tongue. She examined the remains of their breakfast: pancakes with bacon and maple syrup, good coffee and eggs over easy. A thrill of pleasure shot through her. 'We really are in America, aren't we?' Clapping her hands together, she squealed. 'I still can't believe it.'

'Believe it, doll,' Will replied, in an exorable attempt at a Boston accent. He looked around for the waitress and signalled for the bill. 'Let's go be tourists then.'

For the next two days, they devoted themselves to making the most of what the city had to offer. They walked for miles. Janey became obsessed with the Freedom Trail, following the red line painted on the pavement assiduously and taking in all the history wide-eyed. Exhausted, they found Quincy Market and joined the throng of other tourists sampling lobster rolls. On Sunday it rained, so they wandered around the Museum of Fine Arts and afterwards ate pizza in a backstreet restaurant where the wait staff were charmingly brusque, yelling orders into the kitchen and sloshing around with great pitchers of beer. The nights were spent exploring one another's bodies until they eventually fell asleep in an untidy heap, entangled around one another.

All too soon it was Monday afternoon and time for Janey to head home. Will took the day off and went with her in the taxi to the airport. They held hands and sat in silence. Janey watched the passing scenery without interest. Every mile was taking her further away from Boston and from Will.

'I'm just going to go,' he said, when it was time to say goodbye. He swallowed. 'I'm not going to hold it together otherwise.' And then he kissed her hard and left.

Janey didn't really notice Mel, who guided her through Logan, and barely registered getting onto the plane. Rain spattered against the window as it took off and headed back to Heathrow. Back to England. Back to a Cheney House, which would no longer feel like home. Tears crept down her face and blurred her last view of the runway. 'Goodbye, Will,' she whispered and pressed her fingers pointlessly onto the window. She had no idea when she'd see him again.

Clare met her at arrivals, and casting a worried look at her face, took her arm and led her to the car. Leo was in the driving seat so Janey, wordlessly, got into the back. Clare shrieked as Leo pulled away. 'On the left remember! Drive on the left.' He cursed in Italian and steadied the car. She looked back at Janey, slumped miserably in the back. 'Didn't it go well, darling?'

'It went perfectly. I love him. He loves me.' Janey blew out an enormous sigh. 'I had the best weekend ever. *We* had the best weekend ever.'

‘Well, that’s marvellous. Isn’t it?’

‘But Clare, he’s in Boston and I’m over here. How is it going to work?’

Clare shot a fond look at Leo and put a hand on his knee. ‘I don’t know, my dear but I’m sure it will. Love has a way of making things happen.’

Janey snorted and lolled her head against the headrest. ‘I’m just going to have to emigrate,’ she declared.

‘Well, it may not come to a gesture quite that dramatic,’ Clare responded drily. ‘Let’s just wait and see what happens, shall we?’

Chapter 50

The Galloping Galanthophile: December

December is a special month at Cheney House. Bring the kids to meet Father Christmas in our magical grotto, or rebel against the dark days by browsing our lights – we have both indoor and outdoor and this year's selection are especially pretty. We also have a full range of greenery on offer, with holly and mistletoe from the estate grounds, specially made wreaths and, of course, a wide selection of Christmas trees.

Each weekend Kit Oakley, from Fairbairn Farm Animal Sanctuary, will be bringing over reindeers Ethel and Mavis. You can feed and pet them and find out all about these amazing creatures. This won't include Christmas Eve though – they might have another important job to do that day.

Don't forget to pop into the gift shop for present ideas. We have a new range of craft beers and local gins on sale.

Graham can testify that the beer is excellent and Gwen has been sampling the gins and reports they're all good, her favourite being Slake Hill Gin, which is about as local as you can get. It's made in a new distillery just outside Berecombe. And we have lots of plant-based present ideas with a new range of Bonsai trees just in.

If you insist on trying to work off a few mince pie induced calories, it's a good time for digging as the ground is generally still soft, and have a look at any trees to see if they need a tidy up. Graham is on hand to offer advice on the best ladders and we stock a wide range of books on pruning methods and general gardening advice. Again, great presents for those who are tricky to buy for.

As ever, happy gardening and may I wish you, on behalf of all of us here at Cheney House, a very Happy Christmas!

GG

Cheney House was hectically busy in the run-up to Christmas. Graham sold out of trees by the third week of December and had to order in more. Leo was an enthusiastic, if slightly eccentric, Father Christmas, the gift shop was rammed and Gwen and Tana were rushed off their feet in the restaurant serving roast turkey lunches with all the trimmings. Janey would be more than happy never to see another holly wreath, amaryllis bulb in a festive box or poinsettia again. The only consoling thing about being so busy was not having too much time to miss Will. They texted and Skyped and even tried a bit of phone sex until they got the giggles and had to stop. The time difference took any spontaneity out of it all as they had to plan when they got in contact. It left Janey frustrated in more ways than one. Whenever she asked when he was coming to see her, he demurred and said to trust him, he'd sort something out. He was unlikely to be able to get over for Christmas though. The office was only closed for a couple of days and they needed him there.

As Clare expected them to be busy right up to the last moment, the garden centre stayed open until late on Christmas Eve when they ended the day's trading with a carol singsong around the gloriously decorated tree in the courtyard. Gwen passed around mince pie shortbread (a Gwen speciality) and mulled wine and they huddled together against the cold, singing *O Come All Ye Faithful,* their breath misting in the still night air. With the white lights dripping off the old house as a background and the pungent aroma of cloves and Norwegian Spruce hanging in the air, Janey thought it was perfect. Except for one thing. Will was missing.

'This is great, isn't it?' Graham enthused as he put a warming arm around her. 'I love Christmas. Just love it. How about you and me going down the Star afterwards? Bit of a festive sesh? They've got Santa's Old Knobbler on draught.'

Janey turned to him. Looked up at his handsome features sharpened by the chilly air. She needed to tell him. It was now or never. She couldn't keep him hanging on, it was unfair. 'Gray, I don't know how to say this—'

'What's that then, Janey?' He looked down at her. 'You're looking way too serious. Come on, my lovely, it's Christmas! Once we're finished tonight, we've got three weeks off. How's about a bit of Netflix and chill, if you get my drift? That'll get you in the holiday mood.' He frowned, wrinkling his nose, which was pink with cold and too much mulled wine. 'Not sure I've got that right. But you know what I mean.'

'Oh Graham.' Janey paused, trying to muster the right words. 'I don't ... I'm not ...' She sucked in a deep breath of icy air, 'I don't feel like that about you. I don't love you.'

He chuckled. 'Who said anything about love? I was just on about a bit of a drink and a roll in the sack.'

She breathed out and giggled a little. 'I don't fancy you either.'

That got his attention. 'What do you mean, you don't fancy me?' He stepped away, shocked.

'It had to happen one day. You'd come across a woman who didn't want to leap into bed with you.'

'Not until today I haven't,' he said. 'I always thought you were a dead cert.'

'Well, much as I'm persuaded by that charming thought, I've got to put you straight and tell you while I might have been a dead cert, as you put it, a few months ago, I'm not any longer.'

'Fair enough.'

Janey stared up at him in astonishment. 'You're taking this surprisingly well.'

'To be honest, ever since Becca did the dirty, I suspected you were cooling a bit. Always thought you'd be up for a buddy bonk though.'

Janey reined in her giggles. She couldn't help it. She'd thought Graham would be heartbroken and was relieved he'd taken her rejection so well. He really did wade in the shallows. She suspected he hadn't a deep bone in his body. It was all most peculiar. The setting might be romantic and straight out of the climax to a romcom but the conversation most certainly wasn't. Suppressing a longing sigh, she thought the scene might play out very differently had it been Will standing next to her.

'Not even a buddy bonk, I'm afraid. I'll always be your friend though, Gray. Although without the bonking privileges.'

'You got someone, Janey?'

'I have, as a matter of fact, Graham. I have.'

He gave her a hug. 'Then I'm made up for you.' Squeezing her tight, he added, 'And if he doesn't treat you like a queen, then come and get your Uncle Gray. I'll sort him out.'

'Thanks Graham.' She reached up and kissed his cheek.

'And if you ever fancy a friends with benefits gig, you know who to call.'

'I do,' she replied on a laugh.

'What you up to for Christmas?'

'I'm flying to Spain to see Mum and Dad.'

'Hey, way to go, Janey.'

'I know. Global traveller, me, these days. Couldn't get a flight until Boxing Day though. Back for New Year's. Clare helped me book it all.'

'Lucky you, getting some sun.' Graham shivered violently. 'And if you want, they put on a good craic down at the Star to ring the new year in. Do a buffet too. As many sausage rolls as you can eat.'

'Sounds tempting.' How she had changed! Once upon a time a night in the local pub in Graham's company would have made her heart soar. Now all she wanted to do was wait in for a call from Will.

Graham missed her sarcasm. He waved to Tana, who gave a coy wave back. 'Now, if you'll excuse me, I've been on a promise all day. If you don't fancy the pub, I'll have to rearrange my schedule.'

'Off you go.' Janey watched him fondly as he approached Tana, resplendent in an elf outfit and tinsel crown. They disappeared into the night together.

Gwen came up to her and handed her the last piece of shortbread. 'We'll see you tomorrow then, Janey. Lunch at one o'clock sharp so we don't miss the queen's speech. Bring a bottle but you won't need nothing else. Just your lovely self and a daft Christmas jumper.'

'It's a date.' Janey kissed Gwen. 'And if I don't get a chance to say it tomorrow, Happy Christmas.'

'Happy Christmas, my lovely. And you're probably right. You won't get a chance to hear yourself speak tomorrow. We'll be twelve at the table. It's ruddy chaos in our house at Christmas.'

'But you love it,' Janey said affectionately.

'You're not wrong there.' She pulled up her collar against the cold and hurried off, calling Happy Christmas to everyone as she went.

Chapter 51

Janey had thought she'd conquered her fear of flying but a no-frills flight to the Costa del Sol at Christmas tested even the toughest traveller. No First Class privileges for her this time and no obliging Ewan to cosset her path through. Once again, Clare had furnished her with some comprehensively written instructions and it was just as well. Janey found the whole thing bewildering and incredibly stressful. Once she was gathered up at Malaga Airport and driven to her parents' house in Fuengirola she managed to relax. Her brother, Martin, was there too, with new girlfriend Stacey and everyone was ecstatic that she'd made the effort. On the day after she arrived, they took her into Malaga town to see the famous lights and for some tapas. In a side street off the Plaza de la Merced, Janey ate and drank, quietly triumphant that she had come this far.

The flat was cold and unwelcoming on her return. The Devon day was drearily dark after the warm Spanish sunshine, so she added two jumpers to the one she was already wearing and drove to Cheney House and her beloved gardening shed. After boiling the kettle for tea and switching on the portable heater she changed her mind and headed out to the woods beyond the lake. Ever optimistic, she hoped the first snowdrop leaves might be showing. She loved the way the waxy grey-green foliage pushed up from the frozen earth all tightly furled and secretive. She wandered aimlessly for a while, enjoying the cold air and the solitude. Aware that the light was already fading, even though it was barely past three in the afternoon, Janey turned to go back. As she did, she glimpsed a snatch of white to one side of an old silver birch. Nearly tripping in her excitement, she began to run towards it. She was right; in amongst the decaying leaf mulch, a patch of snow-white flowers gleamed in the lowering gloom.

'You little beauties,' she cried. 'My fairy flowers, my Candlemas bells, my fair maids of February. Hang on, it's not even January yet, you don't normally show until well into February.' Ignoring the mud, she fell to her knees. 'It's not possible, is it?' Fishing under her layers for her phone, she yanked it out from her dungarees' pocket. Flicking on the torch, she held it to the nearest tiny flower. It reflected a pure icy white with the palest of pale green stars in its middle. If you didn't know what you were looking for, its beauty and uniqueness would easily be missed. 'Oh,' she breathed. 'I've done it.' Tears pricked at her eyes. 'I've only gone and done it!'

She walked back to the shed in a daze. She didn't notice the lights on in Clare's flat in the big house, missed the sleek silver Jaguar parked on the carriage drive. The hand on her shoulder, as she opened the shed door, made her jump a foot. Turning, she couldn't believe who it was.

'Will!' She flung her arms around him and hugged the breath out of him. 'You're the second-best thing to happen to me today.'

Disentangling himself, he kissed her hard.

'That's nice.' He paused and reconsidered what she'd said. 'I think.'

'Why are you so out of breath?'

'I've been running around the place for the last ten minutes trying to find you.' He jerked his head at the shed. 'I knew you weren't far away, it's as hot as the tropics in there and the kettle is still warm. I was getting worried. Couldn't find you anywhere. I even looked in the boathouse.'

She took him by the hand and led him inside the shed. Shutting the door firmly against the freezing December air, she turned and faced him in triumph.

'I've done it, Will.'

'You certainly have. You always do it to me.' He came closer and kissed her again, his lips excitingly cold against hers. 'Oh, it's been too long, Janey. It seems ages since you came to Boston.' Rearing back, he frowned, as he took in her meaning. 'But just what have you done?'

Flourishing the picture she'd taken on her phone, she cried, 'I've created a new variety of snowdrop. A brand new, never seen before, totally unique and guaranteed to make our fortune new variety of snowdrop!'

He screwed his eyes up at the photograph.

'Janey, that's fantastic!' Taking a second look he added, 'I'll have to take your word for it, I'm afraid, as they all look the same to me but that's incredible.' Then her news really sank in. He gasped. Lifting her up and twirling her round, he yelled, 'It's just got through the air travel brain fog. I can't believe it.

You're a genius, Janey Trelawney. An absolute bloody genius!' Dropping her, he kissed her yet again. 'I take it that's why I'm the *second-best* thing to happen to you today.'

For a second she was nonplussed. 'Come again?' Clapping a hand over her mouth, she realised what she'd said. 'Oh glory. I'm so sorry.' She giggled. 'I'm on a bit of a high. It's been years of work and I didn't really believe it was ever going to happen. The odds were against me.' Grabbing his face, she brought his mouth closer and kissed it. 'I didn't really believe you were ever going to happen either. I'm sorry,' she mumbled through a kiss. 'How can I make it up to you?'

He didn't give the answer she expected. 'Has that kettle boiled?'

'Yes, why?'

'I could murder a cup of tea. I haven't had a decent one for over two months.'

Giggling some more, she released him. 'Sit yourself down and I'll make a brew. A celebratory one. I could do with one too. It might just bring me back down to earth.'

Once the tea was made, they sat side by side, catching up.

'How was Spain?' he asked.

'Pretty good. Once I'd got there.' Janey grimaced. 'The flight was awful though. No leg room and the coffee was terrible.'

Will laughed. 'No champagne this time, then?'

'None whatsoever. I'm going to have to save hard to fly out to see you again. From now on, it's First Class only for me. Or at the very least Premium Economy.'

'Get you,' he teased. 'The seasoned traveller.'

'That's me,' she said, smugly. 'It was really good seeing the folks again. I had a lovely time. I liked Spain and the food was incredible. I got addicted to *patatas bravas y aioli.* I'm going to try to get out there again at Easter. Apparently, Easter in Spain is really something.'

'Again, get you.'

'I know,' she said airily, slurping tea. 'I'm quite the global citizen these days. I'll have to start collecting Air Miles, however you do them. Haven't a clue, to be honest.' She put her arm through his and rested her head on his shoulder. 'Oh it's so good to have you here. Why didn't you tell me you were coming? It's going to be a magical New Year's with you.' She sighed happily. 'It'll be just like the climax in *When Harry Met Sally*. You are staying until the New Year, aren't you?'

'Oh, you know, thought I'd surprise you and yes, I'll be here for New Year. I can't wait to see it in with you.' He turned and kissed the top of her head.

'When will you have to go back?' She settled more comfortably against him. 'I've got to say, that company you work for is very mean with their holiday allowance.' She felt a chuckle vibrate through him.

'I'm not going back. This is my Christmas present to you, my darling Janey. I'm back in the UK for good.'

Janey leaped up. Banging her mug on the workbench with such force the handle fell off, she yelled, 'What?'

He took her hands in his. 'I'm going to stay here. I'm going to manage Cheney House on behalf of Gran.'

'What?'

'You're looking at your new boss, Janey, and I have to say I'm not going to stand for any of your nonsense.' He grinned.

'What?' Janey repeated, stupidly. 'How did this happen? It's always been your dream to work for that all-tootin' fallootin' company in Boston. You said all your ambitions had come true.'

Will drew her to him and sat her on his knee. 'And, at one point in my life, I would have said that was absolutely true. In fact, I'd go as far to say until I set eyes on this mad woman dancing under the chestnut trees in February, it was the only thing that mattered.' He shook his head, smiling. 'But not any longer.' He took her hands again and kissed them. 'Everything I want is here at Cheney House. With you. I can't imagine anything else I'd rather do than work with you and Gran.' One eyebrow rose. 'She's rather persuasive when she gets going, is my grandmother. She kept pointing out how daft it was that I was pining away in Boston missing you and you were here missing me. So I wriggled out of my contract and here I am.'

Janey flung her arms around him. 'I can't believe it. I can't believe you're here and you're staying. Oh Will I love you!'

'And I love you, my darling Janey. I love you so much.'

They kissed. Wonderingly. Passionately.

Eventually Will broke away. 'There's only one problem.'

'What?' Janey said, yet again. 'There can't be any problems. You have me. I have you. We have a new variety of snowdrop to put Cheney House on the galanthophile map. No problems whatsoever.'

'There is one,' Will began. He adopted a serious expression. 'I don't think I can manage you. I said I couldn't put up with any of your nonsense.' He shook his head glumly. 'I think it might be beyond me to be your boss.'

Janey looked stricken. 'Are you going to make me leave?' she asked, horrified.

'Not exactly. I'm offering you more of a, shall I say, co-management role. Then we could work together.'

'Okay,' Janey said in relief. 'That could work.'

Will, with difficulty, as Janey was still perched on his lap, reached into his jacket pocket. He took out a small box and flipped open the lid to reveal a solitaire diamond ring. Lifting her off him, he sat her in his chair, went down on one knee in the dust and said, 'It would give me the greatest pleasure to make you my wife.' He gazed at her lovingly. 'Marry me, Janey. Be my wife. Be my partner in life and love.'

Janey nodded, unable to speak. Tears rolled down her face as he slid the ring on her finger. It was the perfect fit.

After they had kissed until their lips were numb, in the absence of any champagne, they toasted their engagement with another mug of tea.

'And now there's only one thing left to do,' she said, turning to him, challenge in her eyes.

Will met her look. 'And that is?'

Clare went to pull the curtains on her sitting room window against the cold night. 'Oh Leo,' she cried, 'I think it's begun to snow. How marvellous.'

He came to her and put his arms around her waist. 'Marvellous,' he echoed and kissed her neck. 'English snow.' Then he stiffened and peered out at the night. 'Who is that?'

'Where?'

'Under the trees. The big chestnuts by the lake. There are two people.'

Clare followed his look and began to laugh. 'Oh my darling boy,' she cried, 'you've done it. Welcome home Will. And welcome to your Janey.'

'It is Will?' Leo asked incredulously. 'But what is he doing out there in the dark and in the snow with Janey?'

Clare watched for a moment longer. 'He's dancing, Leo. He's dancing with Janey. He's dancing for joy. And for love.' She pulled the curtains shut, turned to him and kissed him.

(Not) The Galloping Galanthophile: January

Well, hello everyone and Happy New Year. Biddy Roulestone here. I hope you don't mind a guest blogger taking over the website for this month. Janey, beloved head gardener at Cheney House and Will, the new general manager are up to their ears busy organising a party. An engagement party! And, as my dear Arthur is always reminding me, if I haven't made myself clear, it's their engagement party. Yes, Janey and Will are getting married. Couldn't happen to a nicer couple. I'm a big fan of Janey's, I can tell you. Had to step in when that nasty Becca woman was bullying her. Soon gave her short shrift. Arthur has also asked me to come clean. It's not the first time I've written one of these blog thingies, you see. If you follow Cheney House and all its doings, you'll know what I mean. Yes, I confess, it was me back in June. Oh, what fun I had winding up that Becca.

So, onto the actual blog. Apparently you're supposed to be brief and to the point but I've never been that and I'm not about to start now. A new year brings a new start in the garden and new beginnings for Cheney House too. There's no denying it's been a rocky time for them but I'm sure they'd like to thank all their many loyal customers for sticking by them. I have and I recommend you do too. Use it or lose it, I always say. Janey has asked me to say to keep checking the blog for some exciting news of how Cheney House is going to develop into a centre of excellence for snowdrops, starting with a brand-new variety of her favourite flower. Yes, you heard it here first, folks, Cheney House's very own snowdrop, Galanthus 'Little Cheney Gem' will be on sale, in the green as they put it, from next month. I prefer a nice petunia but there you go. Each to his own.

And I've been asked to pass this on. Why they didn't bother doing this themselves I'll never know but you know what young people are like; busy, busy, busy. This is what Mr William Cheney-Mortimer wants to say:

'I am delighted to be taking over the management of Cheney House from my grandmother, Clare Cheney. Cheney House is a very special place; it has been a wonderful home to me for many years and last year it played a part in introducing me to the love of my life. So, I would like to invite you all to share in celebrating my engagement to someone you know very well – the utterly wonderful, totally entrancing, Ms Janey Trelawney. Come for champagne and canapés in the marquee on the thirty-first, followed by dancing and fireworks.'

Ah, fair warmed the cockles that did. 'The love of his life.' How wonderful. We could all do with more love in our lives, couldn't we? Make sure you go along to the party, it's sure to be a stonker. I've heard tell a major movie star might drop by and I don't need to tell you who that might be! And I'll be there too. You won't keep me away.

I'm supposed to do gardening tips for this month. Quite honestly, with all the snow we've been having (Arthur forecast a hard winter and he's never wrong) my only tip is to forget the garden and snuggle up in the warm with your loved one. Yes, I've got my Arthur, the rumour is Clare has a hot Italian in tow and Janey's engaged to her lovely young man. It really has been a year of the most surprising triumphs!

As ever, happy gardening!

GG I mean BR.

Acknowledgements

No book is written without help. Sincere thanks to Nell Dixon who generously shared her experiences with dyscalculia. Thanks go to Victoria Garland and Andrew at Cranborne Garden Centre for information on how a garden centre runs and details about snowdrop propagation. Grazie mille to Alison Macintosh who, once again, helped me with the Italian characters I insist on writing; one day I'll learn the language, I promise! All mistakes are my own. Huge thanks to Laura Bambrey for the encouragement and to Jan, Alison, Lynn, Liz and Jayne for the Zoom meetings which kept me sane during Lockdown. Thank you also, to Sarah at Goldcrest Books for going over and above, and to Karen for her forensic attention to proof-reading. Grazie to the Hotel Delfino in Massa Lubrense which inspired Clare's lovely hotel; one day I'll return. If Janey has whetted your appetite for all things snowdrop, I can heartily recommend Jane Kilpatrick and Jennifer Harmer's book The Galanthophiles: 160 Years of Snowdrop Devotees. And, finally, an enormous thank you and much love to you, dear readers. I love Janey and hope you love her too.

Printed in Great Britain
by Amazon

31238307R00189